Arabesque

By Geoffrey Household

THE SPANISH CAVE

THE THIRD HOUR

ROGUE MALE

THE SALVATION OF PISCO GABAR
AND OTHER STORIES

ARABESQUE

GEOFFREY HOUSEHOLD

Arabesque

AN ATLANTIC MONTHLY PRESS BOOK

LITTLE, BROWN AND COMPANY · BOSTON

1948

c.10

Published April 1948
Reprinted April 1948
Reprinted May 1948

ATLANTIC—LITTLE, BROWN BOOKS
ARE PUBLISHED BY
LITTLE, BROWN AND COMPANY
IN ASSOCIATION WITH
THE ATLANTIC MONTHLY PRESS

*Published simultaneously
in Canada by McClelland and Stewart Limited*

PRINTED IN THE UNITED STATES OF AMERICA

For

Robin, Oswald

and

F. S. W., M. E. F.,

who will find in this book none they knew
but many they might have known

Contents

	Prologue	3
I	Syrian Shore	13
II	Prayle	36
III	The High Places	48
IV	Security	69
V	Up to Jerusalem	83
VI	Hospitality	97
VII	Zion	110
VIII	The Heathen	126
	Interlude	147
IX	Burnt Offering	161
X	Prisoners of Cairo	180
XI	Escape	199
XII	Mavis and Marthe	213
XIII	Home to Helwan	228
XIV	Mr. Makrisi	256
XV	Captains and Agents	274
XVI	Fight for Freedom	286
	Epilogue	303

Arabesque

Prologue

THE FOUR GRACEFUL SHIPS steamed out of Beirut harbor in line ahead, their holds and cabins packed with the French Army of the Orient. Thin across the water traveled the music of the bands, as the convoy glided from the clamorous docks away into the profound summer sleep of the Mediterranean, until the troops who lined the rails to look their last on the Syrian coast showed only as streaks of brown between the white tiers of the decks.

It was the final convoy. Every week for six weeks past four ships had arrived from France and left for France, loaded with colonial troops, their wives, their daughters, even their mistresses — if long alliance could be covered by any charitable formula — and the mountains of neat crates that contained their baggage.

The transports were a link between Europe and the besieged of the Middle East: a reminder that Europe was still real. For the men who remained on the quays of Beirut there was in the departure of the ships a sadness deeper than the normal and momentary desolation experienced by those who turn away from empty rails or water. Regret, too, they felt at the loss of so friendly an enemy, of a gallant army which should have stayed and fought instead of sailing away, bewildered, by courtesy of the British Army and the German Admiralty, to a lost country. The departure was irrevocable. Few of these men who had made their homes in gay and lovely Lebanon

would ever return. A little world, full of grace, for all its cor-
ruption, and of delicacy, for all its naked power, had ended.
The British and their slender contingents of allies were alone.
In that summer of 1941, though the lands which they gar-
risoned were immense, they felt the close comradeship and
isolation of an invested army.

Armande Herne stood at the window of her hotel bedroom, watching the ships as they passed beyond the horns of
the bay and gathered speed upon their calm and inviting path
to France. She was still and silent, but the tears streamed down
her cheeks. They seemed no struggling issue from her body,
impersonal and inconvenient as raindrops dripping from her
head.

A middle-aged French major stepped out onto the adjoining
balcony, and returned immediately and tactfully to his room.
The slight movement brought back Armande to consciousness
of herself. She had not been thinking at all, and was faintly
disgusted to feel the wetness of her neck and dress. Such an
ecstasy of unanalyzable misery she had not known since she
was a young girl.

She entered the cool shade of her room, and washed and
changed. Then, drawn to see the last of the ships before they
should disappear over the horizon, she returned to her balcony.

The Vichy major was staring after the convoy, his arms
tense, his hands gripping the rail of the balcony as if locked
around the last pulsation of a feebly resistant throat. He too,
it was evident, had not been afraid to weep.

"You are not leaving, *mon commandant?*" asked Armande.

"Yes. But I shall go on a last boat. A few of us must stay
some days yet to tidy up loose ends for the English and—"
he spat the word—"these so-called Free Frenchmen."

Armande did not answer. To her the Free French were

the flower of their nation. True, they were difficult and touchy, but what other manners could one expect from an adventurous little band who had insisted on accompanying the British in a war against their own countrymen? Their officers, in response to her sympathy, made no secret of a belief that only their wits and intransigence could prevent the annexation of Syria by the British. That belief was logical; it was founded on an accurate reading of history; it was precise, closed, French and unanswerable; but to Armande, brought up between the two wars and sharing the spirit and hopes of her generation, it was manifestly and tragically wrong. Little wonder that the Free French had the impatience of trapped men worrying to free themselves from a subtle, imperial plot, so misty that it did not exist at all!

"I am glad of this opportunity," said Major Loujon, "to offer Madame my apologies."

"There is no need. It was your duty, I suppose. And you were always most polite."

"One does not like interrogating a woman of beauty and character. And then — it is so useless."

"Useless?" she asked.

"Yes, for such a woman is above all the stupidities of war. There is nothing to be gained. Even if you had talked, it would have been on quite a different plane to that of my interrogation. I should have known as I wrote down your answers that they did not mean what they said."

"I had nothing to talk about," said Armande, smiling. "I was never a British agent. I might have been, if anyone had asked me. But nobody did."

"That was stupid of them!"

"Perhaps. But they never came across me. And I am easily forgotten."

"Never, Madame!" protested Loujon sincerely.

"Yes, if I wish to be. It's true, I hope, that when people remember me, they like the memory. But I am not — aggressive."

"That is sad, Madame, for you yourself remember — " Loujon waved a hand towards the smudges of smoke on the horizon — "too keenly."

"No," said Armande simply, "there was no one person. It was just that I died a little death. One dies many times, *mon commandant*."

"Then why *did* you stay in Syria?" Loujon asked, showing his professional curiosity.

"I hadn't any really good reason for being here. So I should have been a very bad agent."

"That's true."

"You see?"

"Madame, let me give you some advice," said Loujon earnestly. "Get yourself something to do. Listen — we are all the same, we policemen. If a woman is not living with a husband or a lover and if she hasn't a source of income that all can see, she is suspect. And — if you really are not working for the British — you will be just as suspect to them as you were to me."

"Oh, no!" Armande protested, incredulous and horrified.

"It is certain. They will not believe you are a German agent, for a woman like you does not work for the Boche. I cannot tell you how one knows it. It would be against the whole current of life. But they will wonder whether you are working for us or for the Russians perhaps. Madame, I beg you—get yourself a job and be as everyone. In war one must disappear into the mass."

"I ask nothing better."

"Then you will pardon my advice and—forgive me for the past?"

"It is easy to forgive you, *mon commandant*," said Armande graciously. "You are so intelligent."

She was weary of him. She recognized that she had been treated correctly and courteously both under interrogation and in the internment camp where he had sent her; but Loujon and his camp were all unreal. It was so incredible that she, Armande Herne, whose conscience was tranquil, should have been ignominiously driven away from her flat at dawn in an army lorry with an expressionless Indo-Chinese driver, and deposited in a hut behind a barbed-wire fence. This, in true enemy territory, could have been accepted as the fortune of war; but to be treated as a suspect enemy of France, that is to say, of Europe, had been a nightmare.

The ships vanished. She tried to drug her melancholy by the beauty of Lebanon. Across the bay the mountains rose from the still sea, each peak so long a sanctuary for lonely thoughts that were not, she admitted, very different from Phoenician worship. The great foothills, rounded and green with orchards, were the many breasts of Earth, the peace of the tiller and his villages spreading down their slopes. One mountain was of the Huntress, split by gorges and tufted with thickets where for thousands of years the silent arrow or cheap Belgian gun had brought down the game for Beirut tables; another she imagined as the High Place of Astarte—a gable of rock, terrible and exquisite, which towered over the pine forest with the delicacy of a cathedral roof. Above them all was the merciless golden ridge of Sannine, forehead of the Sun, shimmering like a vertical desert.

Lebanon was so rich, so eminently habitable. The white-walled, red-roofed villages stood on the crests of the hills, compact and poised in air as Dürer's castles. In such villages there was store of food and wine, a church, a friendly inn; they belonged to the Mediterranean, not to the ascetic desert. It was to this landscape — or rather to all the civilized implications of the landscape — that for more than a year she had turned for comfort.

Though to the eye no loveliness was lost, sea and mountain now held no more inspiration for her than the back yard of a familiar flat. On reflection Armande acquitted herself of sluggishness. One could look no longer at the hills without remembering all the alien activity hidden in their folds. The olive groves were full of tents, the inns taken over by the staffs of corps and divisions. Upon the country roads were no longer solitude nor, agreeably to break it, the cars of French officers with their decorative girl friends. The convoys rumbled up and down the mountains; the motorcycles wove in and out between them; and the Lebanese taxi drivers killed or were killed with impartial good humor. The landscape was too full of men who were rootless: British and Australians longing to be elsewhere, displaced villagers longing for them to be gone.

For all her pity of the troops, Armande envied them. They at least knew why they were in this fortress of the Middle East, and their lives were rendered tolerable by the round of duty, by comradeship and by the romance of the East. All of them hotly denied that they found any romance whatever. That, she had discovered, was because romance meant to them either Arab warfare in the style of Lawrence or Arab pleasure as it might be known to the very dissolute son of a very rich Damascus merchant. Yet of the true and sunlit Levant, its ships and its costumes, its dawns and its distances, they were appreciative, though sometimes resentful, as if it were disloyalty, of their own appreciation.

She herself had neither duty nor comradeship. She was in the fortress and likely to remain and had no choice. There was none to give her an order and none but herself to bring up the rations. No doubt if she became a public nuisance some efficient and impersonal machine of the besieged would gather her up into a refugee camp, and keep her safe both from the enemy and from starvation; but that savored of the workhouse. To call herself ironically a parasite was to toy painlessly with a facet of truth; to feel a parasite was unendurable.

Armande had not been born to the privileges of her civilization; that civilization, however, had easily permitted her to acquire them. Her father was a cavalry trooper who in 1915 married the young proprietress of his favorite *bistro* in Amiens. After the doubtful peace he persuaded Madame to sell her falling francs and settle in England. They bought a pub in remotest Gloucestershire, and for a year he indulged the dream of his life: to sell English drinks to English countrymen.

When she came to England Armande was seven. Memories of that candid little soul, formed in café and public house, filled her with amusement and tenderness. She had been happy at home and in the village school, where boys rather than girls had been her playmates. Because she was fast on her feet and scandalously free of speech, she had been accepted into their games and the innocence of their secret societies.

During four long years of peaceful childhood, the fame of Maman's inn expanded. Bed-and-breakfast visitors came back for week ends. Week-enders spread the news of Maman's cooking and talked of her in London. Maman built a new wing and a new kitchen. She advertised. She raised her prices to a guinea a day, and still the house was full, and still there was a waiting list. The bar had Vouvray and Anjou on draught as well as beer. The villagers took their custom elsewhere.

Armande's mental promise, her two languages and, possibly, her cricket attracted the headmistress of Bingham Priory, who was a constant and exacting client of the inn. One evening, masculinely expansive after dinner, she persuaded Madame that a part of her profits should be spent on the education of her daughter. Armande in imagination could still see the headmistress as vividly as that night — one predatory businesswoman with another in Maman's sitting room — standing, brandy glass on the mantelpiece, in front of the fire where Father used to stand, and looking down on her with professional kindness.

When the inn became an exclusive hotel, her father retired to the simple comfort of the harness room where no one visited him but Armande. Maman was not actively unkind to her husband, but she ignored him as an embarrassment that could neither make money nor had the heart to spend it. The guests avoided any mention of him; indeed few of them realized that the ex-soldier seen polishing something useless in the yard was part owner of the hotel. Modest, lonely and drinking more than was good for him, he faded like some gentle animal displaced into an unnatural environment.

The famous boarding school took from him his last joy and his only companion. Even during Armande's holidays her new life was too hurried for her father, her kisses too fleeting. Hour by hour Maman closely managed her, forced her into activities of work and play, threw her into the society of any wealthy guests who were amused by her, compelled her to accept their invitations. To her father she became elusive as a memory of love. When she was fourteen, he died.

Armande, developing late, had still a child's unquestioning

acceptance of events; but the sense of loss remained with her, to be examined in the self-conscious years of early youth when a first pattern of her life, real or imaginary, was visible. Then she could not excuse her mother or herself, until the mercy of protecting nature taught her to tolerate the poison of guilt and to forget it. Thereafter she avoided, instinctively, the storms of emotion, the spiritual revolts, which might, through dissatisfaction with her accepted self, have set the poison working. She gave herself with docility to the life arranged for her by others.

At Bingham Priory she took pains to become a *jeune fille bien élevée*. This was the order of her mother. It was an ideal reluctantly conceded by the school. Solid knowledge she dutifully acquired, and flowered in arts of self-expression. She could turn a pretty sonnet. She mastered the technique of painting, and indulged in fantastic and imaginary landscapes. She worked enthusiastically under a teacher of classical dancing, for she loved movement and yet preferred not to disfigure her growing beauty by public perspiration on the playing fields. So selfish a use of long legs was not wholly approved by the weather-beaten mistresses of Bingham Priory, but was permissible, they told her, provided she considered it serious training for an independent profession.

Armande completed her education in Switzerland and was turned out upon a world which appreciated her fastidious nature more than she did herself. She distrusted the fuller, coarser flavors of mankind that she had known as a child, but since she knew they existed she missed them. To men of her own generation and upbringing she gave at first an eager friendship; then, bored by those very limitations, she would drift away. Her judgment of older men was less exigent, but she felt that they treated her with the tolerance accorded to a spoiled and entertaining child. She was not a spoiled child. She was a mature young woman whose tastes were incompatible, and she knew it. After three years of London and Gloucestershire — and one hundred and fifty-six weeks of complete familiarity with Maman's intrigues to marry her off — she accepted reserve as probably the most natural trait in her character and certainly the most desirable.

She married correctitude. John Herne was less patronizing than his elders, more persistent than his contemporaries. He was so sanely sure of her excellence that she was flattered and happy, so confident of winning her that she could not avoid him. John had only his salary as a budding stockbroker, but that had been enough to support a quiet standard of easy living and pleasant manners. To be *bien élevée,* even in intimacy, became a habit. It had been, undoubtedly, a restful habit. Armande, sidetracked into Beirut, longed for the three contented years before the war, for her exquisite small flat in Kensington, her dinner table, her circle whose artistic, political and intellectual sympathies redeemed the uncouth capitalism of her husband's trade.

As soon as war was declared, John Herne joined the navy. There was a lusty flavor of patriotism in the unthinking speed with which he offered himself to his country, but she could not help reflecting, with an illogical sense of disloyalty, that a man whose home life was as serene as his would have waited a few months for love to be overwhelmed by duty. She herself, angry with the futile dignity of her country's foreign policy, was no enthusiastic patriot. It was France that she had chosen to serve. A month after John's departure she joined the organization of a M. Calinot, national and decorated pundit of the French aircraft industry, and, conveniently, old friend of her mother.

CHAPTER I

Syrian Shore

THE COOL AIR drifted from the still Mediterranean under the awnings of the Hotel St. Georges, and passed out to sea again bearing the fragrance of fruit and wine. The hotel, though run by Greeks and staffed by Lebanese, remained tenaciously French. None of the guests who strolled from bar to bathing beach and terrace to restaurant appeared to have indigestion or to dislike the rest. Neither enjoyment nor activity nor smartness had necessarily any reality, but the hotel created a civilized environment in which anyone who wished could indulge, without effort, a sense of well-being.

Floating in the transparent solvent of French culture were guests of many nations. Casual British officers from the various missions leaned against the bar. Cheerful Australians from the camps under the olive trees ventured doubtfully upon unfamiliar menus. Sliding their round bodies between the tables with the grace of fish were the Greco-Egyptians from Cairo and Alexandria, overwhelmingly obliging in the drinks they were enchanted to stand and the contracts they were prepared to undertake. Christian politicians of the Lebanon, their trusses and intimate machinery creaking beneath natty trousers, presented to each other champagne and compliments, while the princes of Syria and Trans-Jordan, whose robes of chocolate and gold not only concealed but made unthinkable any infirmity of body or soul, scowled with eternal dignity over little cups of coffee.

In and out through this invasion of males flitted a number of discreetly unattached women: young wives of the French Empire whose husbands, Free or dubious, had parked them conveniently in Beirut; mistresses of Vichy staff officers who, enthusiastically as the office cleaners and canteen proprietors, had embraced the cross of Lorraine; unmarried daughters of the Lebanon, modeling their frocks on Hollywood and their conventions on provincial society of the nineties. There were exotic plants of mountain villages, from Ararat to the Alaouite highlands, transplanted to Beirut by their admirers and now well established in the more lenient air. There were the consorts of the Alexandrian businessmen, whose sad and ruminating eyes looked out from the mascara, patiently ignoring the discomfort of too many jewels and too tight a brassière. All these flowery women spent their mornings in bed or on the beach, their afternoons at the crowded beauty parlors, their evenings at the Hotel St. Georges.

Whatever she did, Armande felt herself to be classed among them. Their eternal delicate presence forced her into an infuriating self-consciousness. She might as well be living, she thought, in a dance hall where a beauty competition was being judged. If you dressed with some spirit, you were immediately mistaken for a competitor; if you defied local convention and were deliberately dowdy, you snobbishly set yourself apart. The competitors' relative degrees of virtue were unimportant; they were all so obviously out to catch the judges' eyes.

This lack of privacy was exasperating; except in her room she had none. It was impossible to have a meal or a drink alone, and difficult to pay for either. It seemed to her that she must know all existing faces of the British Army — the kindly, the callow, the drunken, the weather-beaten and horsy, the strong-jawed and imperial, the scholarly with clean-shaven upper lip, the would-be military with neat mustache, the ultra-military with cat's mustache. Their names eluded her, though she knew uncountable nicknames. A mumble on first acquaintance represented the surname, and never thereafter was it repeated.

Such a multitude of her own countrymen carried her out of the slothful life of waiting. A few of these officers she had met casually in London; others had known John or her mother. The return to her husband's kind made her feel faintly dishonorable. It was hard to explain why, like the women of the hotel, she was doing nothing, and what she was doing in Beirut at all. Romantic young officers, finding her account of herself quietly evasive, set her up as the heroine of a false and fantastic legend. From one to another they passed the word that Armande Herne had been a lovely and gallant agent of their army.

It was on the Sunday morning after the departure of the ships that the hotel desk rang her room and announced a gentleman to see her. As the manager was normally at some pains to protect those of his clients who had no wish for unknown callers, she could guess that the credentials of this visitor were beyond dispute; the guarded voice of the reception clerk, quite unlike the tone in which he announced a friend, an admirer or a man of business, left her in no doubt that the caller was some kind — and, oh God, how many kinds there seemed to be! — of civil or military policeman.

She spoke to the gentleman on the telephone. His voice attracted her. It was deep, decisive and with an odd musical rhythm of its own. He introduced himself as Sergeant Prayle of Field Security and said that he wished to talk to her.

Armande was reluctant to be seen answering all the usual questions in a discreet corner of the hotel lounge. She told Sergeant Prayle to come up to her room in five minutes.

She used those minutes to arrange her black hair in the Madonna parting which had always impressed such callers with the purity of her motives and morals. Her large gray eyes looked back at her sedately from the mirror; then lit and twinkled at the passing thought that she dressed for security men very much as for a poetry reading in her Kensington flat. Armande felt a fraud, but since at the moment she had no doubt of her beauty, conscience was amused rather than reproachful.

Sergeant Prayle's appearance belied his attractive voice. Armande realized that she had seen him on several occasions chatting to the reception clerks; she had taken him for one of those seedy and indefinite Englishmen who might be living precariously on language lessons or the dowry of a foreign wife. He was tall and well made, but wearing flannel trousers that did not reach his ankles, and a sports coat that had never recovered from being packed into too small a space. His lips were thin; his witch's nose was long and one eye was slightly larger than the other. His complexion, too fair to tan, was blotched with red and peeling from overexposure to the sun.

"Do sit down," said Armande, offering him a comfortable chair near the window. "What is Field Security?"

"A racket," answered Sergeant Prayle with relish.

"What sort of a racket?"

"Unfair to the workers. I share this suit of civilian clothes with three lance corporals and the sergeant major. And anyway it belongs to the skipper."

"But why not wear uniform then?"

"Avoids embarrassment. Too many brigadiers popping in and out of bedrooms."

"I understand you want to talk to me," Armande reminded him, primly ignoring his last remark. "But I really cannot imagine what about."

"Softly, softly, catcha da monkey," he murmured, and then added, seeing her bewilderment: "That means I really don't know myself."

There was charm in his crooked smile, but Armande had long ceased to have pity for mysterious males who wanted to ask her questions. Moreover, French Security had never visited her in a lower manifestation than captain, and a good-looking one at that.

"If you are some sort of policeman," she said sharply, "you ought to know."

"I don't think I'm any sort of policeman. Just an ordinary egg."

"And if you want all the details about me, they are in my dossier at the Sûreté Générale."

"I know they are," he answered. "That's why I only want to talk to you."

"But conversation with you is so difficult," said Armande, relenting. "It's all bits and pieces. Surely that isn't the best way to find out what you want?"

"Well, you know, afterwards, when one thinks about what the other person said, there's something that sticks in the loaf."

"Is there?" she asked kindly. "And do you enjoy your work?"

"Yes. I like to deal with people without trying to get money out of them."

"Money?"

"The dibs. Yes. Have you ever noticed that when you really use the loaf on a stranger in civil life you're always trying to make money?"

Armande froze at this vulgarity and its implication.

"I don't mean you," he explained. "I meant all of us — all of us."

"I think you must have been a commercial traveler."

"Sometimes. And once I roosted in a crook employment agency. Didn't know it was one till I'd been there a month."

He laughed ironically.

"So you can run straight now?" she asked.

"Oh, quite straight! The army is like a socialist republic, you know. No temptation to make money."

"I should have thought you had considerable temptations."

"But you don't take 'em. That's what I mean."

"I think I see," she replied, "though you said just the opposite to what you mean."

"I usually do."

"Isn't it awkward?"

"Not a bit. It has the advantage that damned fools can't understand what I am talking about."

"Is that an advantage?" asked Armande, at last interested.

"Yes. For one thing you can classify the fools and the intelligent straight off."

"But lonely."

"All alone in one's own bughouse," he agreed. "Still, it is one's own."

Armande relaxed, and curled herself more gracefully into her chair. Her small head resting on one hand, she watched him with her individual and unconscious intensity of gaze. She was, by this time, beginning to be a fair judge of security men, though her experience had been wholly of the French.

This sergeant, she thought, could surely not be typical of the British service? Where were the keen eye and the professional leading question? Where indeed was anything at all save a puzzled soul with some originality of expression? He hadn't the faintest idea how to come to the point. She felt discomfort and pity as if a blind man were groping to touch her; she wanted to make the interview as easy for him as possible.

"What was it you really wanted to know?" she asked.

"Nothing."

"But you must have come with some idea?"

"I did. I haven't got it any longer."

"May I know what it was?"

"Cats!" he exclaimed, his odd-sized eyes staring at her, as if fixed in a moment of merriment.

"Yes?"

"I was only reminded of them. Intelligence tests. The doc says *curiosity* and you say *cats,* and then he makes a note on your card: 'Will be fit for brigadier in later stages of war if beard not too long.' "

"What are you thinking of now?" she asked invitingly.

"You know."

Casually, abominably, he waved his hand in a gesture that included her room, her bed, herself, as if the disposal of the lot were a mere convenience.

Such coarseness produced, always, a cold anger in Armande. Her normal reaction was to shut up and be conscious of good breeding. She might lose a shade of color, but indifference, untouchability, were as obvious to the offender as to her. She was therefore horrified to feel herself blushing.

The sergeant watched her gravely. His attitude was more exasperating than ever. He had the impudence to look protective — the sort of swine, she thought, who fails to make physical contact and then starts a sort of mental pawing.

"You know, you go all luscious and motherly," he said, ignoring her embarrassment as if it were of no importance, "and then are surprised at the trouble it causes."

"I do not!" snapped Armande, angry with herself for answering at all.

"Damn you!"

"Are you mad?"

"No, no," he explained. "I was only helping. 'I do not, damn you,' was what you wanted to say."

"I never thought of it."

"Then you should have thought of it."

Armande rose.

"Tell your commanding officer," she said, "that I shall be very pleased to give him any information he wants."

"We only discuss such matters with the firm's principals," murmured Prayle. "Now pack up your little Hoover, and the office boy will see you safely past the hatstand."

Armande smiled faintly and politely, and then found that the corners of her mouth were quivering. The smile would not contract.

"I've tired you," he said. "I'm sorry."

She hesitated, and then answered simply:

"I am very tired. None of you leave me alone."

"I suppose not. Well, *we* shan't bother you any more."

"Oh, come again if it's your duty," she said with weary courtesy.

"No need. I told you I hadn't got my idea any more."

"Good-by then."

"*Très bien!*" he exclaimed in an execrable French accent.

It was annoying to be patronized, but she did want to know why he had come.

"Tell me," she said.

"It was just that all your young men — no, not fair, that! — all these young men will have it that you belong to the British Secret Service as they call it."

"I have never said or implied — " she began indignantly.

"I know you didn't."

"How do you know?"

"Because I've talked to you. You haven't that kind of vanity. And you aren't interested in money."

"And suppose I wanted to get information out of them?" she suggested.

"Then a security sergeant would be a very useful friend. My approach was abrupt of course. And beastly true. Still, if you had been expecting something of the kind . . . As it was, your gentle response — seven wise virgins with seven large lamps. Bang, bang! Crash, crash! All on your uncle's noggin!"

"You are a vulgar beast," said Armande with a half laugh.

"Yes. It's a pity."

"Stop it, then."

"Stop it? Why should I stop it?" he answered with sudden bitterness. "What else is there?"

When Sergeant Prayle had left, Armande settled her aching head on the pillows and lay still, staring at the ceiling. She was exhausted by Prayle and the military in general. These men all gave her a sense of being on the defensive, morally and sexually. Yet what on earth had she done? Stayed in Beirut when she should have left. That was all. Loujon thought she was a British agent. Prayle thought — God knew what he thought! This ridiculous Prayle did not think at all. He jumped from one intuition to another.

Loujon was right. It was certainly time to do something.

But what? She had two offers from senior officers at G.H.Q.
who wanted personal private secretaries. When she pointed
out that she knew no shorthand and was a two-finger typist,
they didn't seem to think it mattered. Secretaries in Cairo
were evidently very personal and private.

Nursing was attractive: intimate, and balanced and gentle.
And scarlet and gray suited her — though she suspected that
only regular nurses might wear them. She would have liked
to give herself to the care of sick and wounded if only there
had been a chance of serious training in the Middle East. She
could no doubt be useful washing dishes and sweeping the
wards, but such humble employment was a waste of her
education and ability.

John was always asking her why she did not join one of
the women's services. There seemed to be any amount of
them at home. In the Middle East they did not exist. Englishwomen, in fact, were not supposed to be in the fortress at all.
The wives and daughters who had managed to avoid evacua-
tion were all passably efficient secretaries, or running indispensable canteens and funds.

Was there, she wondered, any sort of amateur intelligence
work that she could do? Everyone assumed that she was
fitted for it, though the opinions as to who might employ her
apparently varied. She remembered a hint thrown out by
David Nachmias. He had only made a casual remark to the
effect that there were interesting jobs around if one looked
for them, but Abu Tisein was not conversational without a
purpose.

Although he was known to everyone and to Armande by
his Arab nickname, he was a Jew, born and bred in Palestine.
Upon his broad and muscular stern, a firm base for opera-
tions wherever he set it down, he sat peacefully in the hotel

listening to his excitable wife. When she disappeared, always in a flurry of smart scarves and feminine business, he sat on listening, equally peacefully, to Moslem and Christian Arabs. His quiet manners, his quality of outward simplicity, appealed to Armande. What David Nachmias was doing in Beirut so soon after the occupation she had no idea. It was pretty evident that the British approved of him. He was said to be one of the Arab experts of the Jewish Agency, and a mine of infor- · mation on the politics and personalities of Syria.

Armande wrote to her husband a letter which was less vague than usual; it gave no very definite news and no more than a suggestion that a change of place and occupation was probable, but she omitted her polished generalities on Life and there was no mention of her soul. The tone was optimistic; she felt, as she sealed the envelope, that John would be pleased with her and that some sort of decision had been taken.

In the afternoon she went down to the terrace of the hotel, sure of finding the Nachmiases. The crowded tables along the balustrade formed a semicircle between the sea and a dance floor. A band played hopefully, but it was too soon after the hour of the beauty parlor for the women of Beirut to risk their complexions in the sticky heat. An Australian officer and a nurse, snatching a moment of civilization after months of disciplined discomfort, were laughing gaily and dancing stiffly, alone on the floor, completely indifferent to the flashy foreigners who watched.

Abu Tisein had chosen a table as far as possible from the band. He was moodily drinking coffee, while his wife's plump hands fussed over the tea, the slices of lemon, the cakes and ice cream. It was hard to guess their nationality or religion. Madame, tightly corseted in body and soul, outwardly expansive, was French to eye and ear. Abu Tisein, with his short hawk nose, clipped mustache and powerful head, looked like a bored and prosperous Spanish manufacturer.

When their eyes met, Madame bowed and gave Armande a signal of round white fingers which the former *jeune fille bien élevée* recognized as a masterpiece. It combined the geniality proper to a place of public amusement with all the etiquette of the upper bourgeoisie, and elected Armande as the only lone woman in the hotel who might unquestionably and without further invitation join Mme. Nachmias at her table.

Armande went over to them, and was almost immediately served by a rushed waiter with a gin fizz. Tea was inadequate to deal with her odd combination of lightheartedness and a headache. She approved of David Nachmias. He never appeared to give an order, and he never howled for the maître d'hôtel. While you were engaged with Madame or looking at the sea or criticizing the Assyrian curls of Lebanese women, miniature gestures of thumb and forefinger played between Nachmias and the nearest waiter, and what you wanted appeared.

"How do you manage it?" she asked Abu Tisein.

She had never waited less than a quarter of an hour for a drink when sitting with anyone else.

"I am a Turk," he said solidly. "I understand them."

"*Mais, chéri!*" screeched Madame. "He is mad, my husband! He is no more a Turk than I am."

"But everyone knows you were educated in France, my dear," replied Abu Tisein with lazy irony — whether true or not, Madame took good care that it should be known. "Whereas I am a child of the Ottoman Empire."

Armande was affectionately amused by Mme. Nachmias's excellent imitation of a Parisian lady who had been dragged to the Middle East against her will and only longed to return to Europe; it might even have deceived her if she had not heard Madame deal with an offending chambermaid in a screaming flow of invective which left no doubt that Arabic was her mother tongue. Abu Tisein's wide Palestinian culture did not appeal at all to his wife. It smelled too much of humble origins.

"The Lebanese," Armande remarked, "say that they preferred the Turks to the French."

"Just because those were the good old times. All the world looks back to the days before 1914. Myself, I prefer Palestine and the Lebanon as they now are. But I admit I was content under the Turks."

"You were also younger," Madame reminded him sharply.

"Yes, but it is not only that. In those days we were left in peace. So long as my people are left to multiply in peace, I do not care who governs — Turks or English or Arabs."

"David!" Madame protested. "One would think you passed your life in chewing melon seeds or smoking a nargileh!"

"I like to do both," murmured Abu Tisein.

"He is impossible, Mme. Herne! Do not believe a word he says! Everyone knows that the Jewish Agency could not exist a moment without my husband. And to say that he would not mind being ruled by Arabs! That, David, when you saw what the Arabs did in Safad!"

She tore the white, spotted scarf from her head with a sweep of the arm that expressed tragic exasperation, and fanned herself impatiently.

"Dear Mme. Herne, it was horrible! I, I who am speaking to you, I was nearly violated!"

"But you were not," said Abu Tisein peaceably, "for one recognized you in time. No, Mme. Herne, do not misunderstand me. As things are, we must trust the Arabs to the Jews, rather than the Jews to the Arabs. We are excitable, I admit, but we do not cut women and children into little pieces. I am a Jew and I live and work for a Jewish Palestine — but I permit myself to regret the days when my country was not full of Poles and Germans, and the Arabs were more friendly. Like a good civil servant in England, I do what I am told but I do not always approve of it."

Mme. Nachmias, implying her opinion that the conversation had become impolitely deep for the presence of two fashionable women, began to prattle trivialities. A French officer invited Armande to dance; when she refused on the grounds of heat and headache, he showed a tendency to hang about the table in the hope of being invited to sit down. To Armande's annoyance, Abu Tisein welcomed him and Madame sparkled with conversation, playing the witty Frenchwoman of uncertain age. Such rapid fire would have overwhelmed Armande even if she had wished to compete.

As soon as Madame and her officer had, inevitably, reached the dance floor, David Nachmias said:

"I suppose that you will be going to Cairo soon?"

This was an obvious invitation to talk of her plans. Armande realized that she had watched unsuspectingly one of Madame's disappearing acts, by which, without any collusion between husband and wife, Abu Tisein was left alone with the person to whom he wanted to speak.

"Yes, I may go — though I don't know what use I shall be when I get there."

"Then why go, Mme. Herne?"

"I'm so tired of Beirut, and waiting and watching."

"Waiting and watching is the occupation of half the world," said Abu Tisein. "Till the land in spring, gather the crop in summer, accept the fact that there is nothing to do for the rest of the year. It is a full life."

"I know, but for us it's such a waste. And I do want to help. I was really useful in the first year of the war."

"Not since?" he asked.

"Not to myself or anyone. My spirit was defeated with the French, I think."

"You puzzle us all, you know."

There was no hint of criticism in his slow voice, but Armande was disappointed. David Nachmias attracted her because she pictured herself as a feminine edition of him — a quiet creature, minding her own business, in whose reserve of strength the world naturally confided. Abu Tisein, however, gave an impression of fine simplicity. Socially, he was not puzzling at all; he was restful.

"It's not my fault," she protested.

"No, no. But — well, why not tell me about yourself?"

"Where shall I start?" she laughed, awkwardly concealing her reluctance.

"At Calinot, for example. I am aware, of course, that you came out to the Middle East with Calinot. How did you get to know him?"

"I've always known him. Before he started to make aeroplanes, he was a good little bourgeois manufacturer of racing bicycles and a friend of the family. He was only a tremendously optimistic financier, you see — and when it came to international contracts and dealing with the Air Ministry and the Treasury he was lost. British officials terrified him. So he took me on as his interpreter. I was a sort of elegant dragoman, really — explaining the ways of the natives and calming them down. In London I was quite important. And here too, at first. We flew out here as soon as France was invaded —

Cairo, Jerusalem, Cyprus, Bagdad, everywhere in three weeks. He was looking for possible factory sites abroad. But when the French surrendered, that was the end. We had to stay in Beirut.

"M. Nachmias, I almost wanted England to make peace, just so that the two countries shouldn't be separated. We couldn't adjust ourselves. Nobody could think of France without England. Then we saw that it wasn't the end of the war at all, and Calinot went back to Paris. He paid me a year's salary in cash, and asked me not to mention it. I never have. That leaves me open to suspicion, but I can't help it. Calinot had no right to pay a British subject so much, and he might have got into serious trouble."

"Why didn't you go to Palestine when he left?" Abu Tisein asked.

"Well, his francs weren't any use in Palestine. He was very French, and didn't think of that. It was humiliating to have to wire home for money. So I just waited. I was certain that the army would declare for Free France, and that then I could be in the war again. They let me wait. They were very good to me. I ought to have been arrested when the German and Italian armistice commissions were here, but I was living quietly in my own flat, and my friends saw that I wasn't bothered. Then when we fought each other in Syria, Loujon had to intern me. A beastly army lorry at dawn, just for me, with an embarrassed sergeant and an Indo-Chinese driver. It seemed so impersonal, so useless, just like shipping that magnificent army off to France — " She shuddered. "And now I am free, too free, with all my old world destroyed, and just beginning to long to make another. So, you see, there isn't any mystery about me at all."

"Not to you, perhaps," he said. "But to the — what shall I say? — uninformed, you are a mysterious character. If you are ambitious, if you want to be used, that is the quality to be used."

"I do want to be used."

"Even if distasteful to . . . you are charmingly fastidious, Madame."

"Even if distasteful."

"Do you think you could fascinate a very distinguished old gentleman? No more. Just fascinate."

"Is he married?"

"No. He is wildly romantic, but most unwilling to permit any interference with his liberty. A wife would destroy too much of him. He is wise enough to know it."

The music stopped. Mme. Nachmias did not return to the table. She led her officer to the bar.

"The high stools, you know," said Abu Tisein apologetically.

"Yes?" laughed Armande.

"Madame is the most sociable of creatures, but she has, like all charming women, her little affectations. One of them is to sit on a high stool in a smart bar. She says always that it reminds her of the Riviera. Myself, I seldom give her the pleasure, for I cannot endure high stools; they are too far from the floor where Allah in his wisdom intended us to sit. But I was telling you about old Sheikh Wadiah."

"Is he very old?"

"Verging on sixty, I think. I call him old from respect and affection. He is always young in heart. You will like him. Of course what I am going to tell you is in the strictest confidence."

Armande nodded, without protesting her discretion. She knew that if David Nachmias chose to add himself to the number of people who talked to her unwisely, he was already sure of her.

"In the Lebanon there are a few families," he began, "who are the hereditary leaders of the Christians. They were the protectors of their people against the Moslem. They still take their responsibilities seriously. The heads of these families are not rich, not politicians — just chieftains of clans, as you would say. None of them can put more than a hundred men into the field, but that is quite enough to deal — in their own mountains — with an old-fashioned party of Moslem raiders.

"Sheikh Wadiah Ghoraib is one of these chieftains. He foresees trouble after the war — who does not? — and he has brought his armaments up to date. This little campaign against the Vichy French was a godsend to him. His clansmen are strong in the hills above the coast road, where the fighting was hardest. They were crawling about the battlefields after dark, collecting weapons.

"Wadiah has been buying, too. When fighting is over, soldiers must relax," said Abu Tisein with patient understanding. "They have reached the limit of endurance. They become careless of their arms. So there are plenty in the market. I have known an Arab enter a tent of tired men, and steal eight rifles from under their blankets without waking one of them.

"Sheikh Wadiah has not been content with rifles. He has acquired a number of Hotchkiss machine guns and Brens. They cannot be left with him, Mme. Herne. When an Arab has machine guns — even if he is a Christian and educated in Paris — his one idea is to use them.

"We cannot force Wadiah to give them up. He will just swear that he has no arms, that it's all a malicious rumor. But I think they might be obtained, quite unofficially — so long, that is, as he got his money back. To put it bluntly, he might sell them. Not to Moslem or French or Jew, but to the British, yes — if the right person approached him."

Abu Tisein paused.

"But why am I the right person?" asked Armande.

"Because he will know of your reputation. Everyone does. Weren't you interned as a British agent? He is strongly pro-British and chivalrous. He will consider your arrival a most delicate attention to him. No moral lectures. No violent methods. Just a charming, mysterious operator with a business offer. I know Sheikh Wadiah. If you cannot succeed, nobody can."

"I'll try, if you think I should be any use," said Armande doubtfully. "But buying and selling arms seems to be the most awful crime. All these military lower their voices when they talk about it — just as if arms trading were something supernatural. Won't Sheikh Wadiah think I am just being used to trap him?"

"He will, at first. But when you have his confidence you can assure him, if you like, that the money will be paid by a British officer in uniform and that British soldiers will collect the arms. That cannot be a crime."

Abu Tisein spoke with a casual air of authority that was convincing. Armande saw that it was stupidity to ask him for his credentials. What would they be? And how in the world would she recognize them? Perhaps there were signs and countersigns that would identify him, but not to her. All he could do, if questioned, would be to refer her to some third person; and, so far as that was of value, she could find a third person of her own choosing.

It was, when you came to think of it, obvious that a new civilian recruit for any form of Intelligence must be picked up very much as she had been — watched, tested in many little conversations, and then told the minimum it was essential to know for the job in hand. The relationship was, in essence, intuitive and aesthetic. Character spoke to character. Vague, certainly — but, after all, the way in which real confidence between two human beings, and especially between a man and a woman, was offered, was accepted and grew.

She had never asked Loujon by what right he interrogated and interned her. It was obvious by his manner and authority that he had such a right. Nevertheless it seemed an elementary precaution to ask whether rumor was fact, and David Nachmias was indeed trusted by the British. She suspected that her hotel acquaintances would not know, but would never — least of all the senior officers — admit to a woman that they did not know. Sergeant Prayle, for all the convulsive leaps of his mind, seemed a likely person to give her an honest answer.

For two days Armande failed to find him haunting, as was his custom, the hotel desk and vestibule. She discovered him one morning when, leaning far out over her balcony to see what had happened to a pair of stockings hung out to dry and carried off by the wind, she caught sight of a corner of the service entrance. Sergeant Prayle was sitting on the steps, teaching the tiniest of the Lebanese page boys how to make a catapult.

She went down, and walked around the lower terrace of the hotel. Screams of orders, of protest and of conversation issued from the kitchens, together with a powerful but appetizing smell of onions melting in a casserole. Sergeant Prayle and the page boy were discussing the treatment and use of elastic from the inside of an old golf ball. They spoke in soldier's Arabic and Sergeant Prayle's French, and appeared to understand one another perfectly.

The page boy fled through the service entrance and was swallowed up by the chaos within. Sergeant Prayle remained seated on the greasy top step. With a wave of his hand he offered the remaining length of it to Armande. She compromised by leaning against the balustrade where her head was level with his.

"You'll get him sacked," said Armande.

"Poor little devil!" he answered with a note of real pity and indignation in his voice.

"Why? He seems to enjoy himself."

"That's why. There he is — at his age! — always smiling just as the customers expect. Hell, I say! It isn't right. One ping with that catapult on the headwaiter carrying a pile of plates, and he'll have a memory that will comfort him all his life."

"You will, you mean. It's not fair."

"He will. An egg or a good squashy tomato — most people would feel better for the rest of their lives if they really did throw one. You would, too. In spite of Kensington."

"I should always think of the person at the receiving end," Armande retorted.

"Ah, but the target must be worthy. A social pest like a cinema organist, or a pest in his own right like a politician. But you have no indignation."

"I have a great deal," replied Armande warmly. "I hate injustice, and I do what I can."

"All subscriptions to Mrs. Herne. Light refreshments at 10 P.M. Lord Tripe and Onions will say a few words — if sober. No, no! You need a barrel of eggs in the hall."

"I wish you wouldn't always put me on the defensive," said Armande, smiling at him. "You'll never get the best out of people that way."

"I might get the worst. But you've forgotten what your worst is like. Whom are you looking for, Mrs. Herne, me or the page boy?"

"You."

The sergeant's expression returned to that kindliness with which he had regarded the Arab child in buttons. When his eyes were merry, they were so intelligent. Armande felt regret that she could not like him. It was impossible — or not, perhaps, impossible, but he made it so coarsely and unnecessarily difficult.

"Any trouble?" he asked.

"I want some information. On a person — if you are allowed to give it me."

"We'll stretch a point, anyway. Whom do you want to know about?"

"David Nachmias."

"Old Abu Tisein? Thanked by generals. O.B.E. when there's a handout. Why?"

"Is he really working for you?"

"For us? Good Lord, no!" he exclaimed. "We don't deal in big bugs like him. But he has certainly worked for other departments. During the campaign he used to go in and out of Syria just as he liked, and bring home the bacon every time. He's trusted, and no secret about it. But — be careful, won't you?"

"It's just that he offered me some letters of introduction to Arabs," Armande prevaricated.

"Then you're in luck. They respect him. Let me know what you're up to."

"I will of course," Armande answered conventionally. "Why do they call him Abu Tisein?"

"It means Father of Two Buttocks. Arabic dual. Not two complete bottoms, you see, but both stout cheeks."

Armande disliked the relish with which he gave her the translation, and made no comment. How lightly and amus ingly any of her French friends could have explained these Arab subtleties of anatomy! Sergeant Prayle's deep voice sounded so vulgar.

Under a screen of polite thanks she drifted with Prayle back to the hotel lobby, hoping that she did not show her disapproval, wondering indeed why she bothered to disapprove. His blotched, untidy face, his impossible clothes, were all so uninviting. It was no fault of his own, of course, but he was one of those people who simply had to stick to the rules in order to be tolerated.

CHAPTER II

Prayle

SERGEANT PRAYLE wished that he could express his thoughts to society, but was aware that he could not even express them to himself. He knew that he was by nature as inquisitive as an old hen. Over religion, philosophy and all abstract exercises of the spirit he brooded quietly with no expectation of hatching more than ingenious fantasy; but at the fatness of human nature he would peck eagerly, watching this way and that for the motive under the action, scratching up emotion to discover truth. In the presence of another person he could not be bored, but his satisfaction was, he feared, entirely personal and therefore futile.

He had been transferred from the Yeomanry to Field Security because he spoke French. He spoke it fluently and grammatically, but as if its consonants and vowels were those of his own language. This almost unintelligible accent, above all when employed in idiomatic profanity, greatly endeared him to the French, who considered him less suspiciously bilingual than his colleagues. His Field Security Section had taken him to France, and his own ability to extract anything out of the masses, from chickens to a horse and cart, had taken the section out again through Dunkirk and had advanced him to the rank of sergeant. Soon after his return he had been posted to the Middle East. His section spent an agitated winter up and down the Western Desert, and in the summer of 1941 were moved into the Lebanon to clean up after the campaign.

Sergeant Prayle was still hopelessly lost among the customs and political currents of the Middle East, and knew it; but he was stimulated by the freedom of his job. In England, Field Security had been overborne by the easy stupidity of the military police and the heavy intelligence of the civil. In the Middle East, they knew themselves to be few and to be trusted. Between the sections, the officers and N.C.O.s there was the unconscious confidence of a first-class club. Their mutual loyalty was far beyond that of a secret service; it was that of a secret society. Corps, divisional and area commanders were divided between admiration of Field Security morale, and disgust that it in no way depended on their own orders and personalities.

Prayle's section were housed in a billet of their own choosing, which stood, fifty yards from the coast road, at the end of the blind alley behind a grocer's shop. It was a convenient pull-in for the detachments of Field Security who passed up and down the road from Mersa Matruh to the control posts on the Turkish frontier. Little brown convoys of thirteen motorcycles and a fifteen-hundredweight truck, piled high with the baggage of the N.C.O.s and the section officer, would often park in the yard, and the men, ruddy and fresh from England or brown and disillusioned as the Arabs with whom they had long mixed, would stay a short night in the billet, full of carefully controlled excitement at their movement from one historic station to another. Sometimes a lone sergeant roared importantly down the alley, himself and his motorcycle crusted with coastal dust or mountain mud, and emerged from his wrappings into the bar as a fairly presentable young man; sometimes a shabby individual, dismounting from the nearest tramcar, carried his seedy suitcase through the yard, to be hailed by his nickname and asked whether he had yet forgotten his English.

All these comings and goings spread before Prayle a banquet of curious motives and contradictory characters such as civil life could never provide. He had a sardonic dislike of pretensions, which attracted him to human nature in the raw. Yet, in his own ideals, he was romantic. He tended to seek out and mother the disreputable, fascinated by the scrupulous honesty of those from whom no honesty could be expected — for moral shabbiness, if they were to mix successfully with the dregs of the population, had to be in their very souls.

The sergeant was grossly overworked, and never more content in his life. He spent the mornings checking the arrivals of strangers at the Beirut hotels, their reasons for departure and their reasons for remaining. His afternoons — since he was a competent shorthand writer in French and English — were devoted to taking notes of Captain Furney's interrogations.

In the world of peace Furney had been a don. Prayle, who from childhood had a contempt for the academic mind, was surprised to find him intelligent and, in his comments on their daily grind, irresponsibly amusing. Furney had a passion for minor originalities. His face was precise, and when he wore civilian clothes he looked — perhaps in personal protest against the general bagginess of his educational past — like a successful city accountant; when he wore uniform, it was with eccentric ornaments of his own. Instead of spectacles he bore upon his nose a pair of gold pince-nez retained by a khaki ribbon, and infuriated generals by stretching a gold watch chain from pocket to pocket of his open shirt.

Sergeant Prayle and Captain Furney particularly enjoyed their evening sessions with Loujon. Major Loujon was not remaining till the last boat from choice. He was not, officially, under arrest, but his departure was delayed until he had been sucked dry of information. No sucking, indeed, had been necessary. Facts and opinions sometimes flowed from Loujon as fast as Prayle could sweep a full notebook onto the floor and start another. As a subject for interrogation Loujon was sympathetic. He considered the British the most entertaining of all barbarians and he hated the Boche as only a Frenchman could. Since for a short period he had worked at the same table with an officer of the Gestapo, he was an unmatched source of news from vanished Europe. He had a comforting contempt for the Gestapo; to be a successful security man, he pointed out, demanded tact and mature judgment — two qualities rare in human beings and especially rare in Germans.

The interviews were awkward and unproductive when Captain Montagne of the Free French Forces was present. Montagne considered himself Loujon's successor. The British had no doubt at all that Furney was Loujon's successor. Nevertheless a reasonable courtesy had to be shown to the French, and Montagne had every right to attend, if he wished, at all interviews with the Vichy major. What might have been a friendly and productive chat, ranging over the personalities of the Middle East and refreshed by supplies from Furney's row of bottles, then became a formal and acrimonious triangle.

Loujon and Montagne never spoke to each other except in the presence of a British officer. Prayle watched their faces as they sat opposite to him, one at each corner of Furney's blanket-covered trestle table. Civil war, he thought, gave the participants a sense of guilt unknown to national war; there was not between enemies even the formal code of military courtesy.

In civil war was a man's conscience, ever, wholly at ease? Loujon had obeyed the orders of his government as a good professional soldier, but he must feel bitterly doubtful whether his sense of duty was not cowardly and mistaken. Montagne had given up home and country to continue the fight with the Boche, yet, face to face with officers who had remained loyal to their legal government, he must sometimes wonder whether he was not a dishonorable outlaw.

That evening Montagne was full of complaints. He made it clear to Furney that reasonable courtesy was not enough: that the political quality which the British called tact, the Free French called hypocrisy. His very appearance was a repudiation of all compromise. Like many of the gallant band who had made their way from West Africa to the Middle East, he had a habit of wearing field boots with his pale khaki shorts. In this odd rig, topped by a blue infantry kepi, he resembled a consumptive lion tamer, worn and embittered.

"You English," said Montagne with a pathetic earnestness that revealed his liking for Furney as much as his dislike for Furney's government, "have always been impossible to your allies and too gentle to your enemies."

"Since for most of our history we were enemies, you shouldn't complain of that," Furney answered.

Loujon laughed. He snapped and swallowed a jest like a hungry fish.

Prayle, sitting at his table with poised pencil, could see that Furney was annoyed with himself. He had not avoided repartee, as a correct and neutral British officer should. Montagne, who had no sense of humor whatever, had been placed at a disadvantage.

General Orders, which Prayle seized upon when they arrived weekly in the office and read with ironical delight, pompously and frequently enjoined politeness to allies; they had not said anything about politeness to the Vichy or any other enemy. Probably G.H.Q. considered such a reminder unnecessary. Montagne was right.

Both Prayle and Furney preferred the Vichy officers to the Free French, although, temperamentally, they were in sympathy with the latter. This worried the sergeant's curiosity until he found a surface explanation. The Vichy staff were efficient, wise and courteous. Though they had just fought a war against their former allies and lost it into the bargain, they had no feeling of inferiority. The Free French, who had been on the winning side and now had the rich pickings of Syria and the Lebanon, were uncertain of their standing and aggressive.

"This officer," Montagne stormed, "locked up all the Front Populaire. Yet you put faith in his list of suspects!"

"He was a little hard on all the pro-British. I admit it," replied Furney with a twinkle in his eyes which either Frenchman could take for himself. "But what else could he do?"

"Get on with the war — the right war."

"Of course. Major Loujon knows that I think his attitude was mistaken. But all the same his lists may be of value."

"I don't believe a word of them," said Montagne bluntly.

Loujon leaned back in his chair and threw out his hands in a gesture of patronizing geniality which was intended to be and was exasperating to Montagne.

"But why not? Major Loujon has collaborated perfectly."

"He is at least accustomed to it," Montagne retorted.

"If," Loujon remarked quietly, "I treated the Armistice Commission correctly, it was to save my country from the disasters that a pack of worthless adventurers will bring upon her for the sake of their own ambitions."

"You describe my general as a worthless adventurer?" asked Montagne, jumping up.

Sergeant Prayle with a pretended start at Montagne's vehemence swept half Furney's papers onto the floor. With incoherent excuses for his clumsiness he scrambled for them under the table, joined immediately by Loujon and, after hesitation, by Montagne.

"Herring, sir. Red," gabbled Prayle, without interrupting his apologies.

Vichy and Free France resumed their seats and glared at Sergeant Prayle. In his ill-fitting civilian clothes he looked both sinister and raffish — the sort of hanger-on one might see in the vestibule of any secret police office.

"Major Loujon's lists. Yes, Major Loujon's lists," murmured Furney, as if trying to remember what they had been talking about, and thereby depriving the lists of all importance, or at least of enough importance for the loss of tempers. "Well, some of his suspects are Axis sympathizers whom he had to release after July 1940. He advises us to pick them up again, and we will. Some are just ladies and gentlemen who are likely to be a nuisance. I see he has included, with admirable neutrality, all White Russians and all communists."

"And with reason!" declared Loujon stoutly. "If there were no Russians, a security officer would have time to amuse himself."

"Fascist!" hissed Montagne.

Loujon shrugged his shoulders and smiled patiently to imply that nothing whatever could be done with such people.

"And some," Furney went on, "are just persons whose source of income is unknown."

"Since when is it a crime to be poor in the French Empire?" asked Montagne.

"*Voyons!* Show a little intelligence! These are all people

living comfortably," replied Loujon, addressing Montagne directly for the first time. "In some of the cases," he added delicately, "perhaps Captain Furney will be able to explain the source of income."

"For example?" asked Furney, smiling.

"For example, Armande Herne."

"No. I don't think she ever worked for us. In fact I thought she had Vichy sympathies. She's a perfectly respectable citizen of London who came out here as secretary to Calinot. What does she look like?"

"You must have seen her at the hotel. An elegant young woman with big eyes in a small face."

"Pretty?"

"Exquisite rather than pretty," said Loujon, warming to the congenial task of finding the right words to describe Armande. "I know her well, since it was my regrettable duty to intern her. There are, you know, women who do not flower till thirty. I think, my dear Captain, she is one of them, for she is not yet a whole person. She has intensity of soul, and with it — detachment. I have known such a combination in Orientals; men, of course. But in a desirable young woman the combination is incongruous. I do not doubt that her intensity is real. I therefore think that her detachment is assumed. And since one can have no delicacy in this disgusting trade, I seek a reason. It may be that she is lost, directionless, and standing still while the world goes by her."

Sergeant Prayle agreed with this description, but found it unnecessarily complex. Intensity, yes. In any moment of interest and excitement, Armande seemed to flash out of the frame; then the black and white of her little head, the nervous outline of her body, were sheer loveliness. The frame? She always had a frame. She had a mothlike quality of merging into her background, especially in a half-light. Her gestures and movements were so swift and quiet.

For more than a month he had watched her in the hotel, at first with mild professional curiosity, then with fascinated interest. He imagined for her a character capable of passionate loyalty and love — though she certainly had no outlet for either in Beirut. On the other hand, if he rejected (which he didn't) his own romantic insight and judged her on her behavior at their first interview and several casual meetings since, there wasn't any fire in her at all. In fact she was too bloody well brought up. Or, as Loujon more prettily put it, she was standing still while the world went by her.

Then why should he feel such overwhelming pity for her? Why, instead of resenting her patronizing airs, should he so long to bring her to life? Loujon, with his French genius for destroying a thing understood by trying to put it into words, had merely deepened mystery. And she wasn't mysterious in any policeman's sense of the word. She was nobody's agent. She was simply the hell of a long way from home like the rest of them, with no one to look after her and nothing much but her own pride to take the place of a commanding officer. That she was puzzling, that she wouldn't ever do the obvious thing, that she was too conceited to do the obvious thing were no reasons for withholding pity. After all, he himself seldom took the course that was obvious to others.

Prayle chuckled aloud, and earned a gratified glance from the Vichy major. But the cause of his amusement was no subtlety of Loujon's. He had suddenly realized that if Mr. Prayle had been a civilian in Beirut his character would assuredly have made him highly suspect to security men.

"Had you anything against Mrs. Herne, except that she was British?" Furney asked Loujon.

"Nothing. But such a woman is dangerous in war. She knows too much. Every young officer confides in her. And then she stayed on here for no reason."

"There was no charming Frenchman?"

"No. Her reputation is depressingly good. Sentimental friendships, but nothing more."

"I know her well," said Montagne positively. "A woman like that is sufficiently stimulated by sentiment. She is decadent."

"Decadent," murmured Loujon. "All our glorious eighteenth century condemned in a word!"

"What the devil has she to do with the eighteenth century?" Montagne asked almost cordially, forgetting his enmity in the excitement of the chase for definition.

"It was the age of the sentimental friendship," said Loujon. "But accept my excuses. I forgot that for the Free French our history begins with Karl Marx."

"*Ah, ça!* As if you did not know that our Movement is lousy with clericals and monarchists!"

"True? Well, we shall see. Meanwhile I permit myself to observe to my interrogators that it is the hour of the *apéritif.*"

Sergeant Prayle hastened to provide whisky and soda. He had noticed that in English company all Frenchmen looked forward to whisky. They drank it with a rapturous sense of adventure, as if it were some exotic toddy from palm or cactus, and were politely astonished at its excellence; it was to them a traveler's wonder of the world that a northern nation, so far from the civilizing influence of the grape, should have taken the trouble to mature its alcohol.

Loujon mellowed more rapidly than in calmer days when he had not been living on his nerves in tactfully concealed detention.

"And now," he exclaimed with his second glass, "*vive l'Angleterre,* the greatest enemy and greatest ally of the French!"

"But never again your enemy," Furney protested.

"Now and eternally our dear enemy! Without France and England there can be no Europe. And since they are complementary to each other, they must never think alike. They are passionate lovers, my captain, who do not understand each other. In the clear light of day they quarrel, but when night comes down on Europe they cling together. You must be gentle to the English," he added directly to Montagne.

"And if they are not gentle to me?"

"My dear young revolutionary, I knew them when still you wetted your red pants. They are sensitive. They are tortured by conscience. They have never got used to their empire, for they have no tradition of Rome. In their hearts they consider empire as immorality. So when you ask me what to do if the English are not gentle, I remind you that you always hold a trump — and that is to threaten a situation where they may have to shoot some natives. Well, you say, they will shoot them, and so what? No! The English will do anything rather than shoot natives. They will perform the most amazing gyrations of policy. Be frank with them, my little Jacobin, but take care to have the means of troubling their conscience."

"They have no conscience," said Montagne calmly, changing the burned-out stub of his cigarette from one corner of his lip to the other. "What of the money paid to our politicians?"

"Speaking as an old security officer with a passion for reading the dossiers of politicians," answered Loujon, "I doubt if they have paid a centime in the last fifty years. It is curious, but the English are the last people left in Europe who believe that a politician has a sense of honor."

"Hope," said Prayle, admitted to equality by the whisky in front of him. "Not belief."

"My sergeant, with you it is the same. That is why you win wars. I do not think you can win this one, and if you do you will be finished as a nation. But you, you will die slowly."

There was the finality of unanswerable truth in Loujon's words. They seemed to invoke a vision of the natural, gradual decay of every individual in the exhausted state. No one replied. Prayle, before he could cast the prophecy out of his mind, had the sensation, as in action, of nerving himself against all manner of unpleasantness.

"What will you do after the war, *mon commandant?*" Furney inquired.

"If you win it?"

"Yes."

"Ask Captain Montagne."

Montagne looked at his boots, and did not reply.

"Death? Or ten years in a fortress? Or will they perhaps forget me if I retire and cultivate my garden? I have only been important here, and they will have much else to think of. But it is certain you will hear no more of Loujon. He is the end of an epoch. He obeyed his government without bothering about its color. God knows to what the rest of you will be loyal."

CHAPTER III

The High Places

BEIT CHABAB was outside the range and interest of troops. The track, which zigzagged up for a thousand feet, through scrub and dwarf oaks, from the bottom of a gorge, led to the village and nowhere else. Beit Chabab lay along the crest of a ridge that pointed seawards from the watershed of Lebanon and ended in a bold wedge-shaped bluff on which stood the white church and squat tower of the Maronites. At the eastern end of the ridge was a Greek Orthodox monastery, its low domes just showing above powerful walls. Wall of Catholic and wall of Greek were joined together by a line of low cliffs, overhung by the rough, wooden balconies of houses. To the traveler gazing upwards from the gorge, so much rock and masonry gave the impression of a medieval town compactly built for defense.

Beit Chabab, however, was anything but compact — a tribute to the peace of the mountains under French rule. On the top of the ridge, among scattered pines, tiny single-storied stone villas were set wherever a pocket of soil among the rocks lent itself to the creation of orchard and vineyard. The village street itself straggled for half a mile along the side of the ridge, flanked by a few houses of great age, by shops of rough timber and corrugated iron, by Roman buttresses and foundations which continued to support whatever ramshackle buildings succeeded one another through the centuries.

The only house in the street which appeared to have been built at one period and from a single source of material was the inn. It was a simple, one-storied block, set around three sides of a red-tiled terrace, high above the road and approached by a flight of steps. Tall, arched windows gave it a commodious and solid demeanor. The massive platform held it firmly in the mountain air, safe from the chickens, pigs and children who fed and scrambled on the dusty cobbles of the street.

In time of peace the inn had been the favorite summer resort of a few French families, attracted by its silence and its cheapness. Even in 1941 Armande's primitive room and three good meals cost her only some five shillings a day. Nothing was clean but the red tiles which covered the floors of rooms and terrace alike, and were proudly scrubbed every morning by a Lebanese Cinderella, twelve years old and already mature beneath her rags. Beds, wardrobes and chests of drawers held deep pockets of black dust in their old-fashioned curves and moldings.

Armande's aversion was overcome by her sense of adventure. An occasional bug could not be allowed to interfere with the equanimity of a secret agent. If sleep were too soon ended, she stood at the great window of her room and watched the sunrise come raiding over the high passes from Damascus and scatter through the valleys to the luminous sea.

When insect life and her initial horror had somewhat abated, she was extremely comfortable. The only other visitors at the inn were a Rumanian cabaret girl and her mother who lived quietly and cautiously in the hope that no one would think it worth while to intern them. The innkeeper, Anton Ghoraib, a humble member of Sheikh Wadiah's clan, treated all three of his guests with generous hospitality. Armande doubted if he could possibly be making a profit, and determined to ask

David Nachmias whether Anton would be reimbursed by
Sheikh Wadiah (for whose honor she was being overfed) or
whether she herself should give him a lordly and Oriental
present.

Sheikh Wadiah Ghoraib paid a formal call at the inn the
day after Armande's arrival, driven in the village car — an
immense Renault which was used for weddings, funerals and
the more important movements of the chieftain. A rider followed the car, his mount, his tarboosh and his Turkish breeches
of neat gray cloth showing him to be a retainer of consequence.
He was Fouad, Wadiah's major-domo. Two humbler retainers, with black scarves round their heads and dusty black cotton
trousers, detached themselves from a near-by café and squatted against the wall of the inn as soon as Wadiah had entered.
The car and its owner-driver, the horse and its rider, the two
poor relations, remained at the foot of the steps in dignified
idleness, supporting by the mere fact of their presence the
prestige of Sheikh Wadiah in Beit Chabab.

As Wadiah Ghoraib mounted the steps to the terrace, Armande had no doubt who he was; there could be no other
person of such distinction in the neighborhood. He was decently dressed in black, like any comfortable French bourgeois,
with a resplendent watch chain across his sleek waistcoat. His
face was round and of a healthy red. His blue eyes twinkled
between the waxed points of a fair and lusty handlebar mustache. Except for the red tarboosh he might have been a prosperous East Anglian auctioneer. So must have looked his crusader ancestors, she thought, when they retired from carving
up Mohammedans and settled down beside the ex-enemy as
landowners and boon companions.

Anton Ghoraib strode up to the head of his clan with a more
manly and independent approach than he ever allowed himself

towards his guests, and then, with a surprising gesture, bent to catch and kiss Sheikh Wadiah's hand. Wadiah swiftly and gracefully prevented him, his face expressing protest and astonishment. Armande assumed that the innkeeper's greeting must be quite exceptional; it turned out, however, to be normal. Sheikh Wadiah's little feudal tableaux never lost their air of spontaneity.

Wadiah introduced himself in perfect French, and, after Armande's conventional responses, launched himself upon a flowery address which nicely balanced the compliments due to an attractive woman and the habitual tributes due to an inscrutable and possibly dangerous visiting pasha. To the limit of informal eloquence he expressed the loyalty of himself, of all his people and indeed of all the Christian Lebanon to the great British Empire.

"When I heard from our friend, M. Nachmias, that you were coming," he added, "I wished to place at your disposal a house of your own with women to wait on you. But would that, I wonder, be *convenable*? You must forgive us, Madame, if in our mountains we have forgotten the finer points of European delicacy. So, till I hear your wishes, I have ordered my good Anton Ghoraib to look after you. If you do not care for Lebanese dishes he will give you French, and if you do not care for French he will give you English. Anton!" he called. "Were you not taught to make an English plum pudding?"

"Yes, Sheikh Wadiah," said Anton, appearing instantly upon his terrace.

"Then you will give Madame a plum pudding every day. And whisky. You will give her all the whisky she requires."

Armande did not like to seem boorish by limiting the quantity of plum puddings — that could be done later in private conversation with Anton — but she felt compelled to enter a mild protest against whisky.

"I am half French, you know, Sheikh Wadiah," she said. "I drink a little wine, and that is all."

"Anton," Wadiah ordered, "you will obtain some of the Archimandrite's wine from Mlle. Pitescu. And, Anton, Mlle. Pitescu must move elsewhere."

"Oh, no!" Armande entreated. "She is such a lovely thing. I like to look at her."

"That, Madame, is truly Parisian! You have a delicacy of thought which one misses in our women of the Lebanon. I must admit that I also like to look at her — as an old man, with benevolent interest, may observe the moon even in the presence of the midday sun."

"When a man is beyond doubt a man," replied Armande, plunging boldly into the Arabian Nights, "even a — a heavenly body forgets his age."

"Charming, Madame!" Sheikh Wadiah chuckled, giving a gallant twist to the ends of his mustache. "Charming! That does not belong to Europe at all. Do you not speak Arabic?"

"Not a word, I am afraid."

"You must learn. Arabic is the language for a witty woman. I was educated in France and I speak French, they tell me, like a Frenchman; yet I assure you there is no language to be compared with Arabic. You can express a shade of meaning so tenuous —" he held up finger and thumb before his eye as if they contained a microscopic gem — "or beat your phrases with a hammer out of molten thought. Arabic! I adore my language! The Moslem, Madame, does not understand the richness of his own tongue. It is too free for his narrow mind. He is limited by his religion. To speak Arabic one must be a Christian. For the generous spirit that enters a man with

— 52 —

good wine, Madame, there is only Arabic — for the verse, the eloquence, the flowers of speech which spring into his head. It is the language of the arrow that pierces the target, and the arrow that flies towards the sun. And believe me, Madame, the sententious arrows that the Moslem launches from his cups of water fly very little way."

Armande responded to enthusiasm. She found herself liking Sheikh Wadiah, and felt a tinge of regret that their relationship was founded on insincerity. She had feared that her victim would be distasteful to her, and deliberate fascination that much the harder; it was now evident that the obstacle to duty would not be his manners or appearance, but her own conscience.

"Will you teach me Arabic?" she asked.

"Willingly, Madame, if you stay here. But I do not think that in wartime you will remain long with us at Beit Chabab."

Such a response to the invitation of her eyes was unexpected. Wadiah had warned her that he was not a child, and that he knew perfectly well she had come to his village for a definite object. His reference to wartime, however, was comforting; it suggested that he had picked up whatever rumors had been laid out for him, and that he did not question her bona fides.

Sheikh Wadiah transferred his whole interest and attention from Mlle. Pitescu to Armande. This, she decided, was due to the romance of her reputation rather than her looks, for Floarea Pitescu had a warm classical beauty with which, on the basis of sheer appeal to the senses, there could not be any competition. Floarea herself showed no jealousy; indeed she welcomed Armande's influence. She frankly admitted that she was under the temporary and most discreet protection of the Archimandrite of Tarsus and Philadelphia, chief drone of the local Orthodox monastery, and that she had no desire to draw attention to herself by becoming involved with a prominent Lebanese.

"The Church," explained Floarea apologetically, "is in no way exigent. He is very mild, my Archimandrite."

"But — but too hairy," Armande protested.

She was shocked at herself for taking anything but a passive part in so intimate a discussion; yet the Archimandrite's hair and beard, ritually uncut, were of such an uninviting luxuriance that they compelled remark.

"My dear, he takes a lot more care of it than we can." Floarea shook back her auburn hair, which was badly in need of a wave and had returned to its original black at the roots. "I tell him that he must lend me his monk."

"He has a monk to do it?"

"I'm sure he has. He swears he does it all himself. But do you believe it? All those corkscrew curls down to his shoulders? He's a dear Archimandrite, all the same," said Floarea sentimentally.

Armande found it hard to admit that any woman whom she liked — and she liked, was interested by, Floarea — could be indifferent to her paramour. Some reserve, even some self-deception, might be demanded by good taste, but the emotions had to be involved. She saw the relationship between this glorious girl and an Arab ecclesiastic as tragedy. Since it could end neither in marriage nor in any real companionship, it must lead to pain and frustration. Thus, being five years older than Floarea, Armande felt protective, and probed tactfully to see if there were a wound of any depth.

"Will you be able to see him often when you leave Beit Chabab?" she asked.

"But he belongs here. And I — to the world," answered

Floarea wonderingly. "It's most unlikely we shall ever meet again."

Her tone completely excluded the possibility of any suffering.

"I want to be a great dancer, and I shall," she went on, trying with her slow, lovely smile to thaw Armande's frozen expression. "I *can* love, my dear, but Mama says not yet."

"Your mother —" began Armande severely.

"She is not my mother really. I just call her Mama. Romanova is my teacher. But for the public we are mother and daughter, and in our hearts."

To Armande, Romanova was a rotten old woman — a retired dancer who gave herself all the airs of a former star of the Imperial Russian Ballet, but in fact was neither Russian nor had ever risen higher in her profession than the cabarets of Balkan capitals. She was, on Floarea's admission, nearly a procuress; at any rate she shared any funds her so-called daughter might acquire. She was plastered with layers of dirty powder, and she gave the impression of spending all her leisure in an unmade bed. All that could be said in Romanova's favor was that she trained Floarea industriously and with faith. For three hours a day she hammered on the evilly resonant piano in Anton Ghoraib's empty winter dining room and bullied her pupil until the pair were mutually exasperated, the sweat shining on Floarea's clear skin and forming a pale mud in Romanova's wrinkles. To Armande dancing was a pure art which she loved and once had practiced with the jealousy of the amateur. The professionalism of cabaret seemed to her vulgarity. Romanova was developing Floarea into an acrobat, not a dancer — and all against the girl's natural instinct for smoothness and grace upon the points.

Even dislike of this Romanova was, however, positive. Armande had lived a year without caring enough to dislike anyone. The mountain air after the sticky heat of Beirut, the sense of useful adventure, the society of two such original characters as Sheikh Wadiah Ghoraib and Floarea Pitescu, snatched her in a week out of the miasma of depression. From mere watching and waiting — which might be virtue for Abu Tisein's casual Orientals, but for her was shameful — she had returned to the enthusiastic activity of the European. The grapevine of rumor had it that she was recuperating from the agonies of internment. In a sense that was true.

Sheikh Wadiah was continually and delightfully gallant, but showed no signs of falling in love. She suspected that he was explaining both her and himself in terms of the novels of the Second Empire which he had read in youth. He considered her, as indeed she liked to be considered, a brilliantly intellectual woman, and evidently felt himself to be at last the intimate of a creature of salons, of international society, of discreet political power. Fascinated he certainly was, but by a romance and a legend that he himself had supplied.

Day after day she talked politics with Wadiah, or rode or lunched with him — when he had gathered together enough Christian notables of the district to do honor to them, to her and to his house. She dreaded these lunches beforehand, found them an interminable effort for the first half hour and ended by enjoying herself.

Wadiah's house was an old, untidy building on the main street, presenting, like the inn, a massive and windowless lower story to the road, within which were the stables and storehouses. On the first floor was a tiled entrance hall, thirty feet square, empty except for a long upholstered bench, like that of a theater foyer, across the far end, and half a dozen plain chairs just inside the front door; on these was seated, under the command of a gloriously sashed and trousered Fouad, an ever-changing group of Wadiah's humbler retainers, whose only duty was to rise at the approach of a guest and exclaim their welcome and compliments.

Wadiah met her at the foot of the steps, and ushered her past the gesticulating retainers into the summer sitting room. There would be gathered some eight or ten of his rivals, friends or relations with their wives and daughters. The men were intolerably polite; the women drearily arch, all pretty, all badly and heavily painted. They sat on furniture of the eighties, covered with red plush and cushioned in imitation leopard skin. Tinted photographs of Sheikh Wadiah's parents and uncles stared from the wall in blank disapproval whenever a sentiment was expressed or a response returned which might not be in accord with books of etiquette. Armande, replying brightly to the conventional questions of the women and the tiresome gallantry of the men, felt, to her furious annoyance, like a lady of fashion who had been asked to tea by her former cook.

The chatter lasted half an hour: a desert of time wherein only coffee was served. Then Sheikh Wadiah would give his mustaches a purposeful twist and lead his party across the hall for lunch. The appearance of the table was enough to raise Armande's spirits. The only vice that remained with her, conscious and admitted, from early days was greed. She could and, in London, often did make do with a diet suited to her soulful eyes and ethereal body, but the Frenchwoman in her frankly liked its lunch.

Sheikh Wadiah's table was always decorated with a vast cold fish at one end, and a variety of Oriental creams and salads at the other. When those had been eaten, the main dishes were all placed on the table simultaneously: chickens, pigeons, crisp *Koubbé* made of meat and pine cones, a whole sucking pig or lamb. The men and their wives sipped araq, their daughters, water; but for Armande and himself and any guest who was interested Sheikh Wadiah produced a specially selected local wine. This he would set on the table with a small speech of introduction, deprecating its quality in comparison with the wines of France, but giving the history of the vineyard or shop or family where he had discovered it.

Under the influence of Sheikh Wadiah's beaming face and of the pleasures his table offered to eye and palate, society manners began to fall away. Men and women forgot to speak their stilted French and settled to the laughing, exaggerated Arabic. Even their daughters occasionally squeaked what they thought rather than what they ought to think. Questioning of Armande became outrageously personal, but merry and sincere. She felt that she was liked and that approval of the lone European woman was no longer merely the admiration accorded to some new arrival at the zoo.

It shocked her that all Sheikh Wadiah's circle should hate the French. They sensed the French contempt for them, and they responded. They were like the Indians, she supposed. (Oh Lord, those arguments with John in Kensington!) The British had given to India justice, the principles of democracy and the means of independence, yet they were hated as a ruling and superior race. In Syria and the Lebanon the same gifts had been dutifully delivered by the French, with rather less of justice and a deal more of the arts of living, yet hardly was there a Lebanese who did not accuse them of selfishness and chicanery. The Christians were all loud in praises of the British, even of British rule in Palestine. They laid their hands upon their hearts, and desired Armande to accept the Lebanon as a crown colony.

Since she was a person of supposed importance, Wadiah's

friends pestered her with small requests — a job for a nephew, a box of sporting cartridges, a minor army contract, even a witness of standing to swear in the Beirut courts that a smuggling Ghoraib had been somewhere where he was not. These importunate demands, confidentially and with much earnest gesticulation brought to her notice at a first meeting with some fawning Lebanese, would have disgusted had not David Nachmias warned her that the granting of minor boons was the very warp and woof of Eastern life, and that she should always, as a matter of politeness, promise to do her best for the applicant; if she really attempted to fulfill one in five of her promises, he said, her credit would stand high. Apologetically she passed on the requests to Nachmias, and was amazed to hear from the gratified suppliants that some had been granted with Western promptitude. The nephew got a job in the customs. The Ghoraib's case was dropped before it ever came to court. Beit Chabab was at her feet.

Wadiah himself asked nothing — possibly arranging through his guests and clients, so that his own dignity remained unimpaired, for the small change of Ghoraib requirements. He stayed within his part of benevolent aristocrat, ready to confer any favor in his domain. Indeed it was more than a part; it was an ideal to which, within the limitations of unavoidable intrigue, he tried to live. Armande waited for her moment, not without impatience, knowing that sooner or later it would arrive.

Sheikh Wadiah was a frequent visitor at the inn, calling to keep an eye upon Anton's activities and menus, or sitting for a while with Armande whenever he fetched her or brought her home. On these visits he never moved from the terrace, so that the inhabitants of Beit Chabab, whatever cheerful lies they might invent, should have no open evidence for scandal. Once

— 59 —

Armande formally invited him to lunch, and after long consultation with Anton produced a meal that was a marvel of delicacy in its marriage of French and Arab cooking; but at the end of the week no bill was presented to her. Wadiah had unobtrusively settled the reckoning.

It was disappointing to take so much trouble, and then to find that as a weak woman she was not allowed to pay. The following week she circumvented the hospitable plots of the Ghoraibs by ordering French champagne and sweetmeats from Beirut, and leaving only the insignificant sandwiches to Anton. To her party, as ever on the terrace, she invited Wadiah and a picturesque bachelor cousin who was a captain of Levant irregulars, Floarea Pitescu, her Archimandrite and the Romanova.

The September dusk in Beit Chabab was still warm as an exceptional English summer evening, and silent save for the murmur of voices in the street and the rushing of the stream through its gorge a thousand feet below. In such a setting she knew that she need no longer accept Floarea as simply *hors concours,* and could use her as a foil for her own beauty. What quality it was in her which moved men to poetry in the dusk she could not analyze; certainly, as she could observe in any half-lit mirror, her eyes, like those of some night-loving animal, seemed to give out a light of their own. Whatever her enchantment of glow and shadow, Floarea could not compete with it. Floarea was always slap in the center of the stage, her beauty protesting against any darkness which would not let it blaze.

For a remote mountain village the party had an air of distinction. Wadiah was wearing native costume, and in most courtly mood; he looked as if he were riding on his way to argue the case of the Christians with the Caliph. The Archimandrite of Tarsus and Philadelphia was exquisitely Byzantine. His curls, lustrous as a Jewess's ringlets, fell from his brimless, chimneypot hat to his shoulders, whence his great beard carried on the formidable cascade of hair, black even against the blackness of his robe. Over his champagne, his sandwiches and Floarea he made little hieratical gestures with beautiful hands, dedicating the fleshly pleasures in the spirit of a poet rather than a priest.

Floarea herself was demurely dressed, but quite obviously wearing nothing of importance underneath. Whenever she passed in front of a lamp — which she did more often than was needful — the Archimandrite approved the revelation with a paternal smile, and the captain of Levant irregulars looked wildly from Floarea to Armande, like an untutored Phoenician peasant caught on a mountaintop between Lilith and Astarte. In desperation he clung to the Romanova, who listened, with the professional patience of one who had passed her life as a receptacle for champagne and men's idiotic confidences, to a long and incoherent story about his horse.

Wherever she moved, Armande felt Wadiah's eyes upon her; they were not desirous, but almost tearful in their tenderness. So young and so unworldly, yet with so much on her shoulders — that, she knew, as sentimentally as it could be expressed in Arabic, was what the old boy was thinking. On the whole, after trying her own champagne, she agreed with his opinion.

They drifted to the edge of the terrace, and Armande leaned against the parapet, her face in shadow. Wadiah, who lounged only upon cushions intended for the purpose, stood bolt upright at her side. Solid and in the flower of his age, he grew upwards from the level tiles, tarboosh and mustaches pointing to heaven.

"How can I serve you, Madame?" he asked gently. "I feel that you are here for a purpose and that you are ready to tell me. Well, you are right to delay. There is a coarseness in approaching the desire of the heart too hastily, and your courtesy is greater than mine. But remember I was educated in France. I too can be direct as a European if it is expected of me."

Armande looked down at four of Wadiah's dusty retainers, who were clustered at the foot of the steps drinking the coffee and araq she had sent to them.

"We are not very private," she murmured.

"They do not understand enough French. If we do not raise our voices, there is no better place to talk. Tell me — what do you want from me?"

"Your friendship."

"Answered like a princess of Damascus! You have it, and my devotion. What use can I be to you?"

"Will you serve my country?"

Sheikh Wadiah forgetfully raised his voice in reply, and the retainers looked up at the ring of pride and command, familiar though in a foreign speech.

"Madame, I have fifty men who will obey me absolutely, and each of them will bring ten more. Say the word, and I will lead my Ghoraibs against the Germans. They shall learn to drive and fight in tanks. By the Glory of God, but they shall learn!"

"Men we do not need," Armande answered, and added tactfully: "Not yet, at any rate."

"What then?"

"Arms."

The word crashed into the pool of romance and shattered its fair surface. Wadiah did not move, did not show his distaste for the forbidden and mercenary subject, but she felt his spirit walk away from her, lonely and disillusioned, into the companionable lanes of Beit Chabab.

"Arms? Madame, believe me, we have none that matter. Our few old rifles — what are they to the great British Empire?"

Armande turned to the light and to him, eyes and body materializing from the dusk in one appeal to listen and to restore their intimacy.

"I have not been there, but I have talked to so many who were in the desert," she said. "I know what they need. Remember that we are besieged, we are in a fortress, even you and I. And there are no arsenals. Every weapon has to be brought from England, round the Cape and up again to Suez. Every weapon costs the lives of seamen who bring it and soldiers who wait for it. Even — even a dozen machine guns make a difference, now, in the desert."

"So few?"

"So few — really."

The ring of passion in her voice almost persuaded her that her words were true.

"Then . . . but I thought there were thousands of tanks, that battles were fought in monsters I cannot imagine," he said. "For the fighting man, is war much as always?"

"As always, so they tell me. We are attacked on all sides, and they fight for us with what they can."

"If I had arms, if I had any arms," cried Wadiah enthusiastically, "I would do what you ask."

Armande was silent. In his voice too was a note of truth, although unduly masculine and rhetorical. But David Nachmias had been very sure; and to her, knowing Wadiah's vanities as she did, it seemed unlikely that he could not arm his men at need, and arm them well.

During this disapproving pause, Wadiah paid some attention to his mustache.

"Is it true you will give us independence after the war?" he asked at last.

"So far as I know, yes. But I thought you wanted to be a colony."

"That was a compliment, Madame, and perfectly sincere. All the same, we know that you will keep your word, and give us independence."

"The promise might be a compliment, too," said Armande mischievously.

Sheikh Wadiah chuckled.

"Really, Madame! Sometimes you make me think I am dealing with an old Turk. You paint a beard upon your lovely chin, as a little boy defaces an advertisement."

"And with no more skill," said Armande, holding out her hand as if to show its inefficiency.

Sheikh Wadiah bent and kissed it. How perfectly, she thought, he managed every gesture! The touch of the mustache was firm and positive, utterly different from the conventional flick of the French officer, or a passing passion that spent itself upon her hand.

"You will keep your word, Madame," he repeated. "And for a generation we shall regret it. But independence is the way of the world, and must be taken. And then? Then we shall be robbed by our own politicians instead of by the French, and just as ever we shall revolt. Revolt will end in war between Christian and Moslem, because it always does. War will mean alliance with the Jews against the Moslem — and the Jews, because they are worse fanatics than either, will be the only gainers. We are mad to want independence; but since we do want it we need arms."

"All that may be true," said Armande boldly, "but you are like the French. You think too far ahead. The other wars may never happen. Help your fellow Christians now."

"Madame, is this truly a Crusade?" Wadiah asked thoughtfully.

"The Archimandrite says that Hitler is Antichrist."

Sheikh Wadiah glanced at him. Unfortunately the Archimandrite was permitting Floarea to examine his ring. Both displayed a reasonable degree of piety, but their curls were touching.

"The Archimandrite can say what he pleases," answered Wadiah with dignity. "He is Orthodox, and therefore superstitious. But we, the Maronites, Madame, are not children. We are of the body of the Catholic Church except that we appoint our own Patriarch and use Syriac instead of Latin."

Sheikh Wadiah, letting himself drift upon a convenient tide of indignation, began to lecture on the history of his ancient church. Armande knew well that he was avoiding any further mention of arms. Negotiations had been broken off smoothly, and without a trace of discourtesy.

Armande re-entered the general conversation of her party. Then she removed Floarea's ecclesiastic and, from both pique and curiosity, monopolized him. Wadiah, wearying at last of light cabaret chat with his cousin and the two Rumanians, delivered a flowery speech of thanks and farewell, and clapped his hands. Instantly Fouad clattered up with the horses out of the night, and escorted his chieftain home.

The next morning, while she lay in bed and let the cool air of the mountain dawn drift across the pillow, Armande considered that on the whole her opening move had been successful. Though without experience, she had a sure intuition that to extract ill-gotten arms from Christian, Moslem and, probably, Jew was the most difficult assignment in the Middle East. The subject, however, had been mentioned, and no damage done. True, she expected more frankness from Wadiah. A definite *no* would have been more easy to handle than this Oriental diplomacy. Yet there had been indications of the way to Wadiah's heart — by chivalry, Christianity or a mixture of both.

At their next meetings she treated him with a new coldness; not deliberately, but because it seemed impossible to recover their former intimacy. This was evidently the right policy. Sheikh Wadiah showed himself hurt, and a little worried.

He made several attempts to fish for what Armande and the military would do if he did not give up his supposed arms. As she had not the least idea what threats were likely to be believed, she was unresponsive. She implied that nothing whatever would be done, that the hierarchy of the army was indifferent to yet another neutral — Wadiah's prestige would merely be a little less. She reminded herself of a schoolmistress dealing with a problem child. No punishment, my dear, because you are not important enough.

Wadiah's first appeal for forgiveness came in an impetuous assertion that he had consulted the leaders of his church — which Armande doubted, having seen in Beit Chabab no Maronite ecclesiastics but the parish priest — and that indeed Hitler might be held to be inspired by the devil. Armande again dropped the word "Crusade," and left it to work.

The end came, quite unexpectedly, one afternoon upon the terrace when Wadiah had led the conversation to the war and asked how long it would go on.

The first wind of autumn wailed up from Beirut between the crags.

"I think for years yet," she answered, "lost, interminable years."

Sheikh Wadiah patted her hand in sympathy.

"Your husband will be so proud of you when you return."

"Perhaps."

It was not a thought that had inspired her. John was always proud of her for such odd things: for courage that one could not help, for action that was quite obvious — never for patience, or ability to suffer bores or breaking one's own mood at will. Certainly, she agreed, he would be madly proud of what she was doing. And that — that suggested it was all some masculine folly, and nothing to be proud of at all.

"And you will remember. Man and woman alike, we have need of memories when we grow old."

"I shall be old," said Armande bitterly, "and there will still be war. The whole world will be flooded with men and arms and misery before it is over."

She had spoken without any thought of her task; but Wadiah, at his old and beloved game of watching the lightest word of the visiting pasha, answered dreamily:

"And there will be arms to give away."

Armande was shot abruptly out of visions of Kensington and an obscure apocalypse.

"No," she said. "That I cannot promise."

Then she boldly plunged.

"But we will pay you for any you surrender now."

Armande's cheeks flushed with excitement. Her eagerness restored the old generosity of their friendship. She felt no longer a prim young nuisance to an older man. Sheikh Wadiah rested his eyes on her with delight.

"Pay? Never!" he declaimed. "Madame, am I a Jew or a Moslem that I should haggle with arms? I am a Christian chief. What has been taken from Christians shall be returned to them. Let us ride to Jerusalem with my arms and lay them before General Wilson himself!"

"Shall we? Is it possible?" asked Armande, catching his enthusiasm.

"In these days? You think so?" Wadiah hesitated, and then sighed. "Ah, Madame, it was the Crusader in me who spoke. I forgot a lifetime's experience of public officials. We should spend a year in jail before the police admitted the purity of our motives. No, Madame! I will deliver what you require discreetly, but only into sure hands and against an official receipt. What do you suggest?"

"I think a British officer should take them over," answered Armande.

"You are right. In uniform and of the rank of major at least. With his own men and his own transport."

"I can do that."

CHAPTER IV

Security

"YOUR GLASS, sir, is empty," said Sergeant Prayle reproachfully.

He poised a bottle over the specially generous spirit measure which the section used for visiting officers who might be helpful. The Field Security bar was hospitable. Sergeant Prayle, in his daily round of the hotels, managed to supplement the liquor ration by economical buying.

Major Guy Furney — since the French had made Montagne a major, he too had been hastily promoted — was spending the evening with the F.S. Section. This very English Gestapo, with its picked men and a degree of good taste in all ranks, had evolved a social code of its own for the bar. Officers were unhesitatingly allowed the conventional address of "sir" and were treated with deference just in so far as awkward subjects were avoided; rank, otherwise, did not exist, and mixing was so effortless that guests, whether majors or privates, could conform easily to the standards which they found in force.

"Yes, but look here! Do let me do a round!" Furney protested.

Field Security was not under his command. He arranged, as it were, their hunting, but he did not own the hounds — directing them only when he needed their aid in clearing his own political coverts, or when they crashed into those tangled thickets hot on their own line.

"Shall we make him an honorary member of the bar,

Sergeant Major?" suggested Captain Wyne, the section officer.

"Not looking after us properly," answered the sergeant major, shaking his head in pretended disapproval.

"Forks," Prayle explained, as he poured Furney his favorite gin and Dubonnet.

"Wanted for the bar?"

"No, sir. For motorcycles," said the sergeant major firmly. "Four of our bikes have had it, doing your road checks in the blackout, and Sergeant Prayle has written off another all by himself."

"Accidents, avoidance of," said Prayle. "When a collision with a tramcar is inevitable, the experienced motorcyclist will see that he is in the tramcar."

"Going to have a quiet chat with Armande," retorted the sergeant major, "and calling it civil security."

"How is the Armande?" Furney asked.

"Went to Jerusalem a month ago," Prayle replied. "Took her little suitcase and got a lift from a major general."

"But seriously, sir, if you could help with the motorcycles — " began the sergeant major.

His passion was the section transport. An N.C.O. could be smart as any regular soldier or clever as a book detective, but the sergeant major never really approved of him until he could lie on his back in a pool of oil and take down his gear-box.

"I know a chap at Army Headquarters," said Furney doubtfully.

Wyne came to his rescue. It was useless to bother Furney for transport; he was completely unfamiliar with the channels, usual and unusual, by which motorcycles were extracted from a reluctant staff. What Furney did possess, however, was infor-

SECURITY

mation — and Wyne's section were continually complaining
that they were not in the picture.

"But you don't look after us properly, you know," said
Wyne. "We'll make you a member of the bar, Guy, if you'll
spill the beans on the Middle East."

"What? All of it?"

"As seen by an important officer of M.I.5."

"And no bull," added Sergeant Prayle.

"I've had too much gin."

"It's your round, so you'll have to have another."

"Oh, God! Well, half of you will have commissions in a
year, and none of you talk."

Major Furney hoisted himself onto the bar, a stout and primitive construction of planks laid across packing cases, and
covered with gay green linoleum. Prayle, remaining among
the bottles and glasses, found himself, as it were, upon the platform. He felt impelled to say a few words to introduce the lecturer, opened his mouth and shut it again. If Furney were
really in a mood to talk, any interruption might wreck his
spontaneity; and, in any case, what Prayle wanted to say
couldn't be said. It was the purest alcoholic sentimentalism.

He was suddenly full of overwhelming affection for the faces
which were turned towards Furney and himself. They varied
greatly in age, in refinement, in experience, yet all had a common denominator of humorous cynicism. If these journalists,
schoolmasters, clerks and commercial travelers had been
dressed to fit their civilian trades — Prayle's imagination vividly clothed them in solemn array of striped ties, umbrellas and
bowler hats — he would never have noticed, he thought, any
collective quality to be loved; but when faces were framed alike
in the sweat-stained collars of battle dress . . .

"The Middle East," said Furney, "may be divided into two

— 71 —

parts. There is the Western Desert where an unpleasant war is being skillfully fought. Most of you have seen it for yourselves, and know as much as I do. It is an unconventional war which suits British troops but frightens British generals out of their wits. Since we cannot change our troops, but can change our generals, we shall win.

"Then there is the Base—the huge base from Turkey to East Africa. We haven't any troops to keep it quiet by force. Chaps like you and me have to keep it quiet by watching every move and thought of the local inhabitants, and giving warning of trouble in good time.

"First of all there is Egypt. It is full of officers who issue orders and other ranks who type them (I need not remind you that in the British Army an officer is considered incapable of using a typewriter). All ranks, when they think of the local inhabitants at all, think of women. This is due to (a) climate and (b) the provocative appearance and diaphanous dresses of the European colony.

"Gentlemen," said Furney, slipping into the normal address of his university lectures, "do not let that bother you. Fortunately the diplomats can handle Egypt. The Egyptians are a kindly people, but in such a continual state of panic and excitement that their opinions are negligible. That was also so under the Roman Empire. I would much rather talk to you about it. But really there is little difference. Their secret police had just the same troubles as we have.

"We pass up the coast road, the only road, I remind you, connecting one half of the Mohammedan world with the other, to Palestine. Palestine is normally inhabited by Arabs, Jews, government officials and the British Army.

"The Arab, contrary to what most of you believe, is not a

fanatic. He is equally willing to accept British or German rule, whichever is the stronger.

"The Jews are wholeheartedly in the war. It is not always easy, however, to know which war. They have one against the Germans and one — just political warfare — against us. The first is for freedom, internationalism and racial equality; the second is for dictatorship, nationalism and domination of the fellow Semite. They keep both wars entirely separate in their minds. In time you will learn to do so too. Our own policy in wartime is to defeat the enemy. And that is all. All. A paradise for the intelligent man. He can . . ."

"Guy, your duty clerk is on the telephone, and says it's urgent," interrupted Captain Wyne. "I'm awfully sorry."

"Oh, damn duty clerks! Have any of you realized that if there were no duty clerks there could be no war? Get the women's clubs to take it up. Hell!" said Furney, descending from the bar.

He dropped his neat and unmilitary pince-nez to the end of his nose, grimaced at his audience and went out to the section office.

"Balmy!" the sergeant major pronounced. "And we could do with a few more like him."

"A pity he's going," said Prayle.

"Going? How do you know?"

There was a chorus of regret and disbelief. The F.S. were usually well-informed, but nothing had been heard on the grapevine of Furney's departure.

"Because I use the loaf, bo. Would he talk to us like that if he wasn't going?"

The section digested and considered Prayle's latest bit of fortunetelling in silence.

"How do you spell *diaphanous?*" asked an earnest young lance corporal.

"I shouldn't bother to take notes," said Bill Wyne kindly.

Furney returned to the bar. His step was jaunty as that of a city clerk leaving the office for lunch. The professional lecturer, annoyed at interruptions, had evidently given place to the industrious officer with a new problem.

"Anybody know where Beit Chabab is?" he asked.

"At the back of beyond, off the Damascus road," Wyne answered.

"Have you got a detachment anywhere near?"

"No."

"Little doings was there in September," Prayle remarked. "Holiday with an old wog."

"Little doings being?"

"Armande Herne."

"And wog?"

"Wadiah Ghoraib."

"Well, you'd better come along. Are we reasonably sober, Sergeant?"

"Duke of Wellington, sir."

"What stage is that?"

"Sober enough to beat the enemy."

"May I take him with me, Bill?" Furney asked. "Montagne is at my office in a flap. A flap rampant, when the French start sending signals to London."

Prayle changed into the section's civilian suit. His natural and courteous instinct was to avoid disturbing the illusions of others; as Montagne took him for Furney's *âme damnée,* he preferred to look the part.

He dipped his head in a basin of cold water and toweled it vigorously. The skin no longer came off in patches. His face had become a uniform red. He observed, with a resigned thankfulness for very minor mercies, that it even showed signs of tanning to a pleasant shade of chestnut. Prayle never quite forgave his face for its appearance; since he only saw it goggling at him from a mirror, he had no idea of the lovable liveliness it could take on when twisted by humor or lit by generosity.

They found Montagne waiting in Furney's office and watched suspiciously by his duty clerk. Prayle gave him a sinister nod as from one conspirator to another, for he rejoiced in Montagne. Those preposterous boots, the bush shirt, the very short (and somewhat ragged) shorts were so entirely right; if Montagne's gaunt figure had to be clothed in uniform, though built for the shabby tie and jacket of the agitator, then the uniform should have, as it did, the irregularity of the barricades.

"*Mon vieux,* you do not look as if you had enjoyed your dinner," said Furney.

"Eating," Montagne answered, "is an unwelcome interlude when there is no opportunity to smoke."

He detached from his lower lip a yellow scrap of paper, and helped himself to another cigarette from the box which Furney offered.

"Otherwise, *ça va?*"

"It would if not for the rats. They are worse than Loujon."

"Which rats?"

"Nibbling away our sacred movement — all these damned Catholic, royalist, fascist sons of bitches. The poor general!"

"Well, he's a Catholic himself," Furney remarked.

"An exception, my dear man! God, it's the dictatorship of the Church and the Families over again! But you must not make me talk politics, Guy, when I have come with a very serious complaint."

— 75 —

"Official?"

"Not yet."

"Thank God! Well, let's have it."

"I tell you, it is serious," said Montagne severely. "Was it not agreed that the French should collect all the arms in the Lebanon? We need them, you know."

"That was the arrangement," Furney admitted. "We don't like your methods, but it's your funeral."

"Bah! These Arabs only understand force. What I want to know is: why the devil are you collecting arms yourselves?"

"We are not," Furney replied positively. "Have our Australians been up to something?"

"Nothing! They are brave children, your Australians, and more honest than you." Montagne drew a sheet of typed paper from his wallet. "No, it's the R.A.O.C."

"Ordnance? Well, they would be the right people to receive any arms, but only on orders. May I see?"

Montagne handed him the sheet. It read:

This is to certify that Sheikh WADIAH GHORAIB of BEIT CHABAB has delivered to me for surrender to the proper authorities:

> 12 Hotchkiss M/G
> 20 charged belts
> 4 Thompson S.M.G.   French Army Marks
> 8 magazines
> 15 Bren L.M.G.
> 15 magazines

Furney passed the receipt over to Prayle.

"First impression — quick!" he demanded.

It was signed by a major with the usual illegible and fairly cultured scrawl. The orderly room stamp was genuine. The paper, in size and texture, was a Stationery issue; the typewriter, an army Oliver. The descriptions of the arms did not seem to have quite the professional exactitude of the Ordnance at leisure, but then the whole transaction was unprofessional.

"Stage property," said Prayle.

"Why?"

Sergeant Prayle hated to take the sense out of his own remarks by explanations.

"Just in the noggin."

"How did you make Sheikh Wadiah give up his receipt?" Furney asked Montagne.

"He replaced it in his pocket a little carelessly."

"But who on earth and . . . how much was he paid?"

"He said that a detachment of British soldiers took the arms away in a truck and that the British Secret Service knew all about it," answered Montagne primly.

"How many times shall I have the honor to point out to you, *mon vieux,*" asked Furney, exasperated, "that there is no such thing? There are various departments of Intelligence with various jobs to do, just as in your army or any other, and some of their work is naturally secret. But anyone who blathers about the British Secret Service is immediately suspicious. I permit myself to advise you to concentrate on facts."

"*Mon cher,*" said Montagne, unconcerned, "you are not now lecturing little bourgeois in your damned school."

"It's not a damned school. It's Cambridge University."

"*Je m'en fous!* If you want the facts, you must listen instead of interrupting. Are you listening?"

"Yes," said Furney sulkily.

"Good! I went up to see that old fraud, Wadiah. I assessed him at a hundred rifles and told him they must be delivered. I made no threats. He has heard how we collected arms in the south. He knows I would billet twenty men and horses on him and make him feed them until he coughed up his arms. Well, I should have accepted fifty rifles. And to think he had all that merchandise! I am not surprised the English tricked me."

"Ah, shut your suspicious trap!" exclaimed Furney genially. "Who do you think tricked you? Me?"

"I think it was your damned Field Security."

"Bah!"

"You do not know them," answered Montagne very seriously. "It is sure that they obey the Foreign Office and no one else."

"I doubt whether the Foreign Office interests itself in the collection of arms from Beit Chabab," Furney replied. "I admit the Field Security sometimes exceed their instructions, but, honestly, there's no mystery about them."

"That is what you have to say," Montagne insisted, glancing meaningly at Prayle.

"The major looks after me," muttered Prayle with a leer from his larger eye. "I make no reports to my government."

"Both of you disgust me," Furney laughed, seeing that further argument was hopeless. "But what did Sheikh Wadiah say?"

"Well, he gave me an excellent lunch, and after swearing all day that he had no arms at all, he told me at last to go and ask the British. I was not too polite about my allies. I told him that it was with France he had to deal, as always. And then he had the insolence to exchange some remarks with me. When I thought he was about to spit in my face, he produced this paper. There are times, you know, when Albion is really perfidious."

"There are times," Furney retorted, "when some damned idiot in Albion thinks he's being clever."

"Any bad characters been in Beit Chabab?" asked Prayle innocently.

"There are two harmless Rumanians. We know all about them."

Wadiah, then, had not mentioned Armande's visit. That fact was in itself suspicious. Prayle stored it away to be worried later.

"I simply cannot imagine who authorized this," said Furney. "The only people it could possibly be are some of those new commando lads who take their orders direct from Cairo. I promise you I will get on to Jerusalem in the morning and find out."

"My dear Guy," Montagne exclaimed with a sudden rush of emotion, "it is extraordinary how I trust you. You know, there is not another person in Beirut whom I trust."

"That's good to hear. But a great pity."

"You think so? Do you know I am being followed?"

"By the Field Security?" asked Furney ironically.

"It is quite possible — but I shouldn't worry about that. After all, we are allies. No, I am being followed by my own countrymen."

"You exaggerate!"

"Look out of the window then."

Furney got up. In the blazing moonlight Beirut was a black and white chessboard, upon which the cypress trees stood up like giant pawns.

"There is a Palestine policeman in plain clothes," said Furney. "There is a girl talking to one of the batman drivers — who looks very shy about it. There is your own orderly. And there is snot-nose."

"And this good snot-nose, who is he?"

"He is a retired Lebanese gendarme to whom, I fear, you pay

small and quite unnecessary sums for reports on any prominent Arabs who visit this office," Furney replied.

"You are crazy, Guy! I know who comes to see you without
employing a type to stand in your filthy street. But you are
right that he is paid — to watch you and me."

"That is puerile."

"I think so too. But imagine! I, who fought for the republic
in Spain, I, who was in prison at the outbreak of war, I have
the power here. Do you think that is agreeable for the rats?
Do you think I do not report their intrigues? They keep me
under surveillance, and they are right. But they have no money
to do it properly. That is why they employ the animal you
have so rightly christened snot-nose."

"Leave them alone then, and get on with the war."

"Leave them alone? These rats who put politics before their
country? Never! But they will have me out soon. I know it.
And you will not find them so friendly."

"I am going myself this week."

"Going!" exclaimed Montagne regretfully. "Where?"

"Abyssinia."

"My congratulations! It is full of little passionate Italians
without their husbands. But we shall miss you. Who is taking
over from you?"

"Rains."

"Rains? He understands nothing, that type."

"But sound, as they say. A harmless palace eunuch."

"I should like to go with you, Guy. If I stay here, I shall be
found with a knife in my back one of these days. You will see."

"If you really believe that," Furney protested, "you will have
deserved it."

"You will see," repeated Montagne, his deep eyes burning
with a somber delight at being persecuted for his creed. "Well,

you will not forget to let me know about Sheikh Wadiah?"

He looked again out of the window, then picked up his kepi and sprang cautiously into the outer office, glancing, birdlike, to right and left. Even his bony knees had an air of distrusting their own nakedness.

"And now, Sergeant Prayle," said Furney, threatening him with his pince-nez held between finger and thumb, "will you kindly have the blasted goodness to tell me what you meant by *stage property*."

"Just that," Prayle answered. "You know."

"I do not know. Explain."

The sergeant resentfully devoted his brain to analysis.

"Arms," he said at last. "How would you collect them yourself? Hush-hush coves of some sort — security or special service. But Ordnance wouldn't collect them. Not from source, I mean. Ordnance would collect them from the blokes who collected them, if you see what I'm after."

"I do. Yes. Well, it must have been one of G.H.Q.'s private armies which visited Beit Chabab. They never have the sense to tell us what they are doing. They are so bloody amateur that they don't know whom to trust. I'll talk to Jerusalem and Cairo in the morning and find out if there's a simple explanation."

"There isn't," said Prayle.

"Why?"

"It smells."

"What of?"

"Flag days in Kensington High Street. Little doings winning the war with a nice, new brassière and a tray of poppycock."

"If necessary," said Furney thoughtfully, "could you go and interview little doings, as you call her? It's out of our territory, but I suppose no one would object."

"Not if you let Captain Wyne tell the Jerusalem section why I am there. We don't like to have secrets in the family."

"Of course. And try not to look so sinister."

"Mislaid the bow and arrow, sir."

"I don't get it."

"Look like Cupid."

"All right! All right! Come and see me tomorrow afternoon, and I'll tell you anything I've been able to find out."

CHAPTER V

Up to Jerusalem

SERGEANT PRAYLE rode his motorcycle carefully out of the yard. Halfway round the corner he accelerated into the traffic stream of the coast road. A staff car missed him by inches and he fled to the middle of the highway, where he was instantly jammed between a six-ton lorry and a Free French hearse. Having bent his footrest and left the skin of his knuckles on the nose of a golden angel, Prayle wheeled his bike into a side street and sat down on the nearest garbage can. There he cursed all army transport, army drivers and especially the sergeant major who had ordered him to take this vile, self-willed engine to Jerusalem.

He pushed his motorcycle as far as the back yard of an obscure and friendly wineshop and left it in a shed, threatening the anxious proprietor with the loss of his license if the machine should be discovered by civilians or military in quest of spare parts. Then he stood sulkily by the roadside to wait for a lift.

He was in a resentful mood. It was all very well to see Armande again — he had every intention of seeing her again — but he would have preferred an occasion when he could be avuncular and helpful. What the devil had she been up to now that he had to go down and interview — not, for God's sake, interrogate — that luminous, surprising little beast?

Throughout his glum and puzzled thinking, Prayle kept an eye on the traffic. He let all uncomfortable vehicles pass, for he meant to travel in luxury. At last he hailed and stopped a fast fifteen-hundredweight truck with the seat alongside the driver unoccupied.

"Where are you going, chum?"

"Haifa. Any good?"

Prayle climbed into the empty seat, and offered the cigarette of introduction.

"What bunch are you, Sergeant?" asked the driver.

"Intelligence Corps."

"Let's see your A.B.64!"

Prayle pulled out his army pay book which was supposed, by general and quite illogical belief, to prove his identity. The driver gave it a casual glance.

" 'S all right, Sergeant. One of your mates told us always to ask for it before we gave a lift. That's all."

"And do you?" asked Prayle.

"Ker-rist, no!" the driver exclaimed contemptuously. "If I can't tell whether a mucker's an honest mucker when he's sitting in that muckin' seat, a lot of muckin' use an A.B.64 is!"

"True," said Prayle. "But some muckers aren't so bright."

"That's a fact," replied the driver, overtaking a small convoy with a burst of careful speed. "Tell you what, chum. Sergeant, I mean. I often thinks, I thinks, if we weren't all such a lot of bloody muckers, there wouldn't have to be so many muckin' rules."

"Army of the future," said Prayle.

"Just so, chum — if there is any army of the future."

The truck was swinging easily round great curves, through mile after mile of olive. Under the trees were camped the Australians, their tents and camouflage nets blending with the red earth and the sheltering green.

"I was in Greece," said the driver.

"Lucky!" Prayle answered.

"Well, I dunno about that. Ah! To be out of it, you mean," the driver said, suddenly comprehending Prayle's shorthand speech. "These blokes," he went on, waving a thumb at the busy troops, "they must think the whole world outside Australia is made of olive trees. Camped under 'em, fought under 'em and hid under 'em. Cor! The times there's been nothing but an olive tree between me and a Stuka! Well, 'ere we are!"

They shot out of the cultivated land, and away along the sparkling edge of the Mediterranean. On the landward side the coastal plain narrowed to a strip of stony soil. Here and there were the neat rows of temporary crosses and the burned-out skeletons of vehicles left over from the Syrian campaign.

Sergeant Prayle, no longer distracted by the skill with which his driver found a third traffic lane where there was only room for two, returned to his impatient thoughts of Armande. Cairo had made exhaustive inquiries, but no branch of Intelligence, from the very secret to the would-be secret, knew anything about Wadiah's arms. He was thankful that Furney had sent him down instead of leaving Armande to some earnest soul in Jerusalem, who would either bluster or endeavor to extract information from her with provocative and professional tact.

Personally he believed that Sheikh Wadiah's precious receipt was a fake, mocked up to deceive the French, and that no arms whatever had been delivered to any British troops. But if it were a fake, who had put Wadiah up to it, and who had got hold of the right paper and stamp? If not Armande, then Armande must know. She was no fool, and she had been a month at Beit Chabab, tête-à-tête every day, they said, with that damned old wog.

" 'Andy little spot," remarked the driver.

They were approaching an old Turkish inn. On the left of the road squatted the long, low building, and on the seaward side, shaded by a vine, was a tiled terrace with an open-air kitchen where the fresh fish, the ice and the bottles of beer displayed themselves in full view of the traveler. Between house and terrace a light roof had been stretched across the road to give shelter to those who in more leisurely days had pulled up their horses for refreshment.

"Stop?" suggested Prayle.

"No, chum. *Beer, George?* they says, friendly like, and gives you a bill for ten ackers. Must 'ave been all right before the troops got 'ere, though. Nothing like us muckers for muckin' a place up!"

"Browned off?"

"Who wouldn't be? Came out 'ere in 1938, I did. And when will I get 'ome? Tell me that, chum."

"God knows."

"The old woman's 'opped it with a Canadian, and the kids are with Mother."

"Hard lines, chum!"

"Hard lines? Well, it makes yer feel a fool. But I dunno. I got a little piece in Haifa. Pinched her off of a military policeman."

"Should have chosen somebody else's girl, myself," said Prayle.

"Two months for bein' improperly dressed and sockin' 'im —that's what I got. Me improperly dressed! The mucker waited till I was alone and 'adn't got no witnesses. Still, it was worth it. Quite the family man I am now. Wouldn't mind stayin' out 'ere after the war, if I could buy a little place like that and get a couple of wogs to run it for me."

What sort of woman was she, Prayle wondered, that had

reconciled the driver to three years' exile and more years to come? The girls they picked up were all, with important differences of degree, prostitutes — but she was possibly warmer and more generous than the old woman, and certainly more foolish. These Levantine girls seemed to be all half-wits by any European standard, yet there was in them the sincerity of children. They lived from day to day, eagerly and unthinkingly, without bothering about keeping up with the bloody Joneses.

Fortunate driver! He had solved the ancient male dilemma in the way of the East: by choosing a mate who could satisfy his sensuality without affecting his emotions. The West, tortured by the complexities of chivalry, had no such easy solution. If you couldn't put to bed the woman you wanted, she was a nuisance, and, if you could, she was an embarrassment — assuming you were a man quick to pity. Armande, now. Anyone who had held that girl in his arms could not rest till he had made her happy. But was there anything solid to make happy? She bothered altogether too much about keeping up with the Joneses. Or perhaps about the Joneses keeping up with her.

She was self-sufficient, all right, and outwardly self-reliant. It might well be that she was the hand-picked employee of one of the army's ultrasecret organizations. Furney himself had said that he did not rule out the possibility of Armande working for some branch of G.H.Q. which had never taken the trouble to let the security people know what they were doing. And then they raised hell when their agents were arrested!

Ten miles away a great bare headland sprawled across the horizon, and dropped sheer into the sea — Palestine and Armande on the other side of it. Prayle dryly reflected that she would be completely at her ease, back in a nice, smug British civilization. She was difficult enough when foot-loose in Beirut;

now she would be calling on the High Commissioner's wife, if he had a wife, and strongly resentful of interference by sergeants — the more so as she was involved with David Nachmias in some conceited idea of her own.

He felt no guilt at suppressing Armande's connection with Nachmias; until the connection was clearer, it was no business of Furney's. To relate the mysterious behavior of Armande to the general mystery of Jewish activities might be embarrassing for her. The security people saw Zionists under their beds; once Armande had appeared on the files as mixed up in their intrigues, the suspicion might remain for always.

Was she herself a Jewess? He was sure that she was not. She had none of the characteristics — except, perhaps, that she was sometimes unnecessarily anxious to show that she was intelligent. As for David Nachmias, he was above suspicion. Prayle had checked his record, and it was clear. Abu Tisein had risked his life on one journey after another to Syria and the Balkans. He had served most gallantly the garrison of the Middle East.

The truck bounded through the French Customs, waved on by an international committee of Lebanese gendarmes, of French *douaniers,* of British military police, and climbed the bare headland to the British post of Ras Naqura. While the documents of the queue of service vehicles were being checked, Prayle looked down, suspiciously, upon the unfamiliar world of Palestine.

Beneath him lay the whole plain of Lower Galilee, closed in the south by Mount Carmel and the Nazareth hills. On the coast the Jewish settlement of Nahariya suggested a German seaside resort, transported, trees, neat gardens and gabled roofs, to an oasis among the sand hills. Beyond was graceful Acre, and at the end of the sands, twenty miles away, the port of

Haifa, its tall buildings forming streaks of white, through the smoke of industry and the haze of the Mediterranean, against the dark green mass of Carmel. Gunfire rumbled across the bay as the A.A. defenses and the warships in the harbor opened up on a practice shoot or perhaps an unidentified aircraft. East of the city the cooling towers and storage tanks of the great refinery thrust up their huge and unmistakable corpulence as proof of the inefficiency of Italian bombers or the excellence of the defenses. It was a Jewish-British world that Prayle looked down upon, foreign to the Mediterranean. Acre, a miniature city of towers and walls and minarets, was all that seemed to him to have sprung by a natural birth from the historic soil of Palestine.

A security corporal strolled down the line of waiting vehicles and noticed Prayle's cap badge.

"On leave, Sergeant?"

"No. Bound for Jerusalem on special detachment. Is there anything going direct? This friend stops at Haifa."

"Can do. There's a Palestine police truck leaving for Jerusalem after lunch. Come and have a bite at the canteen and I'll fix you up."

Prayle said good-by to the driver, and pressed him warmly to drop in on Field Security when he was next in Beirut. His crooked smile assured him of a welcome, yet showed that he understood how thirsty the driver would have to be before daring to set foot in such a den of striped tigers. The sergeant's sympathetic curiosity led him to wish to see again everyone he met. He loved to settle down in the evening with one of his pickups, and listen to him stolidly endeavoring over a drink to explain the inexplicable.

He ate a dish of eggs in the canteen, and then took his seat in the back of an open truck with three British constables of the Palestine police who were returning to Jerusalem from escort duty.

Their conversation startled him. The contrast between these bitter mercenaries and his late companion in the fifteen-hundredweight was depressing. That driver believed in nothing, but hated nothing; he had the resignation, the inner discipline of the soldier, and an appreciation of vitality and comedy wherever they might be. The police loathed both their service and Palestine. Indeed, Prayle suspected, they would have loathed anywhere but the suburbs of a large town.

His comments and questions could never elicit what they did appreciate, never once during the whole journey. When the road passed through Qiriat Mozkin, lined on both sides by Jewish light industries, there was not a word of interest in the passion that had made toothpaste and textiles grow in the desert, only stories of the gangsterism of Jewish labor. At Jenin, sore and scowling, they laughed in the faces of the passing Arabs. In lovely Nablus they told how the police had at last taught the army to put down the Arab rebellion by bothering no longer with the laws of evidence. Their windy epic of patrol, assassination and reprisal showed that at least they admired the desperate courage of their leaders. Over the hills where the Kings of Judah and Israel had carried on their private warfare, they cursed the fields, wind-swept and glorious to Prayle, because they were not green; and at the sight of Jerusalem, tip-tilted towards the traveler from the north so that the roofs and streets within the walls were defined as in a medieval map, they damned its opportunities and longed for the stews of Tel Aviv where in the tactful control of vice or traffic a man could make a bit of money.

Much of their talk Prayle discounted — after all, a first sight of Jerusalem would soon cease to be any more enthralling than a sight of Manchester — but he was weary of their hatred of the Jews, the more remarkable since all three of them appeared to have Jewish mistresses, and of their contemptuous liking for the Arabs. Lord! And the whole world was open to the humble!

The police dropped Sergeant Prayle in Allenby Square, and directed him to the Field Security office. The sun had gone down behind the tall, stone houses. The pale and very distant sky, ringed with clouds on the horizon, seemed to give out a soft wind that blew from no definite quarter. His first impression of Jerusalem was that the English, shamed by the Holy City into thinking, had been inspired to control and design beauty of architecture that they had not produced in their own country for a hundred years. His second impression was that he felt remarkably well. That, he reflected, might be the cause of a few thousand years of trouble. Too many people had felt too full of beans.

Prayle entered the billet. There was a light in the section officer's room. In the main office there was no one but a Scots sergeant sitting in front of a typewriter and fighting with a ferocious black kitten. Prayle introduced himself and asked for the sergeant major.

"The sergeant major is in Tel Aviv, and we are careful not to disturb him in his meditations," said the sergeant sardonically. "It's myself and the skipper do the work."

"His nibs very busy too?" asked Prayle, nodding to the kitten.

"His nibs is providing me with diversion while I wait for the skipper to complete his weekly report," said the sergeant. "As nothing whatever has happened, he will be thinking up a few dir-rty cracks for the amusement of a headquarters that verra strongly appreciates us both."

Sergeant MacKinnon rose majestically from his typewriter, deposited the kitten in the wastepaper basket and put his head through the officer's door.

"Will ye hold the for-rt, sir, while I take the man Prayle to the canteen?"

"Duty clerk, too, am I?" protested a voice from the office. "All right. And I'd like to see him when he's cleaned up and had a drink."

"A verra good skipper!" said the sergeant. "But he canna see that a man wants his rations at six o'clock and not at the godless hours when he eats himself. Drink, says he! Well, I gie ye a drink, but it's food ye're wanting."

He injected a swift and powerful whisky into Prayle, and then led him round the back of the building into the Y.M.C.A. canteen.

When Prayle returned to the billet, he found three weary N.C.O.s sitting around and talking shop. MacKinnon was hammering on his typewriter and joining in the conversation. The kitten was tearing to pieces a dog-sized joint of beef. The stove was lit and there was a proper army fug, for Jerusalem evenings were cold to those who had come up from the coast or the Dead Sea. Prayle recognized the authentic, tense and easy, atmosphere of his service.

The sergeant entered the C.O.'s office and gave him a cracking regimental salute. It was always best to be on the safe side with unknown officers. Captain Fairfather looked up and grinned appreciatively, faint amusement in his eyes suggesting that he accepted this tribute from one amateur soldier to another at its full worth as evidence of good manners. He was middle-aged, bald, with a spare face, deeply lined. He would have given the impression of a lean, regular officer if it had not been for an air of being continuously entertained at finding himself an officer at all.

"Pull up a chair, Sergeant," he said, "and tell me all about it. How did you get here?"

"A lift to Ras Naqura, sir, and then on with the Palestine police."

"Ah! So you know some of our problems already."

Prayle smiled in silence, not knowing whether he was intended to take this remark in the sense he preferred.

"Well, now — Armande Herne. A soldier's dream, Sergeant. I don't say for all of us, but — it's a long way from home, and we've been here a long time. And when you get an English-woman of undoubted charm . . . Undoubted! Though perhaps a little self-conscious. What do you think?"

"Kensington, sir. She can't get over it."

"With long legs like that? You're unjust, Sergeant Prayle. There's more than a touch of Mayfair in her. Do you remember," he added dreamily, "the legs one used to see in Bond Street between midday and lunch? The feet, of course, enormous, so that one felt that shade of pity which is so dangerous when combined with admiration. And those faces of studied melancholy. But I suppose, after all, that most of them came from Kensington. We must not abuse Kensington."

"No hawkers or circulars," Prayle explained bitterly.

"Nonsense! Really, you don't understand her a bit. You're impatient with her just because she cultivates the society of colonels. Some of them are quite intelligent, and they like to be reminded of those quiet squares of Kensington. She dances beautifully, too. She should with those legs."

Prayle did not reply. He resented conversation about Armande's legs.

— 93 —

"Her face," said Captain Fairfather, "is altogether too spiritual for me. Very hard to live up to. Hard for herself, too, perhaps. Yes, now I see why you find something artificial in her — " He leaned forward, and his eyes, though they did not cease to twinkle amiably, lit with a hard interest. "Sergeant, if that young woman isn't straight, she's dangerous. She's just exactly what we all miss."

"Isn't she straight, sir?"

"I thought so. But I only have what Captain Wyne told me in his letter — that you know her better than any of us and want to ask her some questions about missing arms. Funny word — missing. Down here we either steal arms or buy 'em. Which did she do?"

"Just among those present."

"Well, go easy on her. It's quite preposterous to think of her being mixed up in a sordid arms racket. If she's up to anything at all, it's bigger than that. And she isn't, you know, a snob — though I don't think you quite meant that. Bloomsbury would be a better word of abuse than Kensington — except that for Bloomsbury she is too fashionable. I knew her husband slightly in London. A dull fish, but restful. He'd be very shocked to hear our conversation, Sergeant. Have my chaps made you comfortable?"

"Four blankets underneath, sir."

"Yes, that's where you want them on these damned stone floors. Well, tell me what happens, will you? And keep it all in the family. We don't want them to start fussing higher up as yet."

Prayle suddenly felt that he would be safe in asking for advice. This was not a man to condemn Armande merely because she was potentially dangerous — and he liked her, though his appreciation seemed to be unnecessarily carnal.

"What do you think, sir, down here," he asked, "of David Nachmias?"

"He's a very good friend of mine. Down here? Well, down here we're all much too afraid to think. If we lose the war in the Middle East, the Arabs will revolt, and if we win it, the Jews will revolt. What's the use of thinking? Day-to-day administration — that's what we all do in Palestine."

"Has Mrs. Herne seen him?"

"Not much. And, by the merest accident, I know he is not anxious to be with her. I asked the Nachmiases to a meal with Armande, and Madame accepted with delight. She knew Armande in Beirut, I gathered. And then David turned the invitation down on a flimsy excuse."

"What's your reading of it?"

"The merest conjecture. Armande has contracted an attack of Zionism. Now, Zionism with ignorance is a nuisance — embarrassing to a man like Abu Tisein. He's a most able politician. He has no patience with patriotism without technique. He doesn't think in terms of America and Poland; he thinks in terms of Arabs. A dozen of his sort *could* make a Jewish Palestine."

"Whom does he really work for?" asked Prayle.

"The Jewish Agency first, foremost and all the time. But their interests are often ours. And you mustn't think the Agency is some sort of sinister secret society. Jews — Zionist Jews, that is — all over the world elect their representatives, and the representatives elect an executive to administer the National Home. That executive is the Jewish Agency. Its constitution is democratic; its methods are — well, I've never decided who does the most harm, the Agency orators or the Palestine Government. Our people, you see, have no patience with hysteria. We show our distaste. We don't even like having them to lunch in case they make speeches at us. That's all wrong. Treat a Jew as if he were the Messiah (it's amazing how often he thinks in his own heart that he is) and he'll eat out of your hand. Where does Nachmias come into your problem?"

"Back door, sir, if at all. Shall I talk to him first?"

"God forbid!" Captain Fairfather exclaimed. "If it comes to interrogating Abu Tisein, we'll have to have it done on the highest level."

CHAPTER VI

Hospitality

IN JERUSALEM Armande was happy for the first time since the fall of France. She was back in a tiny apartment of her own: a penthouse on the top of a block of flats in Qatamon. The roof stood high above the modern suburbs, looking east to the scrub and boulders of the barren Judaean hills, and west to the walls and pinnacles of the Old City. She was free to choose her own friends, free of all those cheaply alluring competitors in the St. Georges; and, war or no war, it was pleasant to be back in a civilization that recalled London. At the King David Hotel there were even dinner jackets to be seen in the restaurant.

She had no financial worries. M. Calinot's money was near its end, but her expenses at Beit Chabab had been lavishly defrayed as if Anton's inn were a hotel de luxe. She had therefore decided to rid herself of Beirut, its useless life and its useless memories, and to settle in Palestine where there was nothing exceptional in being British and a civilian, and war work of all sorts for the asking. Soon after reaching Jerusalem she had taken a job at Palestine Headquarters which paid her as yet a mere five pounds a week, but gave her security and self-respect. She was at last a useful member of the fortress, not an idle mouth to be fed.

With all this outward peace she was gay at heart. She had carried out a difficult and secret assignment with such ease and efficiency. One night when she thought of the quiet commendation of David Nachmias she had hugged her pillow and kicked with exhilaration like a month-old infant, until the loneliness of the pillow reminded her that she was a woman, not a child.

Abu Tisein had not told her very much of the end of the story — simply that at the appointed time and place Sheikh Wadiah had met the detachment of troops and led them to a temporary cache where the arms awaited collection; he had been mildly offended because the party would not stay to a considerable cold supper which he himself had carried out into the woods.

She sent Wadiah her Jerusalem address, and at once received a reply from him, written in a magnificent flowing hand on the most expensive paper obtainable in Beit Chabab, which happened to be pale pink and deckle-edged. The letter contained nothing but resounding compliments, yet was delivered confidentially by a Maronite monk. Sheikh Wadiah was too much of an individualist to believe in public services.

At the end of November the same monk, bowing, smiling and disappearing with ecclesiastical smoothness, delivered another letter. For two pages it expressed Wadiah's allegiance to her and her country, and then came to the point:

> You will remember my major-domo, Fouad, who, next to myself, was your most devoted servant in Beit Chabab. He has had the misfortune of some slight trouble in his family, and I have thought it best to send him over the frontier into Palestine. He will come to see you in person. His life is in your hands to do with what you will.

Armande discounted this conventionally exaggerated language. Fouad, she supposed, had some private business with army or government, and she was expected to do him a favor —

certainly a large and disreputable favor, since Wadiah himself made the request. Friendship in the Middle East always seemed to be a banding together against common enemies or the officials of the state; it was not so sincere or disinterested as in Europe, yet carried greater responsibilities. She hoped that David Nachmias would be able to do whatever was required.

Abu Tisein kept clear of her in Jerusalem, explaining that there should be no public connection between them. His influence in the background, however, had been of use. He had insured that she met the colonel who was now her employer, and he had opened to her the Zionist circles of Jerusalem.

She liked the Jews of Palestine. They had the taste but not the conservatism of her husband's stockbroking friends, the energy but not the vulgarity of the smaller fry of European commerce, and they had made Jerusalem a little capital of the arts and of science. Her sympathies were wholly Zionist. To historical rights of Jew or Arab she was indifferent. The right of the Jews, for her, was that they were proud and happy, hard at work and secure. A joyous and intelligent folk had been re-created, and the world was the richer for it.

It was a Sunday afternoon in early December. At the special request of her colonel she had spent the morning at work, and had come from the bare maps and tables of the cheerless military office home to her flat. The first heavy winter rain roared out of the windless sky and capered on the roof outside the windows of her living room. Dry and warm amid a veil of water, she idled happily, still savoring her delicious privacy.

Her bell rang. It was her German-Jewish landlord, Dr. Finkelkraut, who had a habit of calling punctiliously upon his tenants at the most awkward hours in order to announce some meticulous and — humanly speaking — impracticable scheme for the care of the furnace, the use of the water or the hanging-out of laundry.

He bowed with Central European formality, implying that he disturbed her not as a casual caller, but as a responsible land-lord acting under the beneficent state.

"Mrs. Herne," he said, "it is my duty to alarm the tenants." She supposed the water was about to be cut off again.

"I am alarmed," she answered, smiling.

"You have taken notice, yes?" he insisted, as if asking her to sign a receipt. "It is the police!"

Armande had developed immunity to the excited noises that occasionally drifted up from the flats below. She now listened. The block was humming with hysterical exclamations.

"What's all the fuss about?" she asked.

"An Arab murderer has been observed to enter my house," replied Dr. Finkelkraut importantly. "By instantly organizing our microcosm I assist the police. They wish to search the flats. I have alarmed my tenants and instructed them not to be afraid."

"Well, he wasn't here and he can't get in," said Armande, "but the police can look around if they like."

Dr. Finkelkraut trotted across the roof with the heavy steps of a good citizen hurrying from one civic duty to another, and vanished down the stairs.

Before Armande could shut her door, an Arab sprang from behind the housing of the stairhead and rushed towards her. She let him in. Fouad was Fouad, whatever he had done.

Fouad fell on his knees and carried her hand to his fore-head. He was no longer the spruce, gray-clad rider who had honored Wadiah by his attendance. The major-domo was wearing the black cotton of the poor. The wet rags clung to his body. His mustache, a black and proud edition of Wadiah's, was weighed down by rain. Blood dripped from his fingers to the floor.

Armande caught him by the good arm, dragged him to the bedroom and shut the door. Then she dashed outside. There was no trace of blood on the roof; evidently Fouad had had the sense to keep his hand muffled in his rags. In her room there was blood on the parquet. She flung a rug over it. When she looked up, Dr. Finkelkraut and the police were at her door.

There were a British sergeant, an Arab and a Jewish constable. The constables began a thorough search of the roof and chimneys, while the sergeant smilingly addressed her in Hebrew.

"Mrs. Herne is English and works for the army," explained Dr. Finkelkraut officiously — her presence added respectability to his house.

The sergeant smiled with relief. He was a pleasant, fresh-faced young man. Armande's excitement, fear, distress — she had no time to realize what she had done, why she did it or what she felt — began to ease in face of this male innocent. Him at least she could handle.

"Bit of luck finding *you* here!" he exclaimed, as if Jews had neither eyes to see nor tongues to speak. "You can tell me all about it. Mrs. Herne, there must be a man somewhere on this roof."

"There might be," Armande answered. "I've been reading."

"Could he have got into your flat?"

"Not without my seeing him. What's he done?"

"Committed a very brutal murder in the Lebanon. We've been on the lookout for him, and he was recognized while he was asking for this street. Then he ran for it, and the constable is sure he saw him bolt into this house."

"Whom did he murder? Was it political?" she asked, sounding, she hoped, the cool and curious Englishwoman.

"Just one of their blood feuds — and all the usual mutilations with it. Now where can he have got to?"

"Fire escape?" she suggested.

"Impossible. I have a man at the bottom of it."

"Well, he can't be here," said Armande. "But have a look round the flat if you like."

She held the sergeant with smiling eyes; she was oddly terrified lest he should watch her throat and see the heavy beating of her heart.

"I needn't bother you, Mrs. Herne," he replied. "I can see you have only these two windows and your door opening on the roof. So if you've been here all the time . . ."

When the police had left, Armande sprang into the bedroom. Fouad was crouching on his heels in a corner of the room: a wet Arab, pitiable and helpless as a wet kitten. So much of their dignity and grace depended on the free movement of the covering.

"*Merci, Madame! Merci! Merci!*" he murmured in halting French.

"Show me the wound!" she cried anxiously. "Did the police shoot at you?"

"Yes, yes, Madame. But it is nothing."

It was nothing, a mere tear in the fleshy part of the upper arm which she dressed and bandaged. Fouad yelled and moaned as the disinfectant stung him, but held out his arm without wincing. She was sure that any Englishman (or Englishwoman, for that matter, if educated at Bingham Priory) would not have uttered a sound, and yet would have made her amateur surgery twice as difficult by wriggling all over the place with set face. Fouad's reaction emphasized the frighteningly foreign nature of the world in which she had to act. To act! Thinking, watching, learning — those had been easy, even enjoyable.

Armande gave him a drink. Dry clothes? Heaven only knew what was the modesty of these feminine and conventional Arabs! At last she thought of a huge coat of rough sheepskin which she had bought in Hebron. He accepted it gratefully.

She left him to change, and paced up and down the living room, giving Sheikh Wadiah a mental dressing-down that would have shattered his self-complacence for a year. Fouad had slight trouble in his family, indeed! His life was in her hands, indeed! Well, it was. That had been no Oriental figure of speech. What power did Wadiah think she had? What absurd picture had he made of her? It was sheer lunacy to saddle her with a common criminal. It was cheating. This had nothing to do with any intrigue or any service to her country.

She returned to the bedroom. There Fouad could safely stay, and had to stay. The windows looked north to a patch of rocky hillside; the walls were flush with those of the house. So long as he kept to the back of the room, he could not be seen. In the living room he would be at the mercy of her landlord, or anyone else who should visit the roof and glance casually through her windows.

Fouad, wrapped in the sheepskin robe, was squatting on the floor, uncomplainingly awaiting the sentence of his judge.

"Are you hungry?" she asked.

"No, Madame. I eat before I come. But a cigarette — you have?"

Armande sat on the bed, and tried to extract his story. It was difficult, for Fouad had no English and only a hundred words of French. He told his crime frankly and with a modest pride, though he admitted that Sheikh Wadiah had considered it ill-timed, inconvenient and out-of-date. He spoke of his chieftain as a boy of his schoolmaster, recognizing that Wadiah, as a responsible authority, had to hand out hard words but did not necessarily believe them.

Twenty years before, in a savage riot between Moslem and Christian, Fouad's aunt had been raped and murdered, and his father killed while attempting to protect her. The murderer was well known, and wisely disappeared into the Moham-medan world of the Far East. While Fouad was on Sheikh Wadiah's business at Damascus, the son of the criminal was pointed out to him. He followed his man to a quiet street, killed him, defiled his body and escaped to Beit Chabab. Wadiah could not deny his guilt and could not protect him.

"He say to me — escape to Palestine! See Madame Armande. Maybe she use influence. Maybe they not hang you. So I am here."

"But, Fouad, I . . ." began Armande.

She was going to say that she had no influence at all, but that, she saw, was just a form of words for her own satisfac-tion. Why alarm him when she intended to do all she could?

"Madame, I not stay here," Fouad reassured her. "I come only to speak. Madame not to fear. I not tell police where I was."

"You must stay here till I come back," replied Armande decisively. "I am going out now to try to help you. Keep in the bedroom and do not open the door whoever comes."

The Nachmiases' flat was in Abu Tor, on the edge of the bare Valley of Hinnom. It was a lovely suburb, but by no means to the taste of every Jew. There was nothing at all between David Nachmias and any excited crowd of Arabs that might issue from the Dung Gate of old Jerusalem; on the other hand, there was nothing between him and the ancient

City of David, outside the walls, upon Mount Zion. As Armande walked along the edge of the escarpment, the rain cleared; the low evening sun shone upon the walls and towers, and in the water streaming off rock and rubble down to the dry bed of the Kidron. Jerusalem indeed was golden.

Mme. Nachmias was at home, languid upon a sofa, with an ivory telephone, a box of expensive chocolates and a French novel by her side. When she rose to greet Armande, the trim bulges under her smart house coat revealed that even in privacy she would not surrender to the lax and corsetless ease of the Levant.

"But you must wait for my husband!" she cried, when Armande apologized for disturbing her. "He would be desolated to miss you. He is very fond of my naughty little Mme. Herne."

Mme. Nachmias archly implied that it was good for the uncivilized David to have attractive friends, and that she chose them for him with care.

"The general wanted to see him," she added importantly. "But he will not be long. I adore your English officers. They are so precise. Ten minutes, and everything is said."

Armande's experience in an army office had convinced her that British officers talked for the sake of talking, and seldom to the point. Madame's opinion was an illusion. She was right, however, in prophesying that her husband would not be long. Half an hour later Abu Tisein entered the flat.

He showed to Armande the stolid gallantry that Madame expected of him, and then turned to his wife.

"By the way, *chérie,* your cousin Susie is back in Jerusalem."

"David! I must, I must absolutely speak to her!" declared Mme. Nachmias impetuously. "I will only be a moment," she added to Armande, "just while David pours a drink for you."

She picked up the telephone and began an exclamatory conversation. Abu Tisein carried the drinks to a far corner of the room.

"You wanted to see me?" he asked.

"It's a long story," Armande warned him doubtfully.

"Madame and her cousin," murmured Abu Tisein, "have equal politeness. On the telephone neither wishes to be the last to speak."

Armande showed him Wadiah's letter, and explained the sudden appearance of Fouad.

"That is awkward, yes," he said. "But I assure you, Madame, it is an inevitable consequence of such a friendship as you made. In Wadiah's mind, you see, you have become the protector of the Ghoraibs. All the same, he had no right at all to ask this of you."

"He thought he had," Armande retorted.

"Mme. Herne, you romanticize the Arabs! He did not even think he had. It was a last chance for this Fouad, and he tried it," answered Abu Tisein with the first signs of impatience that she had ever seen in him. "You must send the man away at once. If he were caught with you — well, the complications might be disastrous."

"But he ought to see a doctor."

"For bullet wounds the police doctors are the best."

"I can't give him up to the police," Armande cried. "And anyway the police mustn't know he was with me."

"Why should they? Fouad told you he would not talk, and he will not. After all, the police searched your house. They know that Fouad was not in it. He has only to say, for example, that he never entered the house at all, that he crept away through all those geraniums around the door, and they will accept it. Send him away tonight as soon as it is dark! Watch the movements of the police, and see that he is not caught going out! And be careful, Madame — if you fail, I cannot protect you."

Armande waited another ten minutes for the telephone conversation to finish, and said good-by. She returned to her flat, hurt and annoyed. Abu Tisein had not only refused to help Fouad, but he had disapproved of her own perfectly natural action. As for his complications — what were they? Wadiah had done a discreet favor to the British; he had every right to expect a discreet favor in exchange. It was all nonsense for David Nachmias to say that he could not protect her. He was being professionally mysterious in order to force her to do her duty.

It was of course her duty to give up a murderer to justice — that she knew without any officious assistance from Abu Tisein — but it did make a difference that the man had taken refuge with her. Neither law nor crime was quite so clear in this strange Levantine world as at home. There were loyalties between Wadiah and Fouad, Wadiah and her, Fouad and her. Beit Chabab had cherished her, saved her, given her self-respect and happiness. To that dear society Fouad belonged. It was utterly impossible to turn him out into the street, and hear the police whistles blowing five minutes later.

The alternative? To spend an indefinite number of nights shut up in her penthouse with a murderer. She smiled to herself at this dramatic presentation of the affair. Fouad was no more a murderer than a seventeenth-century duelist. And he did not consider her as an attainable woman. She was above his world, his protectress, his princess. If he thought of her as a woman at all, it was as his chieftain's woman, hedged around by more taboos than she could possibly imagine.

She told Fouad that for the present he was to remain. Then she telephoned to the charwoman, an expensive and solemn

Jewess who came every morning to clean up when Armande had left for the office, to say that she would be away for a week and the flat would be shut. She moved her bed and dressing table into the living room, leaving the bedroom and its safety to Fouad.

The first twenty-four hours were full of flavor. It was exciting to answer the smile of the policeman on the beat, and to buy extra food at shops where she was not known. It was a calm and personal jest after her own heart to receive an officer who came to fetch her for a dance, and to imagine his horror if he were to learn that she kept a tame murderer in the next room. Only the sharing of her bathroom, to which each of the two rooms had a door, did she find hard to accept. She shuddered at the thought of a ragged Arab among the intimacies of her toilet — though in fact Fouad turned out to be scrupulously familiar with all the complexities of the Western lavatory.

Fouad was quite content in complete idleness so long as he was well supplied with cigarettes, yet the vision of him sitting still behind closed doors began to obsess her nerves. On the third and fourth days the strain became barely tolerable. Then discipline relaxed. Fouad's arm gave no trouble. He insisted on making a feast for her in the kitchen, on cleaning, on doing little services. Once he was nearly caught by a man who came to read the electric meter, and once he was trapped in the kitchen by Dr. Finkelkraut, who then remained with Armande for an hour, discussing the organization of chamber music groups for flat dwellers and the influence of so social a scheme on world fellowship after the war. The trivial changes of furniture effected by female tenants were, she gathered, beneath his notice so long as nothing was broken.

Armande began to realize that her hospitality was futile;

it led nowhere, for she had no idea how to get Fouad away to a possible future. He himself could offer no suggestion except to go and take his chance. He was still expecting miracles from her influential friends, still looking a question at her whenever she returned to the flat. She saw that he had in no way grasped the truth: that she was helpless. She decided to keep him until police vigilance had relaxed. A week would surely be enough for the police to call off their inquiries and whatever unobtrusive check they were keeping on the immediate district. She hoped to God that it would seem enough to her conscience. As Wadiah said, Fouad's life was in her hands.

CHAPTER VII

Zion

ON THE FOLLOWING SATURDAY Fouad was still in the flat. When
Armande came home from the office, with a free afternoon
before her, hostess and guest lunched together in the kitchen.
Then Fouad returned to his idle imprisonment and his cigarettes, and Armande settled down to write to her husband.

She wrote to him from Palestine with more ease, and her
letters had been consistently cheerful, full of comment on her
doings rather than her thoughts. Dear John, now proudly a
petty officer! It was impossible to doubt that in convoying the
merchant fleets back and forth across the Atlantic he was ful-
filling himself and his dreams. She had been inclined, in the
early days of the war, to consider his abilities wasted; but what,
after all, were his abilities measured in terms of a desperate
nation where every man and woman was mobilized, directed
or persuaded? He could produce nothing the country needed
but his own body and a sure gift for leadership. Dear, gallant
John! When he had learned his trade he might well end up
with a small ship, his own to command — and that for him
would be heaven. She could sorrow for herself or for the
partnership which she missed, but she could not pity his expo-
sure to the cold and danger of the seas. John was so obviously
happier than he had ever been without cold and danger. He
did not need her.

She would have liked to tell him this adventure, but she

realized that — apart from the risk of her letter being read by
the censor — she could not write the story in any terms that
would not shock him. He would cable her to see the District
Commissioner immediately and explain her crazy act. See the
man at the top and trust him — that was one of John's favorite
maxims. Of course he was right. And Abu Tisein was right.
Both were perfect examples of that absolute masculine right-
ness which a woman who was worth anything at all could
only admit and ignore.

The letter would not write itself, for the overshadowing
worry of Fouad's presence made all her cheerful trivialities
inane. The blank white paper became a hypnotic; no longer
could she control the thoughts that slipped back continually
to her haunted loneliness. She dropped her head on her fore-
arm and was sinking into the hazy half-sleep of contemplative
depression when she heard steps crossing the roof to her flat.
Instantly she glanced round the room to see if there were any
trace of Fouad. There was none at all. She opened the door.
She felt wearier than ever at seeing the difficult Sergeant
Prayle.

"Bachelor girl!" said Prayle, when he had been graciously
received and planted in a comfortable chair. "Aprons and ink-
pots! Suits you better than the St. Georges, Mrs. Herne."

Armande remembered that whenever the sergeant had seen
her before she had been dressed for the hotel. So, indeed, had
he. This was the first time she had seen him in uniform; he
had lost completely the air of seediness which surrounded him
when, in his borrowed clothes, he hung about the lobby. Armande could not admire his face, but she admitted that in a
battle dress which was obviously cut to his tall figure — not
merely issued and put on, as those of the sergeant clerks in her
office — he looked competent and fully worthy of his three

stripes. There was even a proper loose swagger about him, though eccentric. She was sure that her colonel would put him down contemptuously as one of those Intelligence wallahs trying to look like a soldier. But he did look like a soldier.

"Beirut? Beirut was a cemetery!" she exclaimed.

"Yes. Well, I don't mind a bit of hide-and-seek among the tombstones. It's lively. This might be a lot deader," he answered, looking round the flat with sad approval. "It's a next best thing."

"To what?"

"To your own home. And that's a mistake. Exiles — we all try to run up Kensington in cardboard. Or the village pub, if you like. But in the long run it doesn't help."

"We aren't all as rootless as you," she protested.

"Rootless? Oh, no! Roots so strong that I flower anywhere. Out on the dung heap or in among the aspidistras. Palestine isn't for me."

"What don't you like about it?"

"Too self-conscious. British, Arabs, Jews — all of them walking about saying what fine fellows they are. Just like the first act of a tragedy."

"There's not going to be any tragedy," Armande responded at once, "unless we British make it."

"Well, I only arrived yesterday. And of course I've been talking to mere cops like myself. But one thing is clear. The Jews intend to collect enough arms and enough immigrants to impose their will whether Johnny Arab likes it or not. Am I right?"

"Yes. And they should be allowed to. They have suffered enough."

"Oh, my aunt!"

"Are you stationed in Palestine now?" she asked coldly.

— 112 —

"No. Just calling in on the Holy Places with a little bag of samples."

"And which of them," she inquired politely, "interest you?"

"Yours."

"Mine? You mean . . . have you come to see me officially?"

"Uncle," said the sergeant apologetically.

Armande felt a rush of anger against all these stupid people, personified in Prayle, with their interrogations and internments and vague minds; but she could not afford to show resentment. Had they traced Fouad to her? She thought it unlikely. Did they want to question her, out of utter impertinence, about some unknown indiscretion with Zionist friends? Prayle had already led her into an expression of opinion more violent than she intended.

"Isn't it time uncle understood the modern generation?" she retaliated.

"Look, Mrs. Herne," he answered gently, ignoring her changed voice. "It doesn't matter what you think of me — we're in the same game. And what I want to know is so simple. Who got the Ghoraib fountain pens?"

"That?" asked Armande, amazed. "Who got them? But, Sergeant, shouldn't this be handled on what they call a higher level?"

"Of course it should! But keep on a low level, and the army runs smoothly. That's what we are for."

"Really I know very little," Armande said. "And what I do know I can't tell you without instructions."

"Whose instructions?"

"I don't think I should tell you that."

"Well, what department?"

"I don't know . . . why do you want to be told everything? Surely you and I don't matter enough?"

"Not a bit," he agreed. "But take away the cardboard, and see me as the village cop. Counting necessity and gaining nothing, like the rest of us. Well, something has gone wrong. I polish the buttons and proceed to the vicarage to take a statement. You've every right to send me to the devil, and to say you'll only speak to Sir Horace. But it saves trouble if you don't."

"What has gone wrong? I really don't see what you want to know."

"I want to know who swiped Wadiah's sword and buckler. We didn't. Nor did the French."

"The French? No."

"Well, it was their business. And they started collecting a month or so after Wadiah had unloaded his stock. That's how the story came out. Wadiah swore to Montagne — you remember Major Montagne? Puss-in-Boots. Guillotines — he swore to Montagne that he had given the lot to the British."

"So he did."

"Sure?"

"Of course! Sheikh Wadiah is the soul of honor," she answered indignantly.

She saw Prayle's face light up with tenderness, amusement, relief — impossible to analyze the emotion. His odd-sized eyes and witch nose were integrated into a merry whole. She was reminded of some half-forgotten French print — of Villon or Panurge it might have been — wherein a crooked face shone with intelligence and enjoyment.

"Then to clear . . . Wadiah," he said, "get in touch with the big cheese and tell him Field Security is interested. He'll understand that if we aren't in the picture there's bound to be a stink. Auntie Catroux and Auntie Spears will start fussing, and we shan't be able to get on with the war for weeks. But drop us a hint, and the whole business can be ironed out without anybody's pet racket being compromised. If I come and see you tomorrow, will you try meanwhile to get permission to tell me more?"

"Yes, but I won't promise."

"Or of course you might try to get it now."

"I have told you that I can't, Sergeant Prayle."

"Hop into the next room and ask him."

"Ask whom?" she replied, imitating the lazy surprise with which she invited him to explain his more abstruse remarks.

"The gentleman behind the door that you keep glancing at."

"I keep glancing at the door," she retorted, "because I want to go in there as soon as you have left."

"That," he said, "was a mean trick."

"You asked for it."

"I didn't mean your very natural response. I meant me. You see, I've been admiring your courage. Not once have you glanced at the door. Not once, all the time."

Armande saw that she was fairly caught.

"Sergeant," she said, "even if you were right, there might be very simple reasons for a man in my bedroom."

"There might. But not smoking cheap Anchor cigarettes. You forgot the north wind, you see. It's blowing the smoke back under the door."

Armande stared at him in silence, her face deliberately calm and neutral.

"What did I say?" he asked suddenly.

"I am not going to be interrogated on my private affairs," she snapped.

"Not interrogating you! What did I say? It gave the whole show away. *You* forgot. That's right. Not *he* forgot. Cash, please! We'd have missed that if the boss hadn't been walking round the shop."

"Sergeant Prayle, I give you my word that whoever is in the bedroom has nothing to do with Wadiah's arms."

"Or with Wadiah?"

"Well — not in the sense that you mean."

"Blackmail, Mrs. Herne?"

"No!"

"You're looking a bit harassed — " he nodded towards the table — "starting off to write a letter, and out comes the first verse of 'Lead, kindly Light.' "

In his voice and his queer phrase was such sympathy with helpless loneliness that Armande could not meet his eyes for fear of breaking down.

"Tell me," he said. "I'm not really a cop, you know."

"But you might be forced to behave like one."

"By what?"

"Oh . . . duty."

"Got two of 'em. One's to the neighbor."

"Beit Chabab," she began. "You know I was there?"

"Of course."

"And if I may I'll tell you why. But — well, Sheikh Wadiah thought I was more important than I am."

Sergeant Prayle nodded. That delusion was not confined to Wadiah.

"And naturally I did things for the Ghoraibs — all the nasty little favors that Arabs ask."

"Human," he corrected her. "Not nasty."

"Yes, I agree really. Only not everyone understands. And then his major-domo killed a man in Damascus. And Wadiah sent him to me, of all people, to get him off. I can't get him off and I won't let him go, and there you are."

"And now," said Prayle, "let's have all the details. How did he get here? And how much do the police know?"

Armande told him the story of Fouad's arrival.

"And still you approve of yourself?" he asked.

"Yes. I don't see what else I could have done."

"Nor do I. But it was so much harder for you than anyone else."

"Why?"

"Laughter isn't one of your vices."

"Laughter? I enjoy things quietly. I enjoyed this for the first two days, but a week is a long time to go on smiling at the respectable Mrs. Herne sheltering a murderer. That's what you meant, isn't it?"

"Yes. And I wasn't fair. I've never had the luck to see you when you were happy."

"Oh, I don't bubble at any time," she smiled. "And one of me is too serious, I know. But the other me has a lot of fun all by herself. An ironical sort of fun."

"Which is the conventional one?"

"Both — if you call good taste convention," she answered firmly.

"Do I? Must apply the loaf to that. Your hospitality, for example. Hardly conventional, even by Arab standards. But in excellent taste. Well, I'll have to make Fouad disappear for you."

"But how?"

"Just wave the wand."

"Are you sure you can do it without getting into trouble?" she asked anxiously.

"Were you?"

Armande called in Fouad from the bedroom. Prayle stumbled through the Arabic greetings, watching the man as he gravely answered. His eyes were merry and honorable. He was neither sullen nor effusive, and showed no sense of guilt. He was as naturally courteous as if he had met Prayle upon his own mountains and were inviting him to enter his house.

The word *devotion* sprang into the sergeant's mind. That was his instinctive summing-up of Fouad. It was no rare quality among the Eastern Christians. They might be easygoing — in every bad sense as well as good — but they could love. It was that capacity for devotion, he supposed, which had appealed to Armande. Her own soul responded.

He smiled into the composed and lovely little face that watched the pair of them so intently. Here was the girl he had imagined, with immense reserves of loyalty and courage. He packed away the knowledge, to be squared sometime, whenever his army life gave him the hour and the solitude for slow reflection, with her exasperating and unreal detachment.

"Hardest, first," he said. "That mustache has got to come off."

Fouad, recognizing word and gesture, looked appealingly at Armande; then burst into sad and passionate Arabic.

"Not quite sure," Prayle interpreted, "but I think he said that if he has to swing, mustache swings too. It would be a proud day, you see, and he ought to look his best. How do you talk together, by the way?"

"Oh, Fouad understands simple French. I'll get his mustache off him. Is there anything else you want?"

"Ravishing blondes," he said thoughtfully. "I had shares in a dance hall once, and we used to make a packet out of selling beauty preparations — whenever our tame chemist wasn't all hopped up. No demand for mouse brown. But can do, I suppose?"

"Can do," she laughed, "if I bleached him first. I'll see my beauty parlor."

"Good. His skin is so fair, you see, that he'd look quite a different person with brown hair and no mustache."

Sergeant Prayle talked himself out of the room, remarking casually that he would see her or telephone her the following evening about their various troubles. He did not again refer directly to Wadiah's arms. Armande, amusedly seeking the cause of his embarrassment, suddenly realized — and her heart leaped up with appreciation of his queer delicacy — that he was eager to impress it on her that there was no bargain, and that he completely dissociated the disposal of Fouad from the answer he demanded and expected.

Since it was the Jewish Sabbath, Armande was reasonably certain of finding David Nachmias at home. He was not religious, but he conformed. The Agency employees, whose personal creeds varied from atheism to a mild infection of philosophical Judaism, were careful as bank managers in a town of Methodists to keep their activities unobtrusive on the day of rest.

She called him up, and guardedly, as she thought, indicated trouble. Abu Tisein abruptly cut the conversation short, and said that he would come at once to see her. Armande was piqued that he should doubt her caution on the telephone. The click of the receiver as he replaced it was sharp as a rebuke from a commanding officer.

She tidied her room and put away the overalls. For David Nachmias she was businesslike — not, however, in the sweater and skirt she habitually wore at her army office, but with the smartness of Calinot's former secretary. Calinot's secretary, she remembered, had been a very model of discretion on telephones, and had not, Repeat Not, changed since.

Her resentment vanished as soon as David Nachmias entered the room. Slow, massive and courteous, it was no wonder that Arabs liked him. He asked her immediately of Fouad, and she lied boldly that he had gone. That was her own business — and she had ensured that there would be no smell but flowers and a faint memory of perfume.

Armande gave him coffee, and told him of the sergeant's visit. Abu Tisein listened unperturbed, changing one cigarette for another so smoothly that his chain-smoking was as natural and unnoticeable as the rise and fall of his chest. He did not interrupt her with a single question. His brown eyes held a mild and fatherly interest.

"We have made a mistake, Madame," he said at last.

Armande felt only pleasure at the *we*. If any mistake had been made, Abu Tisein had made it, but she was ready enough to be associated with him.

"I could not guess that the French would collect arms in the Lebanon," he admitted frankly. "It seems incredible that you, the British, should occupy a country and then allow to others so intimate a detail of administration. Well, well, you could have thought of no surer way of making the French unpopular."

Abu Tisein relaxed into silent contemplation of his coffee. Armande watched him, fascinated; she had never seen a man think with so little outward sign of any mental processes at all. After some minutes she ventured to recall him to her own problem.

"What shall I tell these security people? Can I mention your name?"

"I would rather you did not as yet," he replied indifferently. "I will see them myself."

"As you like, of course."

"After all, it is not an affair for policemen."

"I suppose they have to do what they are told," Armande answered, by her tone lightly defending Sergeant Prayle's interference.

"True. Sometimes they must act. And action in the dark is always foolish. Is he honest, this sergeant?"

"Yes," she said — and then wondered at her unhesitating reply. The odd scraps that she had heard from Prayle of his past life and present opinions were far from a guarantee of honesty.

"I know very little about them," replied Nachmias apologetically.

"It seems so odd that none of these hush-hush organizations should be able to check up on each other. Isn't there any one department which knows all the secrets?"

"Probably. But it is very far away. What is this Field Security? I know their officers. Yet I do not know exactly what they do."

"A sort of comic Gestapo," she answered.

"What? Gestapo? Here in Palestine?"

Abu Tisein looked almost angry.

"The completest amateurs!" Armande reassured him.

"All the more dangerous. The professional policeman is without too much enthusiasm. He is afraid of his job."

"But what did happen to the arms?" she asked, emboldened by his nervousness to put the direct question.

"As you promised Wadiah, they were collected by soldiers in uniform."

"Then what is all the fuss about?" Armande's great eyes caressed him, soft with the tender amusement of a mother at the unnecessary evasions of her sons. "You have only to tell the general what happened."

Nachmias did not respond. His face remained calm as a sultry summer evening.

"Madame, consider what you know. Wadiah is not lying. Prayle is not lying. But is it not possible that Major Montagne is lying?"

"I don't understand. When?"

"I suggest to you that he knew all about the deal. He was lying when he showed surprise."

"But why should he say he hasn't got the arms, if he has?" she asked with some agitation. "I don't understand. You ought to let me know what I have done."

"You are aware, Madame, that the French are divided into two parties?"

"Vaguely. But they didn't matter."

"Perhaps not, when you were at Beirut in the days of their first enthusiasm. Now they do matter. There might even be open, violent collision. Catholics and royalists on one side, socialists and communists on the other. Well, Madame, imagine that I was ordered to give arms to the left wing and not to the right. Do you understand now? Major Montagne can never say that he had Wadiah's machine guns. Nor can we. And the greatest, the very greatest discretion is essential."

Armande felt utter revulsion from what she had done, from Nachmias and from the wasted year of her life, that waste which had been forgotten in triumph — and what a triumph! Then men had time for this kind of ugly intrigue in the midst of a war for life and death? Poor, gallant France still keeping up its suicidal feuds in exile, and her own country encouraging and able and ready to split a helpless ally! Then what was truth, and where in this miserable, needless conflict was it? If this were British policy, then all the accusations of French and German and Jew against perfidious Albion were justified.

Divide and rule, divide and rule — it was no better than Hitler's conquer and rule.

Her eyes filled with tears. They spread upon her cheek before she could stop them.

"Madame . . ." protested David Nachmias.

"It is nothing," she answered. "Leave me alone. I shall be all right."

"But what is it?"

"Leave me alone. It's not your fault. I should have known. These things have to be."

"But what you did was magnificent!"

"Ours not to reason why!" she cried hysterically. "Magnificent? Magnificently filthy! Wadiah is worth all of you."

"He is. I admit it. But still, Madame, I do not understand."

"No? Oh God, David Nachmias, are we living a hundred years ago? It was the fashion then — this beastly, crooked cleverness. But that is not what I thought I was serving. That is not why I am in the Middle East. I haven't a country — I haven't a country any longer after what you have told me. Don't you see that I can never work for you again?"

"As you wish, Madame," began Abu Tisein severely. "But you must never — "

"Never! Do you think I would talk of an indecency like that? Do you think I want to remember it myself? Oh, leave me and leave it, and go and build your Palestine. That at least is clean."

Abu Tisein's eyes were expressionless. There was a hint of pity in them, but neither protest at her emotion nor any fear of it. His very presence was a reminder that nothing mattered. Accept, accept, always accept! She was bitter at his complacence, but that calm made it easier for her to gain control of herself.

"I am sorry," she said.

"I have been very mistaken in you, Madame," he murmured regretfully.

"I dare say. I am sorry," she repeated.

"I do not mean that as a criticism," Nachmias assured her gently, "or only of myself. You were so self-possessed in Beirut — almost Oriental. I thought . . . well, it doesn't matter what I thought. I was wrong."

"A *poule de luxe,* like the rest of them," said Armande savagely, flushing at her own vehemence.

"No! Never!" protested Abu Tisein.

Her angry desire to shake him out of his tranquillity had been well and unexpectedly fulfilled. She was sourly amused to see that he was shocked.

"Never, Madame, I assure you! But I thought that you cared for nothing, you understand, but purposes of your own. That was the impression you gave: that you were waiting for — for power to come to you. Power, yes, I thought you wanted that; but not through the methods of a . . . of ordinary women. And you have power. You are dangerous, Madame."

"I am very weary of being called a dangerous woman," said Armande, her tone deliberately implying that she was bored by such stupidity.

"Then be more open, more European."

"More open?" she asked ironically.

Her respect for David Nachmias was vanishing. Hero of secret campaigns he might be — but to leave himself exposed to such a thrust!

"But that — that is it!" exclaimed Abu Tisein, rising with a slow, yet agitated dignity from his chair. "We are children in your hands. And why? What do you want? I said you must be more open. I do not mean more indiscreet and you know it. Discreet? Of course you will be discreet. You yourself might find difficulties if you were not."

"No daggers, please, M. Nachmias."

"And there again! Will you tell me what you are thinking? Not a word! Not a word!"

"But why so much mystery?" asked Armande. "You call me dangerous. You tell me to be discreet. You tell me to be more open. You threaten me. And all the time I am not thinking at all. I am just listening."

"For what?"

"For nothing at all."

"And when you are alone, what do you think then?"

Armande smiled. There was no answer to so stupid or so deep a question.

"M. Nachmias, I shall not speak a word of what has passed between us. So far as all this official curiosity goes, you will satisfy it. That's what you want, isn't it?"

"Yes. And I shall do so."

"And give my compliments to your charming wife. We shall see each other often, I hope."

"Good-by, Madame."

"Good-by. And do not worry about your secrets," she added with a smile.

CHAPTER VIII

The Heathen

AFTER LEAVING Armande's flat Sergeant Prayle went slowly downstairs, stopping on the three landings to read the cards and name plates on the front doors. He had no conscious professional interest; as a civilian he would have done the same — to the exasperation of anyone walking with him who happened to be in a hurry. He liked to acquire an imaginative picture, which might or might not be true, of how people lived and why they lived where they did.

On each floor there were two doors. On the ground floor there was a third door, facing the entrance to the block and unlatched. This he opened, being curious about the layout of the flats, and discovered the furnace, boiler and oil tank. Only then did it occur to him that if the door had a hole for an eye, an hour or two on watch might be profitable. Should Armande go out to see the secret department for which she believed she was working, she might — though God help him if he were caught! — be followed; and if anybody interesting came, he could tell by listening carefully to the steps whether the visitor had gone up to her penthouse.

The Sabbath peace was over the house. There was not a sound from the tenants replete with lunch and patriotic piety. Sergeant Prayle gingerly opened the furnace doors. It seemed possible to heat a poker in the oil jets. He twiddled a cock in the same abstracted curiosity with which he opened a throttle, and produced a blast of flame that seemed, for a panic-stricken second, uncontrollable. By nervous trial and error he mastered the mechanism, then heated a thin bar of old iron, and bored a hole in the top left-hand corner of the door, above the hinge.

As evening drew nearer, the house awoke. A plump and pretty woman, all smiles and dirndl, came gamboling down the stairs with a merry little daughter. Two old men with beards followed, and hung about arguing in the hall before they surrendered to the winter sun. Then entered four earnest and respectable citizens with portfolios of music under their arms; they stopped at the floor where a Dr. Finkelkraut (of Philosophy) had one flat, and a Dr. Pincas (of Economics) the other. Shortly afterwards came Abu Tisein. He walked straight to the boiler room, threw open the door and looked inside. When Prayle, flattened against the wall, recovered from his surprise at this decisive and evidently habitual precaution, Abu Tisein's steps were traveling upwards. The sergeant waited long enough to be sure of Nachmias's destination, then hastily put a block of buildings between himself and Armande's roof.

He returned to the office in a dream of Armande. There was a smack of youth in this Fouad business, just sheer, impulsive, generous youth. Impulsive and alone — didn't that give the key to the fate of Wadiah's arms? She was an adorable, blazing little fool, for all those mannerisms which provoked him, a fine little fool going her own way boldly up the wrong street. Whatever she had done, he was certain that she was justified by his own standards, but those standards were a damned sight too intangible for the army.

He found Sergeant MacKinnon very ready to leave the office in charge of a duty clerk, and to start the Saturday evening's serious drinking. They settled down in the back room.

of an Arab hotel, which catered specially for quiet and thirsty sergeants. Prayle laid himself out to be entertaining. He found this only too easy, as the double whiskies came in and the empty glasses went out, until the sober observer within him questioned whether he was being amusing to anyone but himself. That bottomless pit of a Scot, however, was at last slowly mellowing, and began to talk Palestine. That was where Prayle wanted him.

"How's the local recruiting going?" Prayle asked.

"More Jews than Arabs we're getting."

"Nice, clean fun for them to be at the right end of a tommy gun for once."

"Well, I wouldna' say that doesna' count for the poor bastards," said MacKinnon judiciously. "But 'tis also a grand chance to hae the Hagana trained by British sergeant majors. A fine little army the Jews will have after the war, Sergeant Prayle, for they've Scots instructors at the depot."

"No trouble in getting a man into one of the Arab companies, I suppose?"

"Verra few questions asked. But what question d'ye think would be hard for him to answer?" asked MacKinnon acutely.

Sergeant Prayle took refuge in obscurities until two more doubles had strengthened the bonds of good fellowship.

"Well," he said at last, "the truth is, bo, that the man's got a good name, but he'd better have another."

"Ye'll answer for him in all that matters? And I dinna mean their national sports of rape and murder."

"He's O.K. He's a fighting man, and he'll take to his officers."

"Now ye shouldna' tell me nor the skipper unnecessary details. Our responsibility for this country is verra grave. Here's to ye, Sergeant Prayle! Ye're a credit to the Corps, mon. Ye'll be wanting some papers for him, I take it?"

"Difficult?"

"If he were a Jew, he couldna' get a false identity without the order of the Jewish Agency. But Johnny Arab is an old soldier — he puts finance before politics, if ye see what I mean. Has your chum five pounds to spare?"

"If I can get a casual."

"Aye, the skipper will do that for you. Well now, I've a friend —" MacKinnon looked fiercely at Sergeant Prayle — "and she's a schoolteacher and a respectable girl, and I'll thank ye not to mention her name in the office, for there's my own reputation to be considered as well as hers. Her father is the *mukhtar* of a Christian village — if ye can call them Christian, for to my way of thinking it's wog popery and naething more. Now if ye see him and say ye come from me, maybe he'll do your dir-r-rty business. And if ye'll gie your glass to the black man with the grin on his face, he'll fill it for ye, and then we'll have a bite to eat."

Prayle downed another double whisky, got up and grimly focused the door. Not for anything would he have it said or admit that he could not mix business with pleasure without passing out. Sergeant MacKinnon rose with no less dignity. He drew himself to attention and stood bolt upright. Prayle's sober observer noticed with admiration that MacKinnon was not even swaying.

"Mon Prayle," said the Scot, "I dinna hold with foul language to foreigners. But —" his indignant voice rang clear and steady as bugle — "there has been ar-r-raq in the whusky!"

MacKinnon, still holding himself with soldierly stiffness, leaned from the perpendicular and crashed full length to the floor; once there, he wriggled twice, curled up his legs and settled down with a comfortable snore to the sleep of a professional soldier who was accustomed, whatever the night had brought, to parade at 6 A.M., smart, clear-eyed and clean-shaven.

Sergeant Prayle took him home in a taxi, receiving sympathetic assistance at both ends of the journey, and put him, still sleeping, to bed. Methodically he wrote down the Mukhtar's name and address, and himself rolled into his blankets.

In the morning he took an Arab bus to the village. He could not read his own writing of the night before, but fortunately remembered the name. It was a peaceful hollow among the hills, some ten miles from Jerusalem, seeming much as the Crusaders had left it, with trees, an eager spring and a church built over the imprint of Elijah's head. From his fellow passengers of all three religions Prayle learned that originally the village had been a Moslem holy place (for to them, too, Elijah was a respectable prophet) and had been handed over to the Christians by one of the sporting bargains common in the twelfth century. The Jews, for once in a position to apply the higher criticism, pointed out that the mark of a head, which really existed, was imprinted in late Roman concrete.

The Mukhtar had an exaggerated respect for Sergeant MacKinnon and all his works; the sergeant's name and the cap badge of the Intelligence Corps were sufficient introductions for any business. Prayle's courtesies were cut short as the Mukhtar plied him with a light white wine, which did a world of good to his aching head, and then hurried out to kill chickens for a feast.

After lunch the identity card had only to be mentioned to be given free of charge. This, as Prayle knew, was mere politeness. He kept the conversation on its level of beautiful altruism, and before leaving produced a fiver "for local charities." The Mukhtar unobtrusively pocketed the first identity card and made out another in the name of George Nadim Salibah — a poor orphan, he explained, who had emigrated to America ten years earlier and had never been heard of since. The document was proof against any ordinary bureaucratic inquiries. Fouad would have a real identity as good as his own.

Traveling back to Jerusalem, Prayle resisted the temptation to find out why the bus driver was wearing bicycle clips round the calves of his riding breeches, and devoted himself to a series of mental pictures representing his future acts. He enjoyed the excitement of being once more, as in peacetime, an individual pursuing his own path through a disapproving society, but he had no right to take any avoidable risk. The police, he had observed, were still taking an interest in Armande's street.

Armande, poor unsupported child, had plenty of trouble coming to her anyway. If on the top of this trafficking in arms she was caught hiding fugitives, she'd be wanting false identity cards for her own use. As for himself, the least punishment that could be handed out would be transfer to some awful station of heat and boredom on the Red Sea. It was scandalous for Security to protect a man wanted by the police — unless, of course, Security needed him. Well, he did need a talk with Fouad. That was a loophole. The army at bottom was humane. Give it an excuse that could possibly be believed, and it always did its best to believe it.

When the bus stopped at the Jaffa Gate, the chain of pictures — Prayle complacently described them as a chain of reasoning — was complete. He dived into the bazaar of the Old City and bought the black outer garment and thin, black veil of a respectable and old-fashioned Moslem woman. Then he reconnoitered the hillside at the end of Armande's street, and found a pit among the rocks, full of filth and rubbish, where he could change out of sight of the houses. He disturbed

Captain Fairfather's Sunday evening leisure to demand the loan of the section truck to take him to the recruiting depot at Sarafand, where, he said, he wanted to interrogate a witness; and when Fairfather let him go, at midnight, with permission to use the truck, a lot of unwanted drinks and a lecture on the contradictory aspects of Jewish womanhood in bed and in politics, Prayle telephoned Armande, woke her up, and told her not to go to the office in the morning. He then went to bed himself, full of admiration for his own swift and efficient staff work.

At nine next morning he emerged from the hollow among the rocks as an Arab woman, carrying his hat and boots in a basket under a neat white cloth. Half an hour's patient waiting was necessary before he spotted the plain-clothes man who was watching Armande's street, and had him where he wanted him — at the far end of the street and about to stroll back. It was essential that the man should see him enter Armande's block, but not too closely. Prayle shrunk his height so far as he could, hobbling along with bent knees and imitating the gait of a worn village woman with the usual varicose legs. He turned into the house when the watcher was looking straight at him from a distance of two hundred yards.

He rang Armande's bell.

"Any rags, bones or bottles today, mum?"

His cockney accent did not get a laugh. Armande smiled, wan and puzzled. Her slim, tense body had no life in it. Hell, thought Prayle, my little ship's in harbor again!

"Just slipping Fouad into something loose," he said, "and then we're off.'

Fouad was not easily recognizable. His mustache had gone, and his hair was a dirty golden-brown. Prayle dressed him in the female clothing and veil, and himself returned to his

uniform. He gave Fouad an exhibition of the gait with which
he had entered the house, and warned him to imitate it until
he was clear of the immediate quarter.

"Walk out of town by the Jaffa Road," he told him. "I'll pass
you in a truck and pick you up in about half an hour."

Fouad said an emotional good-by to Armande, his halting
French made more incoherent than ever by tears of gratitude.
She took his hand, gently smiling, but untouched by the
femininely Arab outburst as if she herself had been some just
and grimly masculine administrator. Prayle was astonished at
her lack of warmth. What had happened to her since the day
before yesterday? Never had been so evident that detachment
of which Loujon spoke. The only explanation was that she
just died and departed into a hell of her own when things
went wrong. That in his experience was a common trick of
sensitive men. Possibly it was equally common among women.
But what the devil had gone wrong?

He looked out of the window. The plain-clothes man was
talking to a shopkeeper halfway up the street.

"Now, Fouad!" he ordered. "Hobble! Let that man see you
come out! Don't forget the basket with your clothes in it!
Imshi!"

Fouad again seized Armande's hands, and then dashed down
the stairs.

"I'll follow him in a few minutes," said Prayle, "and then
come back and see you tonight."

"I can tell you now." Armande spoke with such a cold regret
that it was obvious to him she was hurting even herself. "My
department, whatever it is, will explain the whole thing to your
security chiefs. I'm sorry. It's so discourteous to tell you nothing. But Wadiah's arms were a matter of High Policy."

"Why are you so upset about it?" he asked.

"I am not."

"Then what's the matter?"

"Nothing."

"Mrs. Herne, do you believe everything Abu Tisein tells you?"

"You said I could trust him," she answered, seeing that he knew of some recent connection between them.

"I never told you to take his orders. Who did tell you?"

"I never said I took them. I don't want to discuss the subject, Sergeant Prayle. The whole thing will be settled, and I want to forget it."

"Give me a hint. Did British troops collect Wadiah's arms?"

"I hope to God they did not," she answered bitterly. "I hope the French themselves collected them. And there's your hint, and I am not going to say any more. What are you doing with Fouad?"

"Enlisting him. Private George Nadim Salibah of the Palestine Buffs."

"And you won't be caught? Are you sure?"

"Keeping my fingers crossed."

He went out onto the roof and saw Fouad in the distance, well away from police and stepping boldly. Fouad's slight build made a presentable woman of him; he was unlikely to attract attention.

"The worst is over," Prayle said.

"I am so grateful. You've been an angel, a guardian angel. And I stand here like a stuffed owl," she cried with a flash of spirit, "while you take such risks for me, and gratitude is just another ache that I can't satisfy. I mustn't answer your questions. I can't say a word of what you have done. May I even pay what you've spent on Fouad without it seeming an insult?"

"You'll need it more than you do now."

"Why should I? I can earn my own living."

"Just old mother Prayle foretelling the future in a pool of owl tears. I must go now, Mrs. Herne, and pick up Fouad."

"Good luck, and — and bless you!"

"For your own sake," he persisted, "tell me the story."

"I'd tell you so gladly for your sake," she replied. "But I'm not allowed to. Don't think too hardly of me."

Prayle hurried back to the Field Security office, thanking God for Fouad. If that damned, sympathetic murderer had never existed, his visit to Jerusalem would have ended, just as he had feared, in a straight rebuff from Armande. Well, he had got it; but it was no collision of their prides and their tastes, driving them irrevocably apart. It was merely a straight line, a reluctant line, among the complex curves of their relationship.

The truck was waiting outside the office. He jumped in alongside Fairfather's batman driver, and told him to go to Sarafand. Just outside Jerusalem, where the road began to sweep downwards along the hillside, the truck overtook Fouad.

"Let's give the old girl a lift," Prayle suggested.

"O.K., Sergeant, but she won't take it," the driver answered.

"Very heavy basket. Let's see."

Fouad climbed into the back without a word. Fifteen miles further on, in the wooded gorge of Bab el Waad, Prayle stopped the truck and, to the driver's shocked surprise, led Fouad off into the plantations. There he gave him his papers and a sketch of the birthplace and past life of George Nadim Salibah.

"No thanks needed," he said. "Sheikh Wadiah helps us. We help him, and you too. Didn't you help our soldiers when they came to Beit Chabab?"

Prayle's shot in the dark was successful.

"Yes, *moussié*," Fouad answered. "I guide them."

"Did they speak English?"

"Yes, *moussié,* but not like Englishman."

"You don't understand it, do you?"

"I hear plenty English. English say *urra ovva urra ovva.* Very slow. Always angry. These men not speak like English."

"How do you know?"

"Just as I know you not Frenchman. French say *pang pang pang,* very fast. You speak French, but you say *urra ovva urra ovva,* not *pang pang pang.*"

"The hell I do!" said Prayle, rather annoyed. "What did they look like? Dark or fair?"

"Dark, *moussié,* but not so dark as Arab."

"Did Sheikh Wadiah notice anything?"

"No. He talk only with major and speak all the time. Much welcome."

"No idea what they were?"

"No, *moussié.* Not English. Not French. I not know what you send. Great country. Many allies. Me too British soldier now. Very proud."

"That's fine, Fouad," said Prayle kindly. "And when it wears off, just remember Madame Armande."

The driver stared when he saw Prayle return from the woods with a man. Then he grinned. This was real secret service stuff. It was the first time in all his driving for Field Security that anything dramatic had happened.

"Keep it under your hat, chum," said Sergeant Prayle. "Now off we go to Sarafand!"

He saw Private George Nadim Salibah duly sworn, and whispered to the sergeant who took charge of him a mysterious and quite incomprehensible story of the new recruit's services to Intelligence. Salibah's prestige was firmly established, and Sergeant Prayle was invited to lunch at the mess.

Back in Jerusalem, Prayle gave his whole attention to the investigation in hand. He had solved the problem of Wadiah's private arsenal, but not the problem of convincing his superiors. It was obvious that Abu Tisein had used Armande to acquire Wadiah's machine guns for the National Home and that a party of Jews in British uniform had boldly collected them. Proof, however, was lamentably short unless Armande herself spoke out.

Her hint about the French did not make sense. The French never had those arms. Montagne's indignation had been too real. It looked as if Abu Tisein had already started to lay down a smoke screen. Guy Furney's judgment would never be smothered by it, but Furney was already on his way to Abyssinia, and his successor, Major Rains, was reputed to see no farther than the inside of a file. Nobody except Captain Fairfather, who knew both Armande and Abu Tisein, would easily believe that she thought and still thought she was working for her own country. And Fairfather cut no ice in the Lebanon.

"The skipper got any hobbies?" he asked Sergeant MacKinnon.

"Aye, women!" answered the sergeant with relish. "And whusky! And wor-r-rk! But he doesna' take them seriously. And just when I hae him trained to a decent routine of one or the other, he must start some daft doin's to amuse himself."

"Does he look after the chaps?"

"I will not say he cares for our pheesical condition as well as an officer of the Black Watch," said MacKinnon, "but there's no lie he wouldna' tell for any of us."

This testimonial reassured Sergeant Prayle that Fairfather was, at any rate, more than an amiable eccentric. He decided to report to him, by easy stages, as much as he knew.

"Well, did you have any luck with Mrs. Herne?" asked Fairfather as soon as he entered the office.

"Yes and no, sir."

"What did she say?"

"That she wouldn't discuss the matter."

"Bitch," pronounced Fairfather thoughtfully.

"Mentally, sir."

"God forbid that I should apply so coarse a word to her mere enjoyment of womanhood! I meant her mind. Like Tobias's dog, it seduces but does not perform. What else did she say?"

"That the master would deal with my inquiry upstairs."

"Does she believe that, or is the master just wasting time?"

"Both," said Prayle. "There's a lot of innocence in that little noggin."

"Innocent? Armande Herne?" asked Fairfather skeptically. "A pretentious, sophisticated . . . well but, good Lord, you might be right! Who is the master upstairs? Got any line?"

"Old Joab, sir."

"Do you want a commission, Sergeant Prayle?"

"Baton in the knapsack."

"Well, you'll have to be a damned sight clearer for your men than you are for me. Who's Joab?"

"Abu Tisein."

Prayle told him of Abu Tisein's connection with Armande, and of the mysterious collection of the arms. He left out any mention of Fouad's adventures, merely describing him as reliable informant.

"Joab, yes," said the captain. "It touched him off nicely. I just wonder whether he is doing his Joab stuff or his Lawrence stuff."

Fairfather leaned back in his chair, and relit his pipe.

"By the way," he asked, "when did you know that all arms in the Lebanon were to be collected by the French?"

"Captain Wyne did not know till they started to collect."

"Then there's a good chance that David Nachmias didn't know either. That makes a difference, you see. I can't imagine Abu Tisein doing anything so foolish that he would be caught out. But if he never dreamed that anyone would bother Wadiah for arms, the plan looked dead safe. It was a thousand to one against Wadiah ever having to produce that receipt. Why should he? He might frame it and hang it in his parlor some day, when the whole affair was too old for investigation; but that's all. If the French hadn't suddenly started to collect arms, we should never have heard a word of Abu Tisein's intrigue and we should never have guessed that he used Armande."

"She never knew," Prayle insisted.

"Possibly. On the other hand, she's inclined to take a line of her own, you know."

"Can we get David Nachmias for impersonation of the military?"

"Not a hope!" said Fairfather, obviously relishing the subtlety of Abu Tisein's crime. "Your poor old Wadiah handed over his arms to what he thought was a party of British troops. Who were they? They might be French, Syrians, Cypriots, anything in battle dress. You've no proof that they were Jews. And if we accused the Jewish Agency, they would quite certainly reply that the troops were British and that we were trying to frame them. My dear Prayle, it was a very clever coup!"

"But don't these people care whether they are suspected or not?"

"Not a bit, so long as there's no legal proof. The Agency falls for arms like lesser men for wine and women. Time and again they risk their whole reputation. Two motives, I think. One is common to Hitler, Arabs, Zionists and small boys; they consider lethal weapons to be highly desirable merely because they are forbidden. With the other motive I have more sympathy. They say we have failed to defend them in the past, and they propose to make certain of defending themselves in the future. When you remember the massacres at Hebron and Haifa and Safad and half a dozen small colonies, it isn't surprising that the Jewish Agency prefers to have a rifle in every house rather than a division of British troops thirty miles away. I should myself.

"It's all a question of values, Prayle. They would rather increase their own little force than retain the trust of the British. And then, to make matters worse, whenever they are fairly and squarely caught in an arms scandal, they put up one of their long-haired hot-air merchants to encourage the extremists and to tell us we are anti-Semites.

"Good God, if the Jews were one tenth as clever as we think they are, they could be sure of Palestine merely by playing on the idealism of the British and flattering our profound conviction that we always do God's will!

"Sergeant Prayle, I too am a Zionist, and I weep for Zion like Jeremiah. There's a fine, splendid spirit in the making of this country. Never mind their national socialism — only a rather ruthless government of gangsters could make the desert flower as they have done. Under the surface is real joy and idealism and utter self-sacrifice. And all this glorious, interesting experiment is in danger, just because a people who can be incredibly cunning over trifles like arms cannot learn to be cunning in statecraft."

"You should come and take a Syrian section for a holiday, sir," said Prayle.

"Not me! You take security seriously up there. Palestine is restful. All we can do is to watch and report, and nobody pays the slightest attention to what we say. After all, they have heard it before."

"I meant a simple life with the plain, dishonest Arab."

"Well, there are hundreds of people who understand him better than I do. But sometimes I think that nobody in this country understands the European Jew. You see, our governors have had no chance of learning. They are trained in the Sudan or West Africa or the Malay States. They know how to handle the brown-skinned agriculturist with patience and justice. But that knowledge doesn't make them understanding administrators of Palestine. They should spend a year in a Polish ghetto — if there are any left — learning the influence of atheism on the tribal structure of the Jews, and another year on the East Side of New York studying family life and political mythology.

"And the Jews are completely ignorant of us. Most of these immigrants were brought up under czarist or communist or Polish or Rumanian governments, and they simply can't understand our ways. They won't believe that there isn't any secret police more sinister than you and me. (You and me, Prayle! Creatures of dastardly imperialism! Just think of that when you want bucking up!) As for the Palestine police, they accuse them of unmentionable practices just because they can't imagine cops behaving any other way. Poor, gallant, puzzled, hard-working police force with only its twelve-year-old cunning to pit against them!

"And never, never will they believe that so far from our government being a bunch of able, treacherous intriguers, the only people who have any views on Palestine at all are the harmless, honest District Commissioners (whom, incidentally, they generally like) and a few muddleheaded old boys in the Colonial Office who try hard to be fair to both sides at the expense of all imperial interests."

"Gratitude?" Prayle asked. "No gratitude? After all, we put them in Palestine, and we have just beaten the Arabs for them."

"My dear Sergeant, they don't see it that way. We punished the Arabs so severely that they won't dare move unless Rommel crosses the frontier. Then, when we had smashed their rebellion, we gave them half what they asked for. That was brilliant — sword in one hand, bread in the other — and of course a true Palestinian like David Nachmias appreciates it. But do you suppose the new immigrants do? No, God help them, they think we gave in to rebellion!

"Gratitude? Gratitude is a flower that only grows in a courtly, kindly, settled environment. Gratitude means that you, the recipient, believe that a kindness was disinterested, unnecessary, offered for the sake of love or abstract morality. Now, that is what a Jew finds it very hard to believe of a Gentile. He believes it, of course, of his own folk, for, as I need hardly tell you, Sergeant, the only people who really practice Christianity towards each other are — with the exception, as elsewhere, of their politicians — the Jews. You remind me, Prayle, or possibly I remind myself . . ."

Sergeant MacKinnon knocked, and put his head through the door.

"If ye've finished with Sergeant Prayle, sir, he'll be wanting his tea."

"Ah, yes. Tea, of course," said Captain Fairfather regretfully. "Well, Sergeant Prayle, let me know if I can help at all. About once a year we are not so futile as we seem. Are you all right for money?"

"Conditions in Lombard Street very stringent, sir."

"Right oh! We'll give you a casual for anything you want."

As he left the office, Prayle doubted whether even once a year Captain Fairfather was not futile. It was pretty evident that he did not intend to forsake his fascinated contemplation of Palestine for the hard, perhaps impossible, task of bringing military justice to bear on David Nachmias. Armande would thus remain under suspicion.

He could not suppress the fact that she had admitted some knowledge of the disappearance of the arms, and then who was going to believe that she had not, for money or misplaced enthusiasm, worked for the Zionists? All he could do was to present the straight evidence in his report and to stress his opinion of her innocence.

Sergeant Prayle prided himself upon his business method. He had observed and regretted that his clear verbal communications were not easily understood by any but personal friends; he was therefore the more resolved that any written reports of his should be exact, coherent and compelling. After tea, he provided himself with squared paper and plain foolscap, and settled down in a quiet corner of the billet to write a straightforward account of Armande and Abu Tisein. He laid on the table a fountain pen, a blue pencil, a red pencil and a slide rule. He enjoyed all office gadgets; they were an aid to clear thought, and pleasant to manipulate.

The report was carefully written on the right-hand side of the page; on the left-hand side, separated from the narrative by a vertical line, were conjecture in red pencil and auxiliary facts in blue pencil. Attached, as Appendix A, was a graph neatly drawn on the squared paper, showing Armande's moods in terms of her movements. After two hours of most satisfying craftsmanship, he pinned together the sheets of the report and Appendix A, and looked over its colors and neat handwriting with loving pride. It might, he considered, have been the work of an able and original staff officer. Everything was there, and, helped by judicious color and arrangement, everything was in the smallest possible space.

The Scots sergeant obtained for him a seat in the Signals truck, which started at 5 A.M. and traveled fast and direct from Jerusalem to Beirut. Prayle thanked him warmly, but privately considered such efficiency most unwelcome. He had the amateur soldier's irremediable objection to early rising, and his natural inclination was to accept any form of transport so long as it started after seven. Regular soldiers, however, held that the hours immediately before and after dawn were quite normal periods for human activity; in peacetime, as the French said, they did nothing, but did it early.

The road back, along the coast, was Jewish as the road up, over the hills, had been Arab. Even the smells were different. From Tel Aviv to Haifa the wind carried scents of petrol and acacia and oranges; from Jerusalem to Haifa, it carried sage and dust. The Arab villages by the wayside smelled of donkeys and cooking spices; the Jewish settlements of boiling cabbage and pickled cucumber; or, if a settlement were new and hygienic, its desolate neatness was rendered more inhuman than ever by smelling of nothing at all.

Prayle, lying sleepily back upon the mailbags, watched the orange groves and Jewish colonies reel off behind the truck. It was odd, he thought, how Biblical history — in which he was well and unwillingly grounded at a grammar school of true Puritan tradition — had been reversed. Then the Jews had inhabited the hills, and the Philistines the coast; now the Jews held the coast, and the Arabs the hills. The Jews, in fact, had no historical right to the whole of Palestine. Jehovah might have promised them the land, but, except perhaps to Solomon (and offhand he couldn't say whether even Solomon had ruled over the Philistines), Jehovah had been well content with partition.

The truck roared through Ras Naqura, and over the hill into familiar Lebanon. Under the peaceful pagan influence of the High Places and the sea, Prayle's mind forgot the problems of the Holy Land, pausing only to inquire at the frontier whether Mussolini's claim to the lands of Augustus was not as good as the Jewish claim to the lands of Solomon. He decided that it was not, but that it would be if the Italians still worshiped the Gods of the Empire. Then, in that case, did the Nazi reverence for old geezers with wings on their hats and saucepans on their bosoms improve their claim to all Teutonic lands? And, anyway, what was a Jew? Suppose a man was a churchwarden, but his name was Levy and he looked like King David with a hang-over? Suppose he was of pure English blood, but decided that the synagogue was the place for him?

Sergeant Prayle stopped the truck on the outskirts of Beirut, explaining to the driver, in his most cryptic and confidential manner, that he had reason to enter the city on foot and alone. He then strolled to the wineshop where he had left his motor-cycle and triumphantly rode it, for half a mile and without any sort of incident, to the section billet. In the yard he straightened his footrest, and fussed over his mount with a little oil and water, until the sergeant major came out, attracted by such industry, and congratulated him on the excellent condition of his machine after so long a ride.

Interlude

Major Rains was an honest man; he knew very well that of all the branches of the staff, Intelligence was that which fitted his abilities the least. On the other hand it was his duty, as an experienced regular officer, to do the best he could in any situation to which his profession had called him; and one could not, after all, go far wrong if one worked really hard and took pains to obey orders.

He found it difficult, especially in so complicated a business as this Montagne affair, to follow at short notice such a gifted and, he feared, irresponsible amateur as Guy Furney. Rains did not complain — the first duty of a staff officer was to be able to take over from anybody anywhere — but Guy's handling of the office had been eccentric. The files were excellent and comprehensive, but it wasn't much help to read through the utterly damning dossier of some prominent Arab politician and to find at the end a short minute: *"This is tripe. I know him. G.F."* Furney's personal opinions carried no authority, and were destructive of all system. Both he and the Field Security seemed to have taken their obligations much too casually. Rains himself hoped to set better standards both of obedience and of caution.

Ordered away so suddenly and importantly, Furney had had little time to explain the current investigations. All were vague and unsatisfactory — security cases usually were. About the Beit Chabab arms Guy simply said that an explanation was due to Montagne, and that as yet there wasn't any. It now looked as if Montagne were the only person who knew the explanation.

In the presence of David Nachmias, Rains had no need to look again at Montagne's record. He had already learned it by heart, and it was not impressive. Political agitator in civil life. Fought with International Brigade in Spain. Insubordinate. Suspected of conducting a personal intelligence service. Possible communist agent.

To this last hypothesis — supplied, he observed, by a Major Loujon — Rains dutifully closed his eyes. Since the Nazi-Soviet alliance had ended in the way of all German alliances, army orders were to think no evil. Rains kept upon his desk an ash-tray in the shape of three inhibited apes who neither heard, saw nor spoke the inconvenient. He tried to model himself upon them.

Rains's courtesy visit to Montagne's office had left no clear impression of the man beyond dislike of his appearance. Furney, conducting his successor on a very short tour of files and personalities, had said little of his opposite number in the French Army except that he was a good chap. The two seemed to be on terms of intimacy and affection.

This, however, meant nothing, for Guy was well known to be unusual in his tastes and friendships. Certain it was that the dominant clique of the French were sound, solid folk, and that Montagne was very unsound indeed. The man was reputed to be an intriguer and a fanatic. Such people were a nuisance in any army. The opinion of his enemies among the French was easy to understand. Montagne, in any decent mess, would be an impossible bore — the sort of chap who could never talk anything but his own brand of politics.

"It seems very likely, David," Rains said.

Abu Tisein slowly opened his brown eyes with an expression of patient sadness.

"I hear so much," he complained.

"Of course. Of course."

Before this sturdy Palestinian, Jew, Turk — whatever he liked to call himself — unmoved, uncondemning, tolerant of a thousand Oriental treacheries that would have shocked a European, Rains felt himself to be a perky little fellow of no experience. Self-consciously he smoothed his very fair mustache.

"You're sure Wadiah wasn't in it?" he asked.

"Yes. That is why I advised him to come and see you," answered David Nachmias in his steady, simple English. "He detests the French. Never would he give them arms! Never! Wadiah thought the troops were British."

"And this Herne woman? Where does she come in? Knocking about the St. Georges Hotel for a long time, wasn't she?"

"Yes."

"She knew Montagne?"

"Yes. She knew many officers."

"But, David," Rains protested uncomfortably, "I can't believe this of an Englishwoman. I mean — it isn't as if one didn't know who she was. I mean, she's what one would call a lady. I mean . . ."

"She is half French," said Nachmias somberly.

"Ah! That accounts for it."

"I cannot say that Major Montagne employed her. There is no evidence. It was perhaps coincidence that she was in Beit Chabab for so long. Who can tell? The trouble is, Major Rains, that you put too many people in British battle dress."

"The Jews too," Rains replied, with an awkward military laugh.

"The Jews, of course. We are a fighting people now, Major Rains."

"First-class guerrillas," answered Rains professionally, "but no discipline. However, they seem to obey you people all right."

"For the present. But when the danger to Palestine is past we may not be able to control our extremists. Give us free immigration. Then you can be sure of us."

Rains swallowed. The question had to be asked.

"What is your own connection with Armande Herne?"

"I used her. I use her still. Such a woman is rare."

"It's all very difficult," Rains sighed. "What on earth am I to do?"

"Do? Do? You English always want to do. But there is nothing to do. Leave it all to the French."

"Do they know?"

"No more than I. But the same rumor has come to them."

"I might have to interfere," Rains insisted.

"Why?"

"But really I should have more evidence."

"Of course," began Abu Tisein, "I do not know what control you have over the French Army — "

"None," said Rains hastily. "Aboslutely none! For heaven's sake don't get that idea into your head — it might cause infinite trouble. Their internal discipline is entirely their own affair."

"Then leave them alone. You are a real Englishman. You want to take all troubles on your shoulders. If they believe this story against Major Montagne, what is it to you? If one of your own officers had to be dismissed, would you like the French to interfere?"

"Most certainly not!" exclaimed Rains indignantly.

"Very well. Then look at this affair with the eyes of a

French general. Major Montagne is difficult. Major Montagne has no respect for his superiors. There is now a very strong rumor that Major Montagne acquired arms for his own faction. Perhaps they have found the troops that collected them. They would never say. In any case, they have every right to send Major Montagne to command Negroes in West Africa."

"On suspicion only?"

"An Intelligence officer must be above suspicion. And if he plays politics, he is not. It may be that Major Montagne did not mean to keep the arms at all. Perhaps he meant to raise funds for his party by selling them to Arabs or Jews."

Rains seized quickly upon this hint with a conscious pride in his own cleverness.

"So that's how you know the story, David!"

"Dear Major Rains, I know nothing. As soon as I heard the Field Security had been making inquiries, I came straight from Jerusalem to bring you, as is my duty, a story I had learned — just as I would have done for Major Furney. He was inclined, I think, to trust the Field Security too — well, what do I know? Shall I say he gave them too delicate missions?"

"Bulls in the china shop, eh?"

"Oh, that is too strong! But, if I were you, I should have in-quiries — about people — put through the Palestine police."

"They are not too kind to the Jewish Agency," said Rains pointedly.

Really, David Nachmias had gone a little far with his *if I were you.*

"The Agency? No, I wasn't thinking of that. The Agency can look after itself. I was thinking of women like this Ar-mande Herne. The Palestine police would know exactly how to place her."

David Nachmias pulled out his watch.

"Would you like to see Sheikh Wadiah now?" he asked. "I think you have kept him waiting just long enough to show your importance."

"Yes, yes. Of course. On *those* matters, David, I am always so glad to have your advice."

Major Rains had little conceit. He was conscientiously eager to improve his Arab manners. They were already good. He felt, however, that spontaneity was lacking, and sought to replace it by ever more exact observance of the social customs.

"Will you see him alone?" asked Abu Tisein.

"No, no. You are friends, and you would be a great help to me."

The smooth opening of the interview with Sheikh Wadiah was faultless. The cups of coffee, the cigarettes, the polite, unhurried talk about nothing whatever for a quarter of an hour, all were matters for self-congratulation, more especially since Rains did not, could not, like Wadiah. This so-called sheikh too closely resembled a fatherly bookmaker who had absorbed, throughout a disastrous summer at Sandhurst, far more of young Rains's allowance than he could afford. The bookmaker had had heartiness. The bookmaker had had dignity. He wasn't always pressing hands to head and heart with the graceful and hypocritical gestures of Wadiah, but he used to advise Rains, in the most presumptuous and patronizing way, not to bet on the impossible. And that was offensive. After all he had known that the man was out to make money, just as he knew that Wadiah's protestations of loyalty and affection were meaningless.

Wadiah's account of the whole transaction was quite straightforward. The trick that had been played on him he treated neither lightly nor angrily, but with an impersonal appreciation of its part in the general richness of life. His majestic confidence that it was proper and even right for him to possess arms prohibited all discussion of the means by which they had been obtained. He tactfully referred to Armande as "a certain person" or "a charming agent."

"But what made you believe her?" asked Rains with a short laugh.

"Major Rains, I am older — " Sheikh Wadiah stroked an imaginary beard with a beautiful flow of his hand — "but I am not to be compared with you in knowledge. You have had Englishwomen in your bed, and I never."

Rains was disgusted. *I should hope not, indeed,* he declared to himself.

"Therefore I am a child in experience of them. But men I understand, for I am a leader of men. I know when a man is lying and when he is not. And I ask myself — is a woman very different? If a woman of charm and culture should say to me: 'Wadiah, you are the only man I have ever loved,' I would of course believe her. But that is a lie I want to believe. If, however, there is no question of love, but only of policy, of expediency, of duty, then I can judge a woman's lie from a woman's truth."

"And Major Montagne, Sheikh Wadiah?" asked Rains. "You who know men, tell me — when he came to collect your arms and you informed him that you had already given them up, was his surprise genuine or pretended?"

"He insulted me," answered Wadiah. "He was beside himself — a madman. I cannot judge the afflicted. But I tell you Mme. Herne was not lying. When she said she was a British agent, she believed she was a British agent."

"That is possible, of course, Sheikh Wadiah," Rains agreed politely.

"Have you a file on her?" asked Abu Tisein.

So crude a reference to his secret files made Rains wince.

"There may be a few details about her on record somewhere," he admitted.

"They would show you that she is not stupid," said Nachmias with a melancholy smile.

Wadiah turned his folded hands palms upward, as if offering the whole casket of conversation in order that Rains, out of his exceeding wisdom, might accept and seal it with his last word.

Rains was embarrassed. There was nothing to say. He did not know what Wadiah expected him to say.

"There was once a Pasha in the Lebanon," began Wadiah, smoothly entering the silence before it had time to be a noticeable silence, "who was beloved by all his subjects. What a man said to him he believed. And if a man swore by God and his Greatness and his Mercy, he believed him all the more; for he was a pious Pasha as well as innocent, and he could not think that men who must die would take the name of the All-Merciful in vain.

"There came before him, *ya* Abu Tisein, two *mukhtars,* one of a great village and one of a little, who had quarreled over the rights to a threshing floor. The *mukhtar* of the great village was a man of power and cunning. By God, he was a true leader of his people, and for their sake he knew neither fear nor shame! And he lied boldly before the Pasha, swearing that the threshing floor was his.

"Then the other *mukhtar* was silent, for he said to himself: 'If I lie the Pasha will believe me and if I tell the truth he will believe me, and who am I that I should know whether the truth or a lie is better for my village? Let justice be done to the stronger, that the courts of the Pasha be empty and the country be at peace.' "

INTERLUDE

Major Rains was startled at a certain frank and disrespectful tone in Wadiah's voice as he told his obscure anecdote to Abu Tisein. Neither of them, however, showed any change in the expressions of interest and mild benevolence with which they regarded his desk.

When they had gone, he still puzzled over their motives and their relationship to each other. Had they quarreled or had they not? And what on earth was the meaning of Wadiah's parable? He went on puzzling in the mess, where, he feared, he was thought a dull fellow. But sound. He hoped they admitted he was sound.

Devotion to duty was so easy when it just meant spending long hours in the office; but outside the office he could not stop thinking and thinking and getting nowhere. The Middle East was so full of subtleties; nobody said what they meant, or meant what they said. And at the end of it all there wasn't any clear truth to be found. That Pasha, if he ever existed, had saved himself a lot of trouble.

What was in the minds of Nachmias, of the Herne woman, of Montagne? One kept on putting down headings and sub-headings to compel the case into some sort of order, but nothing happened.

He wondered whether the boastful old Wadiah could really tell whether a man was lying or not. Perhaps he could, at any rate with his fellow Lebanese. What a gift to be envied! Or was it? One might be wrong and disorganize the whole system for the sake of one's personal flair. It was the system that mattered, not the man — the tried and tested system that carried the lame dog along.

Rains hoped that the Field Security report, when it came along, would make sense of this case. Guy Furney had suggested that they were likely to produce a convincing explanation, even if they had no proofs; but Guy had not known the full story. He had already left when Nachmias brought up his rumor against Montagne.

The Field Security report was delivered next day by Captain Wyne in person. Rains considered it most questionable. Without a single proof, on conjecture only, they had built up a case against David Nachmias. And Nachmias was a trusted agent of G.H.Q. That meant that he, Rains, was in duty bound to send the gist of the accusation to G.H.Q. — and what a rocket he would get back! It was poor comfort that he could pass the rocket on to Wyne. And there was Wyne, with his damned, lazy, heavy-lidded eyes, watching him read the report as if he knew just what was coming.

"A very clear piece of writing," said Rains — it was a good army rule always to praise a subordinate when you could — "but you know, Wyne, the only new fact you have is that this Herne woman won't say who employed her. Your sergeant believes she was working for Nachmias. Nachmias admits he employed her sometimes, and that he went to see her that Saturday when your sergeant says he did. But Nachmias seems pretty sure that at Beit Chabab she was working for Montagne. Now what is your own opinion of Montagne?"

"Maddeningly intolerant, of course, but honest as the day."

"That is not what we have on record. How do you know?"

"Damn it, I lunch with him once a week!"

"But, my dear Wyne, that doesn't prove anything. Do you realize he might be a communist agent?"

"So might I."

"But you aren't, you see."

"How do you know?"

Rains was conscious of disliking this officer. It was very

unusual, to say the least of it, to treat a superior with irony. One learned that as a subaltern. Brains were not everything.

"Have you your sergeant's original report?"

"Yes. But it won't do you any good, sir."

"All the same, I prefer to see things in writing," answered Rains sharply.

Major Rains devoted himself to Prayle's report, complete with colored chalks and Appendix A. He gave it ten conscientious minutes, while Wyne sat opposite to him idly glancing through files on his desk. Rains preferred — whatever Guy Furney might have allowed — that visiting security officers should ask for any files they needed. He rang for his clerk, and told him to remove the "out" basket.

"Your men should study the style of the military police," said Rains at last.

"Yes, they used to at one time. We changed that," Wyne replied.

"I don't understand."

"If I may say so, sir, it is not his report to me that matters, but mine to you. Prayle is a sergeant who can only give what he knows in conversation. His written statements are extremely difficult to follow."

"A lot of vague drivel about *urra ovva* and *pang pang!*" Rains snapped. "Clarity is the very first thing one demands in an N.C.O.'s reports."

"No, sir!"

"What then? What then?"

"Intelligence — even if you have to dig for it."

"I don't think we're getting any further, Wyne," said Rains with deliberate patience. "Your theory about these arms is disquieting — and a little irresponsible, you know. Really, David Nachmias is beyond suspicion."

"Why?"

"We have to accept authority, Wyne. Otherwise all work becomes impossible. David Nachmias is vouched for by people who know a great deal more of the over-all conduct of the war than we do."

"Major Furney," remarked Wyne, "used to say that the Zionists had two wars — one against the Germans and one against us."

"Very clever!" answered Rains disparagingly.

"On the other hand your point of view may be cleverer still."

"And what do you think my point of view is?"

"That David Nachmias is far too useful to our bosses to be broken on mere suspicion of obeying his other bosses."

Major Rains saw in a flash that this was the thought which had been hovering around the back of his mind for the last twenty-four hours. Captain Wyne could evidently be a very valuable officer to anyone who knew how to handle him.

"But of course you see the implications of that, sir?"

"Yes, naturally," Rains replied. "Which of them do you mean?"

"Montagne."

"Yes?"

"He's for the high jump, if you let Abu Tisein get away with it."

Rains wriggled.

"I wouldn't like the French interfering with my officers, you know."

"And Mrs. Herne?"

"Well, there we do have clear consciences," said Rains with relief. "She seems to have worked for one of them, and from our point of view it doesn't matter which."

"It would be interesting to find out. Shall we pick her up for interrogation?"

That was a suggestion which Major Rains had been dreading. The possible repercussions might be troublesome to everyone.

"You can't go bullying Englishwomen, you know," he said. "Why, there might even be a question asked in the House about it. Leave her alone. We'll just see that she doesn't have any more opportunities to give trouble. Whomever she worked for, hers was quite a minor part."

"We could ask her unofficially over all the proper drinks."

"You have asked her already, and she wouldn't talk. I think we'll leave the matter to higher authority."

"They'll just pass it back to us again."

"They won't, Wyne, they won't. They'll decide there isn't enough evidence either way, and forget about it. We don't want to go setting ourselves up against G.H.Q., do we? That isn't the way to promotion."

CHAPTER IX

Burnt Offering

RAIN, week after week, danced upon the tarmac of the ancient highway that ran from camp to melancholy camp along the Syrian shore. The red mud of Lebanon, the sands of Palestine, choked the culverts and sucked at the wounds of the road where the wheels and tracks of divisions, relieving one another between Tobruk and the Euphrates, had worn away the level and lovely route of peace. The men, huddled in their gas capes, plowing through the mud under the olive trees, cursing the water that found its way through infinitesimal meanderings into petrol cans and pumps, longed for the cleanliness of the desert. Then came the snow, lying deep upon Jerusalem and the hills, even weighing down for a day the great leaves of the banana groves until it splashed onto the semitropical sand of Beirut Bay.

Armande's lonely mood harmonized with, indeed was in part created by, that of the great garrison of the Middle East. She was doubly an alien, being a woman on sufferance among these soldiers who themselves were utterly alien to their surroundings. In her work there was neither gaiety nor excitement; nor, after the bitter use that had been made of her, did she seek for either. She was checking stores in two languages. The fact that some of the stores were confidential made the job no more interesting. She was checking stores, and probably would continue to check until the war ended.

Communication with home was worse than ever. For Armande there was little comfort in the exchange of letters with her husband. Letters from England answered those that she herself had written four months earlier. Her own words were lost in the passing of time. She had forgotten what on earth the correspondent was replying to, so that the response was either stale or meaningless. Much of marriage, she now thought, depended on the little daily intimacies; those lost, a husband and wife had no live subjects to talk about in letters.

What, she wondered, had really happened to the great lovers of fiction and history when they were years absent from one another? Surely their longing must have been so desperate that longing alone created a bond? Each, deprived of half a soul, lived in darkness, and of the darkness wrote. Longing she had, but it was for the life she had lost — not so much for John as for John coming home from the office, John opposite to her at the dinner table, John fussing about the oddness of her friends. Longing for John as a lover — but of that she did not think. It was inconvenient, difficult and led to disloyalty of thought. Observing the emotional follies of these exiled men and women with no conventional outlet for their capacity to love, she could not believe that she had a passionate temperament, or that hers was a passionate marriage.

Her mother's letters she disliked; they were too full of patriotism and complaint. The hotel seemed to have become an expensive rest home for Free French, and Maman exulted over her dear boys and her profits in successive sentences. At least one page of any letter of hers was abuse of rationing and of a hardhearted food controller who would not accept the morale of her guests as an excuse for breaking the law. Dear boys or not, Maman had been twice before the magistrates —

once for killing her own pigs and once for some complicated
deal in eggs that Armande could not understand. So many
references in letters from England were obscure. Her friends
seemed to accept and be perfectly familiar with a hundred re-
strictions on their liberty that to her were foreign and unpre-
dictable as the laws of China.

One evening early in February, Armande was called to an
interview with her colonel. He was alone in his office, a small,
bleak shed furnished only with a map, a security poster and
the two trestle tables belonging to him and his adjutant. It had
the usual smell of a staff office in winter, compounded of stale
ashtrays, wet battle dress and the fumes of a small, overworked
paraffin stove.

Armande recognized in his eyes a well-known look of yearn-
ing, which meant that he had an unpleasant administrative
job in hand and was longing for the open-air life he had enjoyed as a subaltern, or, alternatively, a tent at Advanced Headquarters in the Western Desert where he might occasionally
hear a bang. Longing for his wife and children produced a different expression, of sultry ill temper, when the sergeant clerks
stuck firmly to the main office, and only Armande and the
typists could approach him at all.

In a voice that he was obviously striving to keep clear of any
note of criticism, indeed of any implication whatever, he told
her that her employment was at an end.

"But why?" asked Armande, smiling.

She had never been sacked before. The experience was incredible. In her surprise she answered the colonel as if he had
been talking of someone else and asking her advice.

"Uniformly satisfactory. Excellent character," grunted the
colonel uncomfortably.

"I know," Armande laughed — after all, the man wasn't

writing a testimonial for his batman. "If it's just because I can't type fast yet, I'll go away and learn."

"Good Lord, no, Mrs. Herne! I say, do sit down! This is quite informal."

Armande sat down. The poor old colonel seemed to call for a more intimate touch than could be supplied while standing opposite to him. Poor old? It was just the effect, she supposed, of being a colonel and sitting important (though reluctant) in an office. He was still in his early forties.

As soon as she sat down, he got up and began to dance round the room, his hands thrust deep into trouser pockets, like an embarrassed schoolboy.

"You — you just have to take it," he told her. "Army orders, you know. Very unjust. Often very unjust indeed. The same for all of us. It will all come right in the end, Mrs. Herne. It always does. But you have to obey."

"Haven't I?"

"Oh, yes. Delightful. And all this discipline is so silly for a person like you. Sportsman I always thought you were. Are, I mean. You take everything so — so sportingly. Oh, damn this!"

"But do tell me in what way I've been a nuisance," begged Armande.

"Not a nuisance. Lovely to see you here. And you've been so very kind to me. And you could do it standing on your head, all we've given you to do. In your place I should ask for a court-martial, Mrs. Herne. Fairest court on earth!"

"But I can't ask for a court-martial," Armande replied, smil. ing at his incoherence.

"No. No, I suppose not. You're a civilian employee. No, you can't, of course. Dirty shame, I call it!" answered the colonel, wriggling off round the room. "But — but you have to go."

"If you won't tell me what the matter is, shall I ask the adjutant?"

"No, no! No, no! He couldn't tell you any more than I."

"But you must see I can't let it go like that," said Armande reasonably. "If you won't tell me, who am I to ask?"

"Oh Lord, it's difficult! Damn these people! I don't know what I ought to tell you. Look here, Mrs. Herne, you have an awful lot of friends in Jerusalem, much more than I have."

"No, I have very few friends in Jerusalem."

"Yes, of course. Expressed myself badly. I mean, there's any amount of people you know."

"To speak to, yes."

"Oh, more than that! Oh Lord, Mrs. Herne, don't tell me that a lovely — well, I don't know. Yes, I suppose nobody knows you really well. That makes it all the worse. Gosh, what a mess! What I was going to say was — well, don't you know any of the intelligence wallahs?"

"What have they got to do with it?" asked Armande, with the clear ring in her voice of an angry but well-bred English-woman.

"Nothing. Nothing at all," said the colonel hastily. "I just thought that . . ."

He anchored himself boldly to a corner of the table, and put his head to the threatening blast.

"Look here — you go and see one of them. You take my advice. I expect some of them are quite decent fellows really. Don't you know any of them?"

"I know a Captain Fairfather very slightly," said Armande with disdain.

"Just the man! I don't know what he does. Sort of policeman, I think. Always running people in for wearing their regimental

badges, and that sort of thing. I don't know — may be a very
nice chap personally. We had a censor in the mess once. Always snooping in people's letters home. But quite a decent
chap when you got to know him. You go and see Captain Fairfather. Just a personal call, if you see what I mean. I should be
so glad to see you back. We all would."

"Then why let me go?"

"Oh gosh, I've told you all about it, Mrs. Herne! You mustn't
be so persistent."

Armande left without good-bys, as if she were to return to
the office next morning. She was dull with anger at the stupidity of — well, not the colonel, but the army. Somewhere, some-
how, this was one of the army's maddening, collective stupidities. It was so futile to be sacked and to be unable to give any
reason.

On the plea of a headache she canceled a dinner invitation
of no importance. At least it seemed of no importance now.
She felt it impossible to listen to army chatter without some of
her indignation escaping, and this was not a matter to be confided to anyone until she understood it herself. She knew the
mess some combative male would make, when charging for
her sake into a delicate situation. Why, oh why, when they
were chivalrous, were they almost always clumsy?

The colonel's advice was sound. Laurence Fairfather was
the right man to see before she or anyone on her behalf could
be permitted to challenge the military. She did not like him,
but at least he was reasonable. Too intellectual, John said. But
he wasn't intellectual at all; he used to lay down the law without having read anything that he ought. He was essentially a
coarse man — coarseness seemed to be unfortunately common
among his brand of policeman — whom John had completely
misunderstood. Laurence Fairfather, it was true, had never

attempted to make love to her, but he made it so casually and revoltingly plain that if she felt the inclination he would be delighted to oblige. The man was a nihilist, morally and politically.

She called him up the next morning, and was immediately invited to lunch. Armande replied coldly that she was engaged for lunch, and then, as was her way, relented.

"It's just that I would rather see you in your office," she said.

Captain Fairfather made no comment. That she approved.

"Five o'clock suit you?" he asked.

"Yes."

There could be no nonsense with Captain Fairfather. He was a man whose compliments were likely to be embarrassing if one looked too attractive. A bloody man — Armande from a child had used stronger expressions to herself than ever passed her lips — with a lewd bald head. Bald heads, she decided in her annoyance at this disturbance of her peace, were always lewd. Italians had bald heads. So did commercial travelers. And bankers. But not people with any real culture and gentleness of insight. What did Laurence Fairfather do in peacetime? She didn't know. Some commercial job abroad which took him home to London at regular intervals. Tweeds and smart tweeds were the right wear to intimidate Captain Fairfather.

"You look like something out of the *Tatler*," he said when she entered his office.

"Yes?" she replied indifferently.

"Point to point. So refreshing after all this local color. A cigarette?"

"Thank you. I was told to come and see you by my colonel."

"Very naughty of him."

"Oh, please!" said Armande impatiently.

"But it was. He's not supposed to indicate to you in any way why you lost your job. Of course it would be ideal if every army employer were a born actor and could pretend, when we order him to sack somebody, that the reason was disgraceful conduct or inefficiency. But they aren't actors."

"So it's true you had something to do with it!"

"I, personally? Nothing at all. Nor your Sergeant Prayle either."

"Then for heaven's sake tell me what has happened."

"Certainly. You have been black-listed for employment by any of the Services."

Armande stared at him. The Jewish and Arab employees in the army offices had talked mysteriously of this black-listing. It was one of the bogeys, like arms dealing, to be discussed only in a lowered voice; and dreaded, since its victims, from the point of view of the humble, seemed to be arbitrarily chosen. They were cut off, then and there, from all further attempts to bleed the army pay roll.

What a phrase! Armande shuddered at her racing, uncharitable thoughts. And yet how many of them had sacrificed anything at all to work for the garrison? If they could get more money elsewhere, they got it. Devotion? Damn you, she exclaimed to herself, won't you allow devotion to anyone but Armande? Not those, anyway! And when it comes to having the impertinence to black-list a British subject of standing (what standing, darling, damn you again?) I'll . . . I'll . . .

"Why?" she asked casually, as if the whole matter concerned some other woman.

"Because, I suppose, we are afraid of you."

"No, you are not. Not a bit. Is this a punishment because I have Jewish friends?"

"As many as I?" he asked gently.

"Oh, you! You can get away with anything."

"So can you. Or at least you ought to be able to. I don't know what has gone wrong. I don't know why you are so touchy on this Palestine problem. Just what is your opinion of Zionism?"

"I think we have broken our word," she exclaimed with a flashing vehemence that sprang from her personal humiliation rather than any political anger. "I think the White Paper was a scandal, and the League of Nations said it was a scandal. We have stopped the Jews building up their National Home. And it doesn't matter in the least what the meaning of National Home is."

"We also kept the Arabs quiet."

"That may be. But if I were a Jew, I'd be an extremist."

"Do you often say things like that?"

"Yes, if I feel like it. Is that why I'm black-listed?"

"No. We aren't quite such fools, you know. Your opinions, of course, might be considered — well, some slight additional evidence. But I don't know if anyone ever bothered with them."

He offered her another cigarette, and lit it. His eyes were annoyingly and steadily returning to hers.

"Good God, what a glowing person you are!" he said with a half laugh. "And we continue to talk nonsense."

Armande, raging internally, kept her temper.

"You think that has nothing to do with it, but it has," he went on. "I wouldn't use those words of some obvious little trickster. You're mysterious, yes. But it's so clear from your face that . . . well, Spenser, isn't it? *For of the soule the bodie forme doth take: For soule is forme, and doth the bodie make.* I can't feel you could ever be harmful to anything I believe in. That sounds conceited, I know. And naturally what I believe doesn't matter to you in the least."

He spoke slowly, and Armande had time to regain an uneasy balance. Her thoughts were too ragged for her to feel any sort of relaxation, but she liked what he said; it sounded sincere. The man might be a nuisance, yet less ordinary than she had imagined.

"Home is so far away, Captain Fairfather. Have we got to fence with one another?" she begged. "What crime am I supposed to have committed?"

"Really I don't know. It's in Beirut that they know, or think they know. It appears that in a moment of carelessness or idealism — not, I am sure, for money — you did a job for the French or the Jews."

"I did neither," Armande retorted indignantly. "Doesn't one department of Intelligence ever tell another what it is doing?"

"Not if one department is Abu Tisein."

"You mean I've been sacrificed to — what?"

"Something worthy, I hope. I'm not in this, you see. Palestine — contrary to what you thought — has nothing whatever against you. My only information comes from Wyne, whom I trust, and he trusts Prayle, and Prayle says — he's far from complimentary for so devoted an admirer — he says you are not only innocent, but a sweet innocent into the bargain."

"Sergeant Prayle said that?" she asked coldly.

"Well, I'm translating his thought into my own words, you know. He may have put it quite differently."

"Something about my little loaf, probably," Armande replied, measuring contempt into every word.

Captain Fairfather chuckled.

"Noggin, I think," he corrected her.

Armande had to smile. Nevertheless Prayle's impudence

was exasperating. A sweet innocent, indeed — she a disciplined, calm, worldly woman, who had taken an active interest in every intellectual movement of her time!

"Why on earth don't you people ask David Nachmias about me?" she said.

"Has it occurred to you that he must have been asked before you were black-listed?"

Armande stared at him.

"Oh!"

It was a cry of pain, childlike and uncontrollable, as if caused by some small, surprising wound. His words opened an abyss of human infamy. And it was no valley through which she had to pass. She was in it. Now. And what he said was true, so obviously and unchallengeably true.

"But then — I'm back where I was."

"Where was that?" he asked.

"Oh, just — Beirut."

"I don't know what sort of hell that means to you. But you aren't back where you were."

"Yes."

"What about friends?"

"Not much use, are they, in this sort of thing?"

"I didn't mean the brigadiers," he said, smiling.

"They would shy off, wouldn't they?" she agreed bitterly. "No, I'm ungrateful. Thank you."

"Don't. I hate injustice too."

"How do you know there has been any?"

"Oh, refer to our earlier conversation. . . . My poor Armande, this is a scandalous thing!"

She accepted the sudden use of her Christian name. So timed, it nearly made her cry.

"What am I to do?"

"Well, if I were you, I should go to Egypt."

"Will I be . . . ?"

She hesitated over the word.

"Black-listed there too? Yes, I'm afraid so. But there are two good reasons for going. One is that you may get home from there. The other — you're better out of Palestine till this can be cleared up. In your present situation you're open to police slanders, exploitation, anything. My driver has an odd story of women changing into men, and I see a man is wanted who disappeared from Beit Chabab. No, don't tell me anything! I liked your Sergeant Prayle. But the connection with you is there to be made if the right policeman reads our black list. Have you a passport?"

"Of course."

"Give it me. I'll fix up your visas."

"I can do it myself, really," she protested.

"Perhaps."

"Only perhaps?"

"Anyway, I could do it much more quickly."

Laurence Fairfather's suggestion that she should go to Egypt was wise. She had certainly no wish to be asked any polite questions about Fouad. And every intimate impulse prompted her to get out of Palestine. It was impossible to sit idly in her flat and put off all the awkward and friendly inquiries; impossible even to talk to her acquaintances while wondering how much they knew.

"Who knows about this?" she asked.

"About what?"

"About what I am supposed to have done."

"Your name is just one among hundreds. If you don't apply for jobs with the Services, and don't come to the notice of officialdom — "

"But how long must I endure this?" she interrupted. "Can't I be cleared? Can't I ask for some sort of inquiry?"

"Yes, I think you could. But would you be any better off? Who really were those troops in British uniform who collected the arms?"

"French. Montagne's French."

"Who told you that?"

"David Nachmias."

"When?"

"When Sergeant Prayle was here asking about it."

"And what did he tell you when you took on the job?"

"That British would collect them."

"Any witnesses?"

"No."

"Did he say why on earth we should waste men and money collecting arms in the Lebanon?"

Armande repeated the explanation that David Nachmias had given her on the terrace of the Hotel St. Georges, and the shocking tale of intrigue that he had told her later in her flat.

"Detailed, and to you convincing," said Fairfather. "I don't wonder. But when one knows the general layout, it's tosh! We have enough to do in Syria without bothering about the armament of an old Christian coot in the middle of nowhere. As for David's second story, we should never encourage these divisions of the French. We would give anything to prevent them. No, Armande, it's as plain as can be that what you did was to acquire some much wanted Hotchkiss guns for the National Home.

"Now, suppose you had your inquiry. It's your word against David Nachmias, and whatever half-evidence and innuendo he can bring to bear. How would you come out? Exactly as you are. That is: probably innocent, but not a good risk. And David Nachmias? Quite certainly guilty, but no legal proof. And still very useful to us in bigger things. You see?"

"But it's the most horrible treachery!" she cried. "I didn't know people really did such things."

"They do. In my job I have seen men's lives and, worse, men's honor mercilessly sacrificed. This is war. Everything goes. To myself I stink. But my excuse is that anything is better than the destruction of my country. Is it surprising that the Zionists feel the same? I doubt if to themselves they stink — they are too self-righteous — but their excuse is that anything is better than a world where Jews haven't a home of their own."

"But to use me!" she cried. "To make me a common little crook!"

"There is one comfort, Armande. A poor one — but there it is. You needn't feel ashamed of your own country any longer. We have so much cleaner hands than you believed. Such a policy towards the French as Abu Tisein described for you is utterly unthinkable."

"Is it? Is anything unthinkable? Even you said that you'd sacrifice honor rather than see your country destroyed."

"Personal, not national. I meant that I am prepared to stink, so long as my country does not. All this is really a back-handed defense of David Nachmias. He has made a mistake, and he is saving his country's honor at the expense of his own — and yours. He has to obey orders, but he would much rather be a quiet Turkish gentleman."

"He said so. And I believed it," replied Armande bitterly.

"Oh, it's true. Abu Tisein loathes all these Central Europeans as much as an Arab. He has no personal ambition, but he is convinced — I think, rightly — that he is essential to his people."

When Armande left Laurence Fairfather's office, Jerusalem was in utter darkness. The heavy clouds of winter made absolute the blackout. The masses of clear masonry which had faintly reflected the brilliant starlight of summer and autumn were not even shapes against the sky or before the outstretched hand. Here and there, under the doorways, were faint blue lamps. Puddles of light appeared and disappeared on the ground as pedestrians flashed their torches and groped their way round the blast walls that obstructed the narrow pavements. In the shuffling silence she could hear the jackals hooting, like little breathless factory sirens, from the valley of Kiriat Shemuel.

Armande walked slowly towards Qatamon, then turned back into the center of the town. There was nothing any longer at home to welcome her; her room was no more a refuge from the ever-present, ever-insistent society of the garrison. That society did not require her. On the familiar streets, the short, well-known thoroughfares of a small but active city, progress through the darkness gave to her just enough automatic occupation to set free her racing thoughts. She ached for comfort, for an older man, a father or an uncle, to whom she could leave, for a time, all the arrangement of her life.

John? Oh, dear John — it would be comforting to have him, but what an intolerable deal of explanation would be necessary. She wanted a sort of Laurence Fairfather, but without his unhelpful habit of seeing two sides to every problem, her own included. Two sides? Ten! And believing none of them. Someone wise, to whom she would always be right. Prayle might be like that, if only . . . but he was crazy, anyway. He was no giver of comfort; he needed mothering. All the same, it would do her good to hear that restful voice, with its odd, jerky rhythms, which she had so liked when she first heard it on the telephone.

What a conceited little fool she had been! That morning when she had found him teaching the page boy to make a catapult — if only then, instead of fussing over his explanation of the nickname, she had told him what Abu Tisein had asked her to do! Too discreet. Can a person be too discreet? No, darling, but she can be on her dignity with sergeants.

The strong scents of oranges and cooking spices called her back to the outer realities. She was approaching the Jaffa Gate. The carelessly hooded head lamps of two Arab taxis and the chinks of light from the windows of Arab cafés revealed, alongside the black pavement, masses of a deeper black which, at a distance of five yards, could be distinguished as sacks of oranges, donkeys and a couched camel. Across the road was the dim outline of the gate. There must, she thought penitently, be some wisdom in this administration if now a woman could grope her way in peace through a city of such burning passions. Three years earlier that darkness would have been the gift of Allah the All-Merciful to raving little mobs of Arabs.

Armande passed under the gate into the Old City, brushing the robes of unseen passers-by, and turned left into the Christian Quarter with the vague impulse of seeking a temporary peace in some church or monastery courtyard; but the heels of the shoes that she had worn for Captain Fairfather, while low enough to suit her tweeds, were far too high for cobblestones in darkness. She sought more earthly but immediate rest in a small Greek restaurant. As soon as she had entered she realized that it was primitive, but also that she was very hungry. She hesitated, and then went boldly to a table.

The place was full of Christian Arabs and a party of young and well-dressed Moslem effendis, who were tasting, with gestures of exaggerated pleasure, the forbidden wine. What a lot of fun they get, she thought with weary envy, these Moslems with their wine, these Jews with a dish of bacon! And to me nothing is forbidden except what I forbid myself.

The customers stared at her with friendly interest as she sat down before a tablecloth matted with oil and egg. One of the younger Moslems spat an obviously insolent remark in Arabic, of which she only understood the word for Jew. He was instantly rebuked by two older members of the party, who bowed and smiled to her an apology, and looked away as if to assure her that their courtesy was wholly disinterested. Did they, she wondered, recognize her as an alien English-woman or didn't they care? She decided that her religion was not in the least apparent — with her black hair and big gray eyes she was sometimes mistaken for a Jewess — but that her class was. Arabs seemed to have a strong sense of class, perhaps because they could afford without jealousy, within so true a democracy as Islam, to pay homage to wealth and education.

Wealth? Well, she looked smart. *Tatler,* damn him! But actually she wouldn't have much left by the time she had paid her fare to Egypt. An income of five pounds a week had been very useful, though she hadn't really attempted to live on it. One couldn't, with Palestine prices soaring upwards. Invitations from the military had accounted for a shameful number of her solid meals.

The Greek proprietor, who kept his belly in a sort of box formed by the cash desk, wine barrels and crates of bottles, moved to her with surprising speed, and whisked from a shelf a less revolting tablecloth. She left the menu to his care. Armande could never understand why people made such a to-do over ordering, eating, paying and tipping. As a child of the trade, it was all familiar to her; and something in her manner seemed to proclaim to any purveyor of food that she was aware of routine, circumstance and what there might be on the ice.

The proprietor brought to her crisp fried fish from the Sea of Galilee. Odd, she thought while enjoying its excellence, how all the good fish in Palestine was Arab, and all the large and tasteless fishes Jewish! Odd that in this filthy little joint — or, for that matter, in Beit Chabab — she felt at home. The frank and kindly stares, the interest of customers and proprietor, were they not more in the ancient European tradition than the neat indifference of Jewish restaurants? All these Palestine British who preferred the Arab to the Jew — was the reason wholly, as the Jews said, that the British liked to be among natives whom they could dominate rather than fellow Europeans whom they could not? The conservative English always disliked the artificial; and Jewish civilization in Palestine did seem, compared with the true Levantine, unsure of itself and brittle.

That's right, she accused herself, blame the Jews just because you have been let down by one of them! A lovely child you are — becoming an anti-Semite and a pest to men busy with a war and a snob to sergeants! Oh God, I wish I were out of this!

She lifted tear-filled eyes to meet, with foolish, unexpected impact, those of the proprietor. With silent sympathy he brought her coffee and a sweet of incredible stickiness.

"War no good," he murmured. "No good for business. No good for Greeks. Most, no good for women."

"No good for business?" asked Armande. "With all the troops?"

"Ham and eggs, George, beer? Beer, George, ham and eggs?" answered the proprietor, imitating the invariable inquiry of the British and Australians. "Make money — oh, yes! But business not all money — business my life. No fun. You understand, yes, no? See him?" He pointed to a Greek major, alone and moodily sipping his coffee. "He cry every night. I make plenty money, yes. But he cry. You cry. War no good. Ham and eggs."

Armande paid her bill, which had been scaled reasonably upwards to suit her personal appearance, and went out. The clouds were dropping a wet snow into the blackness of Jerusalem; at the Jaffa Gate she took a taxi. When she had settled back comfortably into the warmth of the cushions, it occurred to her that in future she had better walk or wait for buses. Taxis and the most expensive dishes — even in cheap restaurants — could no longer be unthinkingly commanded.

CHAPTER X

Prisoners of Cairo

"THERE YOU ARE THEN," said Laurence Fairfather, handing back her passport, "all fixed for this afternoon's train. I couldn't get you a sleeper — they're only for generals and contractors — but the train control will look after you, and you'll be all right. Where will you stay in Cairo?"

"Oh, I'll find a hotel and then look round," answered Armande.

"Hotels are rather full, you know," he said doubtfully. "Well, I've written a note about you — just saying I knew you in London — to a pal of mine, a Major Honeymill. Here's his telephone number. Give him a call if you're in any trouble. He'll be delighted. He has nothing whatever to do except train a sort of Arab legion, and he knows everybody in Cairo society and takes none of them seriously. Just the person to get you a job in — well, civilian life, if there's any left."

"Thank you. And you will do everything you can?"

"To clear it up? Of course. But, as I told you, that depends on Beirut, not on us. However, you have Sergeant Prayle there."

"Give him my love."

"I'll make a point of it."

She held out her hand, and Laurence Fairfather kissed it. Unnecessarily, she thought. It was his casual manner that made him so disconcerting. He never hid the fact that he thought her lovely and desirable, yet assumed, without any real attempt to test his opinion, that their temperaments were entirely incompatible. She left his office full of gratitude, but wishing that, on the tide of temporary emotion, he had either kissed her very lonely lips or played the silent comrade and grimly but tenderly shaken the offered hand.

The long train of white coaches, windows shuttered against dust and sand, drew in to Lydda station. Armande, piloted by one of Fairfather's corporals through the milling mob of bulky, rattling soldiers in full marching order, of porters, lemonade and orange sellers, of passengers and onlookers screaming Arabic in the hysterical excitement of the Middle East over anything whatever that came and went at fixed times, reached the train and found a corner seat reserved for her.

The other five places in her compartment were occupied by an Egyptian businessman and his wife (after so long a stay in the Hotel St. Georges she knew the type), by an indeterminate Latin with an alert, sensitive face, an insolent-looking young man dressed in a new checked suit of boardlike stiffness, and a Levantine whose silk scarves, cap, overcoat and baggage were all so smart and appropriate that they suggested an advertisement of the perfect masculine traveler in an American magazine.

Except for the Latin who gave her a delightful half-smile and some assistance with her coats and baggage, they looked at her with curiosity and resentment, and then continued their conversation in clipped and raucous Middle Eastern French. They talked war and war interminably, till the orange groves gave way to date palms, and the desert, the sea and the dusk closed down upon the railway.

Armande, curled in her corner with an unread book, won-

dered what each of them really believed, for what they said
was so far from any conceivable reality. The Egyptian had it
that the war in the desert was a bluff. The man in the suit of
checked upholstery material agreed, and informed the compartment that he was a Turkish officer and bound to G.H.Q.
on a most secret mission to arrange for the training of Turkish
gunners. The well-outfitted traveler preserved a discreet and
well-informed silence, at intervals approving or condemning
monosyllabically. At last, having aroused the respect of the
others, he stated that he was the local Syrian correspondent
of an American news agency and distributed a number of
visiting cards to prove it.

The compartment's blacked-out lamps gave just sufficient
light to distinguish the faces of fellow travelers. The Syrian
rose from his seat, and with a gold-handled penknife scraped
the blue paint off the bulb above his corner, thus creating a
pool of light in which to read. The Egyptian wife yapped complaint and apprehension, protesting that he would attract all
the enemy aircraft from the Mediterranean. The Syrian assured her that neither Germans nor Italians had any intention
of bombing the railway, since they expected to use it for evacu-
ating their troops from Egypt. He then selected from his bag
an English novel, and settled down to enjoy the admiration
of the compartment.

Armande, utterly disgusted, got up and stood in the corridor. From the blackness of the train, she could see through
the windows the moonlit sand and scrub of the Sinai Desert,
gray emptiness after gray emptiness slowly rumbling past.
After a while the Latin joined her in the corridor, and offered
a cigarette. His eyes were humorous, and indicated that he,
too, preferred the desert to such humanity as the compartment
offered.

"I couldn't hear any more of it," she said.

"Oh, you mustn't mind!" he answered, as if defending the Middle East where he had made his home. "It's not their war."

"Do they really believe it all?"

"Consciously, yes."

"And unconsciously?"

In the dim light she could just see his face crinkle with pleasure at so promising an opening to café conversation.

"At heart they don't believe a word of it. They are terrified, you see, at the nearness of all these modern, Western engines of destruction. That accounts for their wild stories — anything to persuade themselves that the war will never reach them."

"I hope it does," Armande said savagely.

"No, I wouldn't wish that on them — not even if my own country escaped."

"Which is that?"

"Palestine. But I was Italian till Mussolini reminded me I was a Jew as well."

"And do you like it?"

"I love it. Palestine is *my* country, *my* landscape. Our colonists should be drawn from the Mediterranean — Italians, Spaniards, Greeks, North Africans . . ."

Armande resigned herself to listen. A professorial Italian with a gift for eloquence and a woman for an audience could not be interrupted. Moreover, she was in need of masculine chivalry. An hour away was Kantara with all the complications of the frontier, of food and drink, of the ferry over the Canal, of finding a seat in the train on the other side.

All these minor problems the Palestinian Italian solved for her efficiently; and of their former traveling companions only the Syrian correspondent, by now too sleepy to be a bore, was in their compartment on the Egyptian side of the Canal.

At dawn Armande's morale was low. Reluctant examination of her face and uncombed hair in the mirror reminded her that in another three years she would be thirty. A swift and sufficient glance at the lavatory, combined with the sickening smell of the eau de cologne in which the Syrian was cat-washing his face, left every too fastidious nerve offended. The train drew in to the shrieking Cairo station. When the Italian had handed out her bags through the window, she stood on the platform feeling lost and helpless as in a nightmare.

Her luggage was seized and borne aloft through the crowd by a porter whose great height and immense potbelly made him grotesque as a pregnant woman. In the anxiety of following him she lost touch with her Italian. At last, limp and feeling humiliatingly inefficient, she was led by the porter to a taxi. He then stood between her and the haven of the taxi door, yammering for more money. Other porters, scenting the impressionable infidel, joined him, and bayed and pranced before her in support of their colleague's demands. Desperate, she flung them bits of paper until the menacing noise changed to exaggerated and almost tearful thanks. The grinning taxi driver consented to drive away

Not even the warmth of Cairo had any appeal to her; it was too soft a warmth, sweetly tainted as if a beflowered and un-decaying corpse were drying in the sun. At one hotel after another she was bowed from her taxi by a gorgeously dressed luggage porter, and bowed back again. None had a room. She was weary of the polite and natty hotel clerks, weary of well-bathed officers leisurely departing from their rooms to G.H.Q., weary of the whole air of spurious smartness. The faint smell of horse dung in the streets, which greeted her whenever the taxi door was opened, made her homesick, recalling her father and the inn stables when she was a little girl.

She appealed to the taxi driver for the address of a hotel less likely to be crammed to the attics with military. He took her to a pension. Her overworked nose immediately revolted from yesterday's cabbage and a vintage lavatory pan. She decided, as a last resort, to telephone this Major Honeymill.

Again she had to accuse herself of inefficiency. She could make nothing of the complicated welter of military exchanges. She drove back to the most sympathetic of the hotels, where French had seemed to be a native language rather than a mere medium for polite robbery or refusal, and demanded, hating herself for shrillness, that the hotel clerk should get her Major Honeymill on the telephone. He seemed to have no difficulty whatever.

The major's voice was soothing. Armande wondered whether that manner was usual to him, or whether she herself, by this time, sounded like a hysterical patient demanding admission to a psychiatrist's consulting room. He did not bother with unintelligible directions. He put an immediate end to this wandering through Cairo streets in charge of a leering taxi driver.

"Stay right where you are," he said, "and I'll come and fetch you before lunch. Let me talk to the manager."

The manager engaged in smiling Arabic conversation over the telephone, in which there seemed to be a good deal of exclamatory backchat and, probably, of conventional masculine indecencies.

Major Honeymill evidently knew his Cairo. There was clapping of hands at the desk. A brown man in red robes and two black men in white robes made obsequious appearance. Madame would have a bath. Madame would have breakfast. It was deeply regretted that Madame could not yet be given a room, but meanwhile the hotel was at Madame's disposal.

Armande sighed with relief, and suffered herself to be led to hot water and coffee.

After a bath, Armande felt more charitable towards the Cairo winter climate. Beneath the windows of the hotel a café garden was filling with idle and overdressed women, who were obviously not depressed by the Palestine or any other problem and who all looked likely specimens for any black list — if Egypt ever bothered with the collection of such butterflies. Armande dived to the bottom of a suitcase in search of more color and less warmth than had been called for by Jerusalem. The chambermaid was ready with an iron. When she came down to the lounge at midday, she was conscious of being fit to partner the gorgeousness of Major Honeymill.

Gorgeous he was. He wore a tall lambskin cap on his head, a green sash around the waist of his khaki sweater, desert boots, gray gabardine trousers, and bits of chain mail and shiny whistles in unexpected places. He was browned and slim as an Arab youth, though in his late thirties, and had a suggestion of Arab femininity in his sensitive face; of this he seemed to be aware, for he had grown a black mustache of remarkable ferocity which would more properly have given tone to the characterless face of a young cavalry officer. Armande, now feeling more cheerful, thought, as she shook hands, of the belief that where a cat's whiskers can pass, its head can also go. She decided that the whole of Major Honeymill's slender, sweatered body could follow his mustache with ease; so, no doubt (for his eyes were wholly Western and commanding), would his Arab irregulars.

Major Honeymill led her to an enormous staff car with an Arab driver almost as exquisitely uniformed as himself. They drove out to the Pyramids for lunch. Armande, knowing by this time how strongly the generals objected to the use for joy rides of army petrol and transport, was alarmed when the car was stopped by the Military Police. Major Honeymill gave his name and unit without the least sign of embarrassment.

"What on earth will you say?" she asked. "Can I help at all?"

"I shall say nothing," he answered with a grin. "I shall just whisper. After all, it's the Emir's staff car. And I am merely his A.D.C. Is it not possible that I should sometimes escort to His Highness those women whom he delights to honor?"

"And you can get away with that?" she laughed.

"How nice that you have a sense of humor! My dear, the simple soldiery will believe anything. But one must whisper. That is essential."

The major was an enchanting host. His military duties were of the vaguest — mothering an aged and important Emir and training the Emir's considerable body of retainers — and left him free, he said, for the far more important duty of preserving, in spite of all this military austerity, a reasonable standard of living in Cairo. He chatted agreeably of London, of Arab politics and of Laurence Fairfather, for whom he had a great regard. There had evidently been a long history of mutual amusement inspired by alcohol, and of favors done and received, often at a distance and always without question. He was unobtrusively tactful. It was impossible to guess whether he thought that Fairfather had been her lover or merely a good Samaritan. Armande warmed to his liking of her for herself.

"I can put you up," he said, "as long as you like, if you can stand the crush. Don't bother with hotels. Carry will fit you in somewhere."

Armande protested politely but unconvincingly.

"Carry will love to have you there," he said. "I'll telephone and let her know you are coming."

The great car swept them back to Cairo, its driver, mindful of his master's prestige, hooting even at the tramcars. Honeymill was dropped at his office, and Armande with her baggage taken on to his flat.

It was on the ground floor of a large new apartment house, facing a quiet little square with a garden in the middle. The flat had its own front door. Pepper trees across the road gave shade; bougainvillea and flowering shrubs around door and windows allowed individuality. It was just like Honeymill, she thought, to have found the Egyptian equivalent of a bower of roses in the midst of all the comfort of a modern block.

The driver let her into the flat and deposited her bags in the hall. Out of the hall opened a tiny kitchen and a very large living room, bare and masculine, but with a number of feminine garments strewn over the divans and thrown into corners. On the far side of the living room were only two doors. Armande recognized, regretfully, that there would indeed be a crush. She was going to be a nuisance to the Honeymills.

She pushed back a chair, and settled herself to wait gracefully for Carry or Honeymill, whichever should arrive first.

At the noise of her movements, a woman's voice behind one of the closed doors shouted gaily:

"Come in, Toots! I'm only having a bath."

"It's me, Armande Herne," she said.

"Who?"

"Are you — er — Mrs. Honeymill?" asked Armande, feeling utterly foolish, for she was suddenly, simultaneously certain that there wasn't any Mrs. Honeymill.

"I'm Carry Laxeter. Who are you?"

"Didn't Major Honeymill telephone?"

"Oh, God! Toots is impossible," came a despairing wail from the bathroom. "Wait a minute!"

The door opened, and a cloud of steam swept across the living room and out through the muslin mosquito curtains. With the mist about her strode a tall, angular woman attired in the major's silk dressing gown. Her height and the grace of her decisive walk gave her an air of distinction. Her face had a cheerful grin, and her plucked eyebrows were humorously lifted in an expression that seemed to call aloud for Armande's understanding, and alliance against the unaccountability of men.

"Have you come to stay with us?" she asked.

"Well — yes," said Armande, "if — "

"That's lovely. You'll be such a help with Xenia."

"Xenia?"

"She's a distressed Jugoslav. She lives here too. Jugoslavs do get *so* distressed. But I expect you need a drink — we can't be bothered to make tea. There's the gin in the cupboard. Are you any good at a Martini?"

"Yes," said Armande humbly. "I think I am."

"Be a darling and pour me one too, then."

Though it was only half past four, Armande mixed a couple of stiff drinks. The situation at Major Honeymill's flat was, in the cold light of normal reason, incomprehensible; it might, she considered, fall into some sort of recognizable pattern if the outlines were softened by a cocktail.

"Cheers!" said Carry Laxeter. "That's really good. Toots will make you mix the drinks."

"Toots is Major Honeymill?" she asked.

"Yes. Didn't you know?"

"I — well, I only met him this morning."

"Letter of introduction?"

"Yes."

"Maiden in distress?"

"Well — in a way."

"Oh, God!" exclaimed Carry with a ripple of laughter. "Isn't Toots delicious?"

"He has been very kind," Armande replied primly. "But perhaps I didn't appreciate . . . I mean — "

"It's just that Toots is so hospitable. Arabs, darling," Carry added vaguely. "You know."

"But — "

"No, not a harem. You see, he put me up when I'd run away from my husband. And that was a bit awkward. So when Xenia came along, what was easier than to put her up too? And now there's you."

Armande involuntarily looked round the flat. There could not possibly be more than one bedroom.

Carry smiled at her bewilderment.

"Toots sleeps there," she said, pointing to the second door, "and Xenia and I doss down in here. And if you'll join us there's a third divan for you."

It seemed to Armande that the last words had been spoken with unnecessary firmness.

"I'd love to," she answered, "for a day or two. Where is Xenia?"

"She was crying on Toots's bed. But I think she has gone to sleep now. Shall we have a look?"

Carry got up, carefully balancing her Martini, and opened the door of the bedroom. Xenia was huddled up with her back to them, gently snoring. Armande's first impression was of a mass of coarse black hair spread over the pillow and a moun-

tain of fine, peasanty bottom, in the shortest of slips, occupying
the rest of the bed. She put down Carry as a highly civilized
cat, who had known perfectly well that no one, for at least
twenty-four hours, could get over such an unfavorable introduction.

"She's fallen in love with Toots," Carry explained.

"It wouldn't be difficult."

"But don't. It's useless."

Armande smiled sympathetically. A slight bitterness on the
ironical face of her temporary hostess showed that she too had
fallen or, more probably, wanted to fall in love.

"Don't misunderstand me. He's an angel," Carry Laxeter
went on. "But you never know how far it is just pity. And
then there's no privacy. An impossible man. Darling, if ever
there were only one woman here, you can bet two of his pals
from the desert would drop in and camp in the hall."

When Major Honeymill returned from the private staff
work of his private war, he brought with him an Arab officer.
Lieutenant Rashid Abd-er-Rahman ibn Ajjueyn looked more
like a soldier than any man Armande had ever seen. Not for
him were the puzzled, the deliberately firm-lipped, the heartily
virile expressions of European officers in days of science and
Geneva Conventions. He was an Arab d'Artagnan, doubtless
full of religious and social conventions of his own, but obviously capable of whipping off an enemy's head without a
change in his merry, velvet eyes or his straight carnivorous
smile. Armande considered that if Major Honeymill had fore-
seen, as he probably had, some restraint in his domestic relations, he could not have chosen a better diversion.

"But this is delightful!" exclaimed Toots, as soon as the
introductions were completed.

With a wave of his hand he implied his pride at seeing two

such women in his room, and his satisfaction that Armande should be confidently mixing drinks.

"How is Xenia?"

"Xenia is here," answered a thrilling voice from the doorway of his bedroom.

Xenia was very much there, one hand on each portal of the door, her head sunk upon her left shoulder. She was wearing an astonishing negligee of lace and white satin which clung to the more voluptuous curves of her young body, and cascaded everywhere else.

"Grandmamma's wedding dress," said Carry in a stage whisper. "We are clever with our fingers."

"Xenia, my sweet!" cried Toots. "Come and join the party!"

"I vas veeping," announced Xenia solemnly, as if it had been an employment which needed serious concentration.

"Did you have a nice sleep, darling?" Carry asked.

"I dream you come to me," said Xenia to Toots, ignoring Carry.

Armande decided to have no more of this from either of them. Dreams? Who hadn't dreamed? And who had not wept in the morning that love was no longer in her world?

"Xenia and I have not met yet," she reminded Carry.

"Xenia, this is Armande Herne. She has come to this asylum to stay. I use the word in its proper sense, Toots — a refuge from the world."

"It is rather like a bughouse, isn't it?" said Toots proudly.

Xenia stared at Armande for an embarrassing moment; then, as if encouraged by the quiet smile, she slipped a plump arm under the tense, slim muscles of Armande's, and entered the room under her protection.

"You vill be my friend, yes?"

Armande, though faintly disgusted, felt the girl's need

Xenia was ridiculous. She evidently said whatever came into her head, and said it with quite unnecessary drama. Yet that was no reason for dislike.

"I do hope so."

"You are kind. Ve vill both love him, yes?"

Toots and Carry went off into ripples of laughter. Armande, seeing the girl was not in the least offended, squeezed her arm.

Lieutenant Rashid observed the scene with a genial smile. He seemed perfectly at ease.

"Give him a drink, Mrs. Herne," said Toots.

"Make it Armande," she replied, "or I'll feel like a dowager around here."

"Lovely Armande, then. Rashid, you look like a Cheshire cat."

"What is a Cheshire cat?"

"It grins. It remembers all the canaries it has swallowed."

"Do I smile? Well, I was reminded of my father's *beyt*."

"How many wives had he?" asked Carry.

"We don't mention those subjects," Toots warned her.

"Oh, I don't mind!" Rashid declared. "The ways of my host are my ways."

He drained the Martini which Armande offered him at a single gulp.

"*El-hamd Illah!* My father had six wives — what you would call wives."

"And did they get on together?" Carry asked.

Rashid glanced merrily at Armande, as much as to say that she should excuse him for answering silly questions.

"We have a saying that the female of all creatures is the meeker — except mankind," he answered.

"What's in the larder, Carry?" Toots asked.

"I expect Mahmoud didn't leave anything. Shall we go out?"

"I wondered whether Armande mightn't be too tired to go out after her journey," said Toots diffidently. "So Rashid and I brought a porcupine."

"Where's it going to sleep, darling?"

"It's a — well, it's a dead porcupine, Carry. I thought we'd eat it if there weren't any eggs."

Rashid sprang joyously into the entrance hall, and returned waving the porcupine by its hind legs. It was naked of spines. Its nose was very long. Its throat gaped horribly from the Mohammedan knife.

Carry looked at it with resignation.

"They brought home a baby camel last time," she said. "It hung about for days."

"Sucking swine!" exclaimed Xenia enthusiastically. "With fingers! Yes, please?"

"With fingers and on the floor in the Beduw manner," Toots agreed.

"Then I change my dress. You come!" she ordered Armande, compelling her gently towards the bedroom.

Xenia flung off her imperial negligee, and looked at herself in the mirror.

"Am I beautiful?" she asked.

"You are young," Armande replied.

In the contemplation of her own body the girl's vitality seemed to subside as suddenly as it had been aroused by the offer of barbaric and unrecognized food.

"And nobody loves me! Nobody!"

"Oh, I'm sure they do," said Armande weakly, embarrassed by so much flesh and emotion.

"Nobody! He say, come and live with Carry and me! I think first I be servant. Then I think I be loved. I do not know,

I do not care. He is so kind. I come. My mother dead, my father prisoner. What shall I do? I come. Then I find — nothing to do. I am just nice friend. I hate this Carry. I say, I go. He tell me not to be silly. I stay."

"I shall speak to Toots about it," said Armande severely.

Too much kindness — that was what was wrong with the man! Could anybody have too much kindness? Possibly not, towards a person of the same sex; but kindness to the opposite sex — as every woman knew, though it mightn't be so obvious to men — was very swiftly limited by nature or good sense.

This flat, she saw, was by no means the delightfully irresponsible loony bin that it seemed in the first few hours; its eccentricity had developed from Toots's character and his first impulsive hospitality to Carry. Carry was a delightful and amusing companion who could make the unconventional fashionable all by herself; nevertheless, she or he had been strained by so much intimacy. So then, moved one day by Carry's loneliness and Xenia's destitution, he had offered his hospitality to Xenia as well. That upset both of them, and Armande (hadn't he praised her sense of humor?) had been called in to keep order. She hoped that Toots's gift for impromptu planning was of use to G.H.Q. as to maidens in distress.

She returned to the living room with Xenia, now all bouncing in a pinafore. Carry was draped gracefully against the entrance to the kitchen. The two men had removed their tunics and were happily at work: Rashid squatting on his heels by the open back door and blowing at a charcoal brazier, Toots struggling to disjoint the porcupine.

"Let me do it," said Armande. "I'm a professional."

"You? I thought you were so . . ."

"Helpless?"

"Never! Ethereal! Dew and rose petals in the dusk."

"But not for dinner. This is a rotten knife. Rashid Bey, lend me yours."

Rashid grinned and stood up. Armande was sure that so boyish a character would have a good blade in his pocket; she expected him to go to his tunic and fetch it. Instead, he undid collar and tie, and lifted over his head a string of camel hair on the end of which was an eight-inch knife in a soft leather sheath. He laid the knife on the dresser for Armande to pick up.

"Good God!" exclaimed Toots. "I never knew you carried that thing under your shirt!"

Rashid, still grinning, watched Armande. She was absurdly proud to notice that he showed no sign of anxiety as she felt for the unfamiliar joints with the thin and precious leaf of damascened steel.

"And rose petals with it!" said Carry admiringly. "Darling, you are a dangerous woman!"

And from her own sex this time. Dangerous? Incompetent! Drifting to Egypt at the will of the fortress. Drift into this crazy place. Drift into marriage. Futile whenever she tried to strike out for herself, as in her choices of Calinot and David Nachmias. What was the cause of this false impression she gave? Merely because she was intelligent? Merely because she was reserved? What did they think she was keeping herself for? What was she keeping herself for? Nothing.

Armande took refuge in polite detachment. She knew it must be obvious to all of them that her gaiety had vanished, but determined to be an appreciative guest even if unavoidable thinking of past and future prevented her from being a contributor.

The spirits of her companions did not, in any case, require

assistance from her. Rashid carried in the joints of porcupine, aromatic of herbs and charcoal, resting on a mound of rice. They put the dish in the middle of the floor, and gathered round it on a ring of sofa cushions. Xenia, excited by alcohol and great gobbets of the supposed sucking pig, burst into Jugoslav song until, with startling suddenness, she fell asleep. Carry became more lavish with her terms of endearment, the more pungent her wit. Rashid flashed his merry, watchful smile, but said little. Either his habit of downing a cocktail in a single draught, or the pious Arabic exclamation which followed, seemed to act as an antidote.

At midnight Rashid carried on a courteous and conventional argument with Toots — Toots protesting that he must stay the night, Rashid swearing that it was the desire of his heart but impossible. They went at it, partly in English, partly in Arabic when English politeness was inadequate, before and after Rashid telephoned for a taxi, and again when the taxi was at the front door.

Toots was more decisive when Rashid had gone. He came back yawning, and produced for Armande a pair of the finest linen sheets and a heap of rough army blankets. Then he said good night, and vanished into the bedroom.

"What are the arrangements for the morning?" Armande asked Carry.

"We all pretend to be asleep, darling, while Mahmoud brings Toots his breakfast in bed."

Armande unpacked her suitcase, and went to bed. Carry turned out the light, but remained sitting by the mosquito curtains which stirred gently in the night air.

"Good night," said Carry. "And I'm sorry."

"What for?"

"Whatever I said that reminded you. I think that in these

days every woman in Cairo has a word — you know, a sort of talisman — which will spoil her mood."

Armande slept soundly, food and drink overcoming the exhaustion that might have kept her awake. At dawn she saw, though never heard, a Sudanese servant in white robes — Mahmoud, she presumed — flitting back and forth to the bedroom with eggs and toast. Then she fell asleep again, and woke to hear the soft scream of the kites hovering over the pepper trees across the road. It was too gentle and sugary a mewing, yet it reminded her of the call of curlews in her childhood. She was very homesick.

That mood or, at any rate, its keener ache vanished amid the memories of the preceding night. If that was a typical Cairo evening, she was going to like Cairo. Probably it was not at all typical. So often one arrived in a new town or country to be offered, at once, a rich experience of things and people, never again to be repeated. Rashid, she hoped, could be repeated. Though they had exchanged no serious conversation, he gave to her the flattery that she loved best of all; he had looked at her as if she were the only person in the room whose opinions really mattered. By all she knew of Arabs, he ought to have been more strongly attracted by the outrageous Xenia. Damn Xenia anyway! She was crying quietly, and something must be done about the child's hang-over, and Carry, though wide-awake and smoking a cigarette, showed no intention whatever of getting up.

CHAPTER XI

Escape

"I HAVE GOT TO EARN MY LIVING," said Armande. "This can't go on."

"Don't hurry. It seems only yesterday you came here."

Toots leaned forward to flick the ash off his cigarette, and smiled with sudden, charming intimacy as his face passed through her territory at the other end of the sofa.

"It's three weeks since I came here," she insisted.

"What's three weeks in a lifetime? Do take a bit more time to look round."

"I have looked round."

It was true; and the looking round, even with good introductions, had been depressing. The business world of Cairo seemed to be organized into unions for mutual aid. A Copt, a Greek, a Jew, a Lebanese or an Italian — if too harmless for internment — could always get a small salary from a firm of his or her sect and nationality. For an Englishwoman, without any technical qualifications, there was no possible paymaster but the army. Neither to Toots nor to any prospective employer could she bring herself to explain why the army would not do.

"I want you to stay on in the flat when I go," he said.

"No, I won't, Toots, my dear."

"Who'll look after Carry and Xenia?"

"What on earth makes you think that they can't look after themselves?"

ARABESQUE

"Perhaps I haven't thought of that enough," he said courteously, but evidently considering her unkind.

"You haven't thought of it at all, Toots. You're just holding them as prisoners."

"But they are so lost."

"How long will you be away?" she asked.

"I don't know. Depends on Rommel. We might fetch up anywhere."

"Then let Carry stop here alone, and find herself. But Xenia is no more lost than a bird. She sorrows and flutters and mates and dances, and goes through joy and agony every day of her life. Get her a job in one of the Jugoslav camps, Toots. So long as she has a lover and can be useful, she is fulfilled."

"That goes for you, too."

"Does it? Yes, I suppose so."

"And I could get you twenty useful jobs at G.H.Q. tomorrow, only you won't let me."

"And arrange a lover for me, too?" she asked ironically, quickly avoiding all discussion of jobs.

"I'd even leave Rashid behind for you, if you'd stay here," he answered.

"Poor Rashid! He's so easy for a woman to live up to, Toots. A knight, and I am his unobtainable lady. He writes me poems in Arabic which he refuses to translate. He'd never forgive you or me if he guessed you had left him behind deliberately. *I could not love thee, dear, so much, loved I not honor more* — can you say that in Arabic, Toots?"

"Yes, you can, and mean it. Armande, why are you crying?"

She clung to him in sudden terror of the unknowable future, of this lonely passing from one life to another. His lips responded to hers with a gentleness that gathered force and passion, and then faded back to gentleness.

ESCAPE

It should be so easy to be loved by Toots, she cried to herself, so easy to love him. She made a last effort to act what she longed to feel, but there was no release from self-consciousness, from awareness that neither his spirit nor hers was ready to follow the body into a blessed instant of annihilation. All she could capture was a vivid, composite memory of every sentimental, unsatisfactory flirtation in Beirut and Jerusalem.

"That was so sweet," he said.

"What a lovely voice, Toots! I wish you meant it."

"Armande!" he answered reproachfully.

"Oh, my dear! You're kind and exciting, and what more could anyone want than that?" she exclaimed penitently. "It's me, don't you see? It's as if I were always in love and couldn't forget. I'm death to all emotion. Death."

She was exhausted by her struggle not to allow this flat to become another Beirut for her. She knew that the Armande of assured background and easy future was smashed and finished. The alternatives before her were to hang on to unreality, accepting, like Carry and Xenia, any impossible situation so long as it provided shelter with honor, or to enter the Praylean world of adventurous individuals who could take in their stride crook employment agencies and hopped chemists and any other beastliness.

"You must stay here," he insisted. "I can't leave you like this, accusing yourself of all sorts of impossibilities. Get some money from London, and wait till you are surer of what you want."

"I will not get money from London."

"I don't mean from your husband. From your mother."

"Never from my mother!"

"All the same," he persuaded her, "help in trouble is what mothers are for."

"But they blind you. They are ruthless. I never want to be possessed by her again."

He murmured something about her father, of which, in her agonies of self-reproach, she heard only the word amid a blur of soothing sounds.

"Oh, leave me alone!" she cried. "I killed him too."

"What was your father?" he said, his cool hands closing on hers. "Tell me — as if you were telling the story of another person."

"An old cavalry trooper who kept a pub."

"And he married your mother in France during the last war, I suppose?" he asked, refusing to be distracted by her attempt to shock him.

"Yes. And when the franc fell she was ready to get out. I can remember how happy he was the first year in England. And then Maman — for me or for herself? Just because she was made that way, perhaps — turned the pub into a famous place."

"That must have startled him."

"Slowly, if one can be startled slowly. Oh, Toots, I can see him now. He had nothing to do — nothing! Every morning he used to polish the mahogany bar, polish it for hours. It was the only use he was, for Maman's barman served the drinks. And then she covered the bar with zinc like a *bistro*. It was all he had left.

"He didn't have me any longer then. Before I went away to school we would spend hours together. Not talking much. He didn't talk much to anyone. But together and so happy. Afterwards, in my holidays, Maman kept me busy, always with herself or with the guests. He didn't want to intrude. He kept away till I was used to him keeping away. He sat in the stables, trying to be busy. And when Maman covered the bar, he died."

Armande's cheeks were flooded with tears, though she sobbed no longer.

"I didn't understand," she cried. "I was a little fool. Because he kept to himself, I made no effort. I just accepted Maman's way. I could have loved him, spent my time with him, told him that he mattered to me more than anything on earth. But I was allowed no time. No time. Maman dominated us. It's as if everything I am had been made by a human sacrifice."

"How old were you when he died?"

"Fourteen."

"A bit young to run your own small world," he said.

"No. Not for a woman. Not for a tough little *gamine* as I had been only three years before. As I'm going to be again. Not too young to love and show love and make it all that matters to someone who needs you. Oh, Toots, I don't know why I've told you this! I've shed all my life onto you."

He kissed her hair, and got up to fuss with drinks. Armande made running repairs to her complexion. She was weary of herself and her body and her sordid tear-stained face; but Carry or Xenia might come in at any moment. It would be the lowest depth of shame if either of them should see that in an afternoon alone with Toots she had made the usual Cairo scene.

"Why do people tell you things?" she asked.

"I don't know," he replied, and added vaguely: "All these homeless men and women. And then there are one's own chaps. I learn to listen. I wish I could go on learning."

"After the war?"

"If I get to the end. It makes me so anxious to settle all the unhappy too soon. And perhaps all I do, as you say, is to make prisoners."

"It's not your fault. We're just women weeping for Adonis."

"I don't croon or anything," he protested.

"Darling, I was serious, quite serious."

"Were you? Yes. Sometimes it's hard to tell what there is behind all that light in your great eyes. And it's surprising to be called Adonis by Astarte. Appropriate, perhaps — though our great scene failed."

"Toots, that's the second hint. Don't be rash, my dear."

"I must be a little rash. It's what we've been trained for."

"Where are you going?"

"Into the desert," he replied. "And soon. That's why I've had to talk to you seriously."

"Do what I ask about Carry and Xenia."

"I will."

For a week Armande was all brittle courage, which led her only into exploration of Cairo and a few improbable interviews. One morning as she let herself flow through the streets upon the tide of busy human beings, hoping for inspiration from their very variety, she found Floarea Pitescu decorating the Rue Soleiman Pasha. The girl was staring into the window of a drugstore, where a display of beauty preparations, in the deep tints and heavy perfumes that the dusky Middle East demanded, was grouped around the portrait of a movie star. Armande first recognized the Rumanian by her valiant air of concentration. Floarea's pose was quite unlike that of a pretty woman who had stopped to look in a shop window. She was slightly frowning and, as a connoisseur before a picture, standing a little back: undoubtedly to analyze what the star had that she, Floarea, had not, whether it could be acquired, and with how much effort.

Armande carried her off for cakes and coffee, noticing with amused interest the appraisal — a joint appraisal — that they received, and the little silences as they passed between the crowded tables of the garden café. Alone, she attracted no particular attention; nor, she suspected, did Floarea. Floarea's frocks and auburn hair were so provocative that her profession might well be misjudged; the casual glances of other women were more likely to be contemptuous than admiring. When, however, both were together, Floarea drew attention to Armande's good looks, and Armande to Floarea's respectability, or rather — for respectability was too unkind a word — to the fact that Floarea had a private and definite character inhabiting her too conspicuously beautiful body.

While they strolled through the streets, Floarea's enthusiastic chatter, illuminated by an occasional fact tersely expressed, had made it clear that she was in Egypt to get an engagement, that the Romanova was still with her and well, and that times were hard.

"And you?" asked Floarea. "By the way, I have a message for you."

"From whom?"

"Sheikh Wadiah. Before I left he said that if ever I met you I was to tell you that you would always be welcome at Beit Chabab. He was very precise. *Always,* he said."

"How nice of him!"

"Yes, it was. After all the trouble."

"What trouble?"

"I wouldn't know, Armande. I keep clear of politics. But there were French and British officers hanging about (they were very useful to me — I got my visa), and everyone knew it was something to do with you. First of all Beit Chabab said you were a German spy. And then Wadiah told them something. I don't know what. And then they decided that you and Wadiah together were arming all the Christians in the East. It's made Wadiah more of a prince than ever. That's just like

— 205 —

my own country. Any man of influence has to be mixed up in a scandal before he gets real respect."

Armande laughed. She was relieved to learn that Wadiah bore her no ill will. She could imagine him as he twisted his mustaches to heaven, hinting, prevaricating, dropping calculated indiscretions until a desirable legend had been born.

"How do you like Egypt?" she asked. "Have you got no work at all?"

"Just odd jobs as a photographer's model. This sort of thing!"

Floarea hunted in an oversmart bag of white patent leather, and produced a photograph in which she was lying dazzlingly and completely naked on a Victorian sofa.

"Good?" she asked, with the tolerant pride of an artist in a minor but efficient production.

"Well . . ." began Armande, too startled to criticize.

Floarea's face in the photograph was so serious and composed that it gave to the portrait a grave beauty. The pose was not languishing enough to advertise clothes — which indeed it hardly could — or any object of feminine vanity or masculine desire.

"What on earth is it for?"

"Constipation. I never need pills, Armande, do you?"

"Have you got to do that kind of thing?" Armande asked.

"Why not? I am waiting to dance at a smart locale. I will not take an engagement at the second-rate."

"But you're heaps better than all these old turns in Cairo that everybody is tired of. Haven't they given you a trial?"

"Oh, yes. But the conditions, my dear! The proprietor! Even the doorman! In Bucharest one is allowed some choice. But Cairo is a great brothel."

"I am sure it is nothing of the kind for the top-flight turns," said Armande demurely — she had already done the round of the Cairo cabarets with Toots and his circle.

"Do they have to sit at the tables?" Floarea asked.

"I don't think the best do, unless they want to. You ought to be in their class."

"I know I ought, but I haven't the right approach."

"Floarea," Armande suggested, "what would happen if you and I asked for a job together?"

"You?"

"I can dance, you know. Or at least I could."

"That doesn't matter. I could carry you through."

"I did not mean acrobatics," said Armande coldly.

"That's not fair!" Floarea flashed. "How was I to know you could dance? If you can."

"I'll show you. If I can, would I do?"

"Yes, but . . . there might be difficulties."

"What's the matter with me?"

"Nothing."

"Am I sufficiently *snob* for the big engagement?"

"Of course, Armande. But . . . are you all right? I mean, we shouldn't have any trouble with the police?"

"Why should I have?" asked Armande indignantly. "And what about you? An enemy subject!"

"I am a Jewess," said Floarea smugly.

"Are you? I didn't know."

"No, Armande. I am Orthodox," Floarea replied, drawing out from her bosom a small gold cross, and kissing it. "I wear my cross, though I hide it — and may God forgive me for the lie! But Mama found out that artistes were allowed to work and travel if they were Jews. So we learned a prayer in Hebrew, and said that we were. They say it's dangerous in Palestine, that there is a secret Jewish police who ask too many questions.

But here we were believed. After all, any good Rumanian could pretend to be a Jew or a gipsy. Is it wrong, do you think?"

"Not for you," Armande answered. "It's a policeman's world, this — and each of us must do what she can. Is there anywhere with a piano where we can practice? Then you can see how much I've forgotten, and make up your mind."

"Yes. At our rooms. Mama will be there."

Floarea led her to a grim, unpainted apartment house, rising six stories above a row of shops. It was shabby, but in a good street, and looked as if it might be inhabited by small Greek businessmen with large families. Floarea ran up five flights of stairs with a lightness that amazed Armande, unlocked the door of a flat and called loudly for Mama.

The flat looked and smelled as if it had been used by generations of cabaret artistes. The hall was hung with photographs of dancers, their signatures and their affectionate dedications to the landlady scrawled in vast flowing hands, a dozen European languages and green, blue and violet inks. There was furniture everywhere, covered with cheap Oriental hangings and cottons printed with scenes from ancient Egypt. Scattered about this overbearing quantity of textiles were cushions in vivid silks with the heads and feet of dolls. There did not seem to be anything in the house without a skirt except the dancers in the photographs, Romanova and the landlady.

The landlady wore trousers. A roll of fat from her hips, surprisingly bagged in the pink silk of her underwear, emerged from the undone placket like the shapeless materialization from a cheap medium. Romanova, in a flowered cotton wrap, lay among the dolls drinking coffee. She looked cool. Indeed the whole flat, heavily curtained and shuttered, was cool. The same air had been imprisoned for year after year, but at a more gentle temperature than that of the street.

The Romanova greeted Armande with reserve. Her eyebrows, painted in two appealing semicircles high on the aging forehead, were raised more in interrogation than welcome. Floarea explained, in a rush of emphatic and musical Rumanian, the reason for Armande's visit.

"Let us see," said Romanova neutrally.

She led the way to a room which was empty except for a piano and a stool. It occurred to Armande, who was trying hard to think charitably, that this barren space probably accounted for the pantechnicon of furniture everywhere else.

"Can you lend me some clothes?" Armande asked Floarea.

"I got 'im!" said the landlady, bursting importantly into English. "Nice, clean! I know what you like."

She had been staring at Armande with embarrassing approval. She now waddled out of the room, and returned with a neatly ironed play suit, thoroughly practical except for a quantity of fish-fin frills.

"I like English," she said. "When you finish, you come have tea."

Romanova looked critically at Armande's long legs.

"Tap?" she asked.

"Classical."

"Not without more muscles in your calf than that, my girl! But you'll certainly give the clients something to look at."

Romanova seated herself at the piano.

"What do you want?"

Armande, overcome by a flurry of nervousness, could not think of a piece.

"'Tristesse'? That do?"

"All right."

Romanova began to play, watching Armande's interpretation

of the music and sympathetically adjusting the accompaniment whenever she landed herself in a dead end.

"Oh, my God!" exclaimed Floarea regretfully.

"Little fool! After all, you don't know a thing!" snapped the Romanova. "She can manage her arms — which is more than you ever will till you stop thinking how pretty they are. You're hopelessly out of training," she added to Armande.

"I know. How long would it take to get back?"

"Months."

"Well, that's that," said Armande.

"But I thought you wanted to dance with this child, not ballet. You'd be good enough to partner her in a fortnight — if you really worked."

Floarea stood still, her shocked eyes filling with tears. Then she suddenly swooped across the room, lifted Romanova off the piano stool and kissed her.

"Mama! Will you stop trying to take the conceit out of me!"

Romanova, for the first time, smiled at Armande, as if she too must admire the relationship between this impetuous girl and her so-called mother. Armande did admire it. She also began to think more kindly of the Romanova than at Beit Chabab. There was, after all, no real reason why a woman should ever remove powder from her face if she didn't want to.

"Can I train here?" she asked.

"Yes. Two hours in the morning alone with me. Two hours in the afternoon with Floarea. If you do less, I won't take you. Are you eating well? You look like it."

"Very well," said Armande guiltily. "And — and you?"

"On tick. Ecaterina is an old friend — " Romanova lifted her eyebrows in the direction of the door through which the landlady had gone — "but getting restive. Pay for the lessons if you can."

"I can, but not for very long."

"You won't have to for long. You and this child will be on easy street if you behave yourselves."

The landlady had tea waiting for them. She was a Rumanian Greek from Galatz, and passionately pro-British. Her exclamations made it plain that this was partly due to the sympathetic natures of British merchant seamen on the Danube, and partly to enthusiasm for the useless gallantry of British aid to Greece. Mme. Ecaterina understood English, but could only summon up her phrases after some thought. The conversation settled easily back into Middle Eastern French.

Armande, now committed to a future that appalled her, forced herself to ask whether Mme. Ecaterina had a room that she could occupy. Ecaterina had. It was clean, and could have been cheerful if scissors had lopped off the fringes of bedcover, curtains, lamp shades and mantelpiece.

The landlady waddled back into the hall, Armande delicately following in her wake, and poured out more tea.

"But one thing," said Ecaterina, "must be clearly understood. You are not to bring gentlemen here. I will give you a very nice address."

Armande froze. All of them, the flat, the room, the dancing, immediately took on an air of unreality, while she, an intact observer, sat on. Then suddenly she realized that there was no reason in the world why she should not be angry; no reason why here, at the bottom of society, she should not say aloud the things she was saying to herself. Her spirit leaped back seventeen years into the easy past.

"Mme. Ecaterina," she remarked, with an irony that grew through every word of her exquisite French, and culminated in sheer invective, "if I take a room and pay my rent, I demand the right to receive my friends. And if my friends are men, I shall lead them into that bedroom directly under your filthy nose and shut the door and close the keyhole and leave the rest to your disgusting imagination."

"You are English. You can do what you like. I trust you." Mme. Ecaterina surrendered at once, the whole jelly of her body quivering with timidity at this attack. "I only made it clear, as I always do."

"*Bien,*" said Armande, "but I am old enough to assume there is a *vase de nuit* under the bed without you placing it in the middle of the room."

"Armande!" exclaimed Floarea, horrified.

"Armande — I am sick of Armande! What's your name when you dance?"

"Mavis. It's romantic."

"It's suburban — but if you like it! Then I will be Marthe. Mavis and Marthe. Will that do? I will come tomorrow, Mama, for a lesson. And I will take the room, Mme. Ecaterina, at the end of next week."

Armande stormed out of the flat, utterly ashamed of herself, lips trembling with nervousness, but hot with satisfaction in the bottom of her heart at the shocked faces of her landlady-to-be, of Floarea and of the Romanova.

CHAPTER XII

Mavis and Marthe

THE HUNGARIAN and Rumanian artistes who normally staffed the cabarets of the Eastern circuit had been rounded up and dispatched to Cyprus, where, among the limited circle of officers who were fortunate enough to be stationed there and to have private incomes, they preserved the traditions of Aphrodite's island. Egypt was short of high-class entertainers, and had to fall back on its native supply of acrobats, conjurers and stomach dancers. Their exotic feats on stage or floor were of international excellence, but did not suggest to patrons of ordinary tastes that there was any object in getting to know the performer over a bottle of so-called champagne. Troops and contractors with money to burn had little temptation to spend any really substantial sums in the cabarets.

Mavis and Marthe, new, exciting and of prewar loveliness, had no difficulty in obtaining a profitable engagement where they chose. Armande decided on the Casino. It was out of bounds to British troops, and therefore less embarrassing to her first shyness; and it was about to move out of winter quarters into its attractive summer garden by the Nile. At their interview and exhibition, the proprietor, though a good business Greek, was unable to hide his enthusiasm at this unexpected gift from heaven. Armande seized the opportunity to bargain.

Neither she nor Floarea, she said, had any intention of

taking a contract which compelled them to sit at tables with the clients. Floarea added, to gild this bitter pill, that they would do so if they chose, and that she, at any rate, might often choose if her commission on the drinks were generous. The proprietor turned their offer down flat, with the regretful discourtesy of a bazaar merchant who had been tendered half the real value of his wares. Armande left her address and walked out. The proprietor, as she expected, remained silent for a week — during which she and the Romanova had the utmost difficulty in persuading Floarea not to return to the Casino — and then accepted Armande's conditions.

Their engagement opened at the end of April. Romanova had arranged two numbers designed to show the grace and ease of her pupils, but demanding no more than a beginner's skill upon the points. The artistes at the summer Casino were not confined between tables; there was a good stage upon which to exploit the romance of flowing skirts and swirling draperies.

The first number was a waltz of crinoline period, with Armande in white organdie, Floarea in sea green, and an atmosphere of innocent girlhood at the court of Vienna or St. Petersburg — Armande was never sure which. In the second number they were two butterflies, and dressed in little else than wings attached to jeweled brassière and thigh, wrist and shoulder. Romanova made no secret of her intentions: to show the beauty of Armande's arms to the lover of ballet, and as much of Floarea as the police permitted to the connoisseur of women. Armande agreed only after violent argument.

"But why, Armande," Floarea asked at last, "are you so ashamed of your own body? It's not too slim. It's very pretty."

"I'm not in the least ashamed of it."

"Yes, you are. Yet you wouldn't mind swimming in just as little as you will wear as butterfly."

"That's different."

"But why?"

"I suppose," replied Armande, flushing, "because I am not being stared at by men."

"But you are," said the Romanova. "There are always a lot of cretins on any beach with nothing else to do."

"I'm not being paid for them to look at anyway."

"That's just the point," Romanova snapped. "At the Casino you are being paid for them to look at."

"Well, I won't do it."

"Then you shouldn't take the money."

"And think of your art," said Floarea. "After all a butterfly doesn't wear any clothes."

"But I have not the pretty habits of the hymenoptera," exclaimed Armande sardonically, exasperated by Floarea on Art. "We needn't go into details. For one thing I do not lay eggs. And, Mama, you talk nonsense. I am *not* paid to exhibit my navel. I cannot make it turn in circles like Miss Fatima."

"And you — you dare talk of shame!" Floarea cried.

"All right, my darling, all right," said Armande, wearily surrendering. "Give me my wings. Measure me for my — what do you call it, Mama?"

"*Cache-sexe,*" answered Romanova modestly.

"Well, for heaven's sake see that it does."

Mavis and Marthe were received with acclamation by civilian Cairo. To the military — except security men and others with the right to wear plain clothes — they were comparatively unknown. Any uniformed soldier visiting the Casino fell into the capable hands of the Military Police.

Armande was prepared for the usual questioning. She was certain that the security people would fuss, as soon as they looked her up in their files and found that the British subject practicing so enigmatic a profession had been black-listed. In due course an elderly major turned up at the Casino, and invited her to call at an address in Gezireh the following afternoon.

Never had she been so little impressed. His fumbling futility was the more obvious since he had chosen his own flat in which to question her. His view of life was black and white; it would, she supposed, be a valid view among the dregs of the Egyptian populace, the drug smugglers and politicians and *souteneurs,* but it hardly fitted him to undertake the analysis of all the fine shades of gray in the mind of the intelligent European, especially if the European were an educated woman.

Armande treated him *de haut en bas.* She was, she said, a trained dancer from her youth and entitled to earn her living; she had been unjustly black-listed, and, if he knew anything of the secrets of his own business, he should know that; she was respectable — and she lit up the word by the tone of a woman to whom respectability was a harmless virtue of the lower middle classes. Finally, remembering old days in London, she asked:

"If you were to prevent me from working, would your Minister be prepared to defend such a policy in the House?"

The major at once became tender and fatherly. He offered her a small retainer either to report on any suspicious visitors to the Casino, or, if she didn't like that, simply to come to his flat and talk to him once a week. She refused. She thought him a pitiable, lewd and lonely old man who should have retired long since to grow roses in England. She did not appear, however, to have forfeited his good will, for Marvis and Marthe remained untroubled by any but small fry of the Egyptian police. Their halfhearted attempts at blackmail were contemptuously dismissed by the experienced Romanova.

Toots and Rashid had vanished from Cairo. Armande received a number of visits and telephone calls from their friends, but was deliberately evasive. She writhed under an intolerable sensation that everyone was staring at her, that women despised her and that men would congratulate each other, with great guffaws and warnings to be careful, upon the entertainment of that pretty piece from the Casino.

Carry Laxeter refused to be dropped. She did not hide her love of Armande and was adored in return. She assumed that Armande was starting, or rather continuing a serious profession as a dancer, and accepted her surroundings as amusingly eccentric rather than sordid. Armande could not really bring herself to believe in Carry's fiction; she knew too well that she had no intention of making a career of dancing, that the whole hated business was partly an angry protest and partly a provision for eating and living in comfort. It had to be that, or else a life like Xenia's, existing on the wealth of her emotions and other people's kindness. Even for Xenia Armande had not allowed such a course to continue. Toots had found the girl a job in a Jugoslav camp. She served tea in the canteen, and had taken to communism with the hysterical fervor of a convert. After a vain attempt to proselytize Armande and Carry, she ignored them as lost and parasitic souls.

Carry treated the Casino as if it were a smart London restaurant with a floor show. At least once a week she would sit with Armande, Floarea and the Romanova before and after their dance, and mischievously encourage Armande to accept an occasional invitation from the tables. The unreality of Carry's capricious lightheartedness shocked Armande; to exhibit one's body to fat Levantines, and to listen to their suggestive conversation (thank God most of them didn't dance!) was a horrible way of earning a living, and witty irresponsibility made it no better. Still, Carry's humor was a refuge. Armande clung to her as a companion, and loved her as the last existing bond between herself and her past life.

Seen through Carry's eyes, two at least of her fellow performers were engaging; but Carry, she knew, would only laugh if Miss Fatima ended in jail and Mlle. Joliette were pulled in for compulsory medical examination. They were objects for pity and sympathy, not for laughter. Yet, if one were thrown into their society, were, in fact, to the outer world their equal and colleague, an understanding laughter was the only possible working attitude.

Miss Fatima was a pure Egyptian with the morals of the Old Testament. Her ambition was to become the concubine of the highest in the land, in order to gain power for herself and security for her relatives. Yet she — with the possible exception of Floarea — was the only sincere artist of the Casino. Fatima spent hours every day in a practice of muscle control that would have done credit to a Yogi disciple. Her object was to move breasts, stomach and abdomen in ever-increasing circles, sometimes clockwise below and anticlockwise above, while reducing the movement of her feet to a mere suggestion of action as delicate as a Chinese poem. Armande realized that it was art of the highest standard, but to European eyes it did not seem sufficiently integrated. It was so hard to watch the exquisite nuances of emotion expressed by Miss Fatima's ankles and toes, while appalled by the gyrations of her torso.

Mlle. Joliette's technique, on the stage or at a table, was wholly Western. The base for her attack was not the Moslem promise of curious and amatory acrobatics, but the Christian appeal of innocence to chivalry. She was a blond little angel, largely French, who had lived the first fifteen years of her life in Tunis and the last five in artistes' hotels. Joliette was ut-

terly indifferent to men and to sentiment; she did not care
whether a client had known her an hour or whether he had
been buying her champagne for a week, whether he was mod-
erately white or definitely brown; her price was 3000 prewar
francs, neither more nor less, and before yielding, with a delicious simulation of shyness and terror, to romance in any cur-
rency she would work out the exchange to insure that she had
really been offered the magic sum. Had Joliette delivered her
will-o'-the-wisp beauty for 2800 francs she would have considered herself both dishonored and a bad mathematician.

As a result of Carry's humanizing or demoralizing influence
— Armande called it one or the other according to her mood —
she began to make a few acquaintances among the less boring
of the regular clients and, if so disposed, to sit with them.
She needed evening frocks which would not depart too far
from the showy fashions of the Casino, and would yet be
bearable. Carry helped her to choose them, and also named
them.

There was Churching of Women, a pious little thing in black
and white which gave her the bosom of a nursing mother. Well
of Loneliness was a tube of twilit green and gray, easy to get
into and the devil of a job to get out of. Public Bar, so called
because the customers were inclined to lean over it, was of deep
crimson velvet with no straps. Fate Worse than Death was an
Empire frock of pleated white marocain, which suggested a
half-ravished vestal virgin. That was the only purchase which
made Floarea jealous; she complained that when Armande in
Fate Worse than Death descended from the dressing rooms
down the wide steps to the trees and soft lights of the garden,
all her favorite clients became wistful and melancholy.

Floarea was happily excited. After the war would come an
engagement at Budapest, where the Eastern and Western cir-

cuits met, and then the night clubs of London, Paris and Berlin. To her, war was merely a temporary nuisance. She was a neutral spectator, without any love for her country's allies, and certainly without hatred for its enemies.

She could congratulate herself on reaching the top of her profession in her own territory. Only visiting artistes from the Western circuit and of international competence ever obtained the privilege exacted by Armande: that they were not bound to sit at tables or to dance with clients. Floarea's contract was a useful advertisement, and evidence for any management that she was a serious performer. That was its only value to her, for in fact she spent nearly as much time at the tables as she had in days when attendance was compulsory. She liked to dance; she liked to be complimented; and she hoped to find a sympathetic protector to whom to be faithful for the duration of her stay in Egypt.

Armande, however, decided that Floarea could not be allowed any of her half-mercenary, half-sentimental attachments. The Romanova, whose wants were amply supplied by the Casino contract, agreed. It was really Carry who had the most influence. She raked Floarea's half-dozen candidates — who ranged from a solid detective of the Military Police to an Egyptian newspaper proprietor — with devastating ridicule. Floarea worshiped Carry's aristocratic mixture of honesty and eccentricity, and took her for a model, even copying Carry's graceful stride. This intrigued Armande, who perceived that in truth Floarea was imitating Floarea. The unconventional good manners and casual acceptance of anything that life might send up from the basement, which in the Rumanian were genuine, Carry had always cultivated as a pose.

In the middle of June the Casino was as packed as ever, but the character of the audience had changed. Armande found the place more tolerable. The regular habitués, young moneyed and idle sons of Christian and Moslem business, were disappearing. The rich Greeks and Jews had gone. Joliette complained of hard times. Talk on the floor was of nothing but Rommel's advance and the fall of Tobruk.

The civilians comforted themselves by rumors. All the Arabian Nights imaginings about the course and object of the war, of which Armande had had her fill on the journey down to Egypt and daily ever since, increased in fantasy. Some pinned their faith to secret weapons in the Western Desert; others to an Egyptian Empire which, they said, Mussolini intended to establish. Then came the day when the chimneys of G.H.Q. poured upwards a volcano of black smoke, and the ash of burned paper settled on the roofs and streets and gardens of Cairo's diplomatic quarter.

That soldiers should burn the paper they so industriously produced rightly seemed to the Egyptians as clear evidence of impending defeat as if they had thrown away their arms. There was little comfort in rumors. This was it — the dreaded end. The German and Italians were coming, and the café politicians realized in sudden panic that they had no notion what the victorious armies would do, and what they would not — it was pretty generally admitted that there was nothing they would not.

The following morning Carry called on Armande at Mme. Ecaterina's flat. She said that all British women, except essential workers, were to be immediately evacuated to Kenya, that she had been ordered by the Consulate to round up any who could not readily be reached through husbands or employers, and that she and Armande would leave together and stay together.

"But what about Floarea and Mama?" asked Armande.

"Darling, they'll be all right. Even Hitler doesn't know whose side the Rumanians are on."

"Yes," said Armande doubtfully. "I suppose they will be all right."

She had kept the secret that they were officially Jews. That was their business. She wondered whether there were any Egyptian police records from which the S.S., scavenging in the wake of the Afrika Korps, could justifiably decide that Jews they were.

"I don't know what to do, Carry."

"Darling, you can't dream of staying."

"Have you talked to anybody? What do the generals say?"

"They smile confidently," Carry replied, "and say that the situation is hopeless but not desperate."

Armande hesitated. Was there anything in this defeatism except the rotted imaginations of all these planners and administrators living at ease in the scented heat of Cairo? Impatiently she accused them of being as like soldiers as those sweetly calling kites were like curlews, and then accused herself of having the futile optimism of ignorance.

But was she ignorant? After all, she and Carry had talked in casual contacts to troops from divisions mauled in the recent fighting. They were no longer so spruce, no longer the gay and skillful warriors of a private war far out in the desert, but their morale was unaffected. They felt that they had been outgeneraled, not outfought, and were confident of their power to defend any reasonably sound position.

Perhaps this wretched, trembling giant of a G.H.Q. really thought the same. Perhaps the office officers were eager to defend the Canal, rifle in hand. That, in her experience, would be just what they called their cup of tea. But in that case why in God's name weren't they private soldiers instead of colonels and brigadiers? The war couldn't be won by grown-up boys, full of courage but incapable of thought. What a country was this Britain in miniature at Cairo! It had no guts — beyond those necessary to die. Children! Anybody could die. To live and win — that was what mattered.

"Carry, I'm not going to run away," she said, utterly inconsistent with her own thoughts. "And what on earth would I do?"

"I suppose they'll put us in camps. You know — stew for breakfast and the things they call latrines."

"Distressed Englishwomen!" Armande exclaimed bitterly. "Like Xenia. What a kick the army will get out of being gallant and chivalrous!"

"Oh, darling, don't be so morbid! We have to be sent away while there is still time. They say that if Rommel gets Cairo, he'll go right through to Syria."

"I don't believe it, Carry. And even if the whole Middle East collapses, why should I go?"

"But if you stay, you'll be interned."

"I've been interned, Carry. It's not so bad as all that."

"What a soulful Armande! Be sensible and come with me!"

"Where to?"

"Kenya, darling," answered Carry impatiently.

"Kenya? That's internment too. Oh, my dear, it would be like committing suicide. Happier in heaven, and all that sort of thing. If the war is lost, what does it matter where I am or what happens to me? Everything we care about will have ceased to exist. I will take it here if I must, but I won't go off and become a useless spectator, and have to take it in the end anyway. What's the magic of Kenya? If Egypt goes, Kenya goes too, sooner or later. You might get Japanese instead of Germans — that's all."

"Oh my God! How appalling!" Carry exclaimed. "You don't really think so, do you?"

"I don't know," Armande replied. "I think I'd rather have them. The Germans would destroy our souls and their own forever. But the Japanese, once they had conquered, might be peaceful and polite. There's nothing to be gained for me in Kenya, Carry. If the world is to be divided up between these brutes, I'd as soon accept my fate here as anywhere. I'm sick of running away. It just isn't worth my pride to go, darling."

"Armande, but they'll make you go! It's an order."

"Who'll make me? Do you think anybody is going to bother about a cabaret girl?"

"My sweet, why are you so bitter?" asked Carry tenderly. "What beastly thing has somebody done to you?"

"Nothing."

"I'll never understand you. One moment you sound like Joan of Arc, and the next as if you hated us all."

"Not you, dear Carry. You've no idea what a help you have been to me. I'd love to come with you to Kenya. But here I am free, and I want to stay free. And I don't believe a word of all this pessimism. I don't believe Rommel will get Cairo. I don't believe we are defeated. Don't tell me we can't beat the Boche when we're on level terms. It's just these serious lumps of staff, who keep thinking of Dunkirk and Greece and want to take precautions."

"Darling, they wouldn't be right to take a chance of never getting the women away."

"Wouldn't they? Well, it's a grand excuse," said Armande. "They must be so sick of us hanging about and weeping and falling in love and getting drunk. But they haven't any rights over me, Carry. I won't go."

"Shall I stay with you then?"

"No, dearest. They would make any amount of trouble for you. As you say, it's an order."

"We may all get back to England," Carry suggested.

"You won't. No ships."

"Armande don't be so absolute! Kenya will probably insist on getting rid of us. If we do go home, is there anything I can do for you?"

"I can't think of anything. But if I do, I'll write to you."

"John?" Carry asked.

"If you ever run across him, don't let him be worried."

"Does he know what you are doing?"

"Of course not."

"Men take letters so seriously," Carry said.

"Yes. They don't understand that if one is miserable, one wants to write, and that the next day it's all over. Oh God!" Armande cried wearily. "Why do we have two sexes?"

"Darling, I can't leave you in this mood."

"That's what Toots said."

"Did he? You're not staying for Toots?" Carry asked suspiciously.

"No."

"Tell him when you see him that . . . well, you'll have it all your own way."

"I should if I wanted him. But I don't, Carry."

"Didn't you ever?"

"I tried. Just tears and confessions. Typical Cairo."

"Is it? Well, of course you aren't Toots's type."

"No. Nor anybody's."

"Oh, darling!" exclaimed Carry repentantly. "I didn't mean to be cruel."

"You weren't. Tomorrow I shall feel I'm everybody's type —

especially in Public Bar. And no you to laugh at it. Good-by,
my darling."

"Armande!"

"My Carry!"

"And we'll laugh at all this," said Carry sobbing. "Lunch at
the Berkeley sometime?"

"London and June and peace. Don't make me cry, my
sweet."

As Armande closed the door and turned away, she was saved
from breaking down by the assault of Mme. Ecaterina. A jelly-
fish stranded on her own emotions, she babbled incoherently
of Greeks and Germans and forced labor.

"Ecaterina, why do you listen outside my room?" Armande
protested gently.

"I must hear. I must know," screamed Ecaterina. "The Germans are in Alexandria. The English are running. Oh, who
would ever have thought it? The English! Mr. Gladstone!
Lord Byron! And to think that they are running!"

"You only hear half the story in a language you don't really
understand, Ecaterina," said Armande severely. "The English
are not running. They are in a very good position with the
navy on their right flank and some sort of depression or desert
or something on their left. And Alexandria will not fall."

"But the women? All the women are going!"

"Of course. We are useless."

"Useless, you and I?" cried Ecaterina indignantly. "No!
Never! Do I not knit for the Greeks? Do you not dance for
the soldiers?"

There was reality in Ecaterina's scatterbrained agitation.
Armande resisted the temptation to retort that she danced for
wealthy civilians who were fleeing from Cairo as fast as trains
and taxis could take them, and that Ecaterina's prickly bala-

clavas were not essential in the heat of June. She envied Mediterranean woman. Screaming and yelling and scenes. Tragedy and vulgarity inextricably mixed together. Yet all the while work or an illusion of work, and a blessed sense of being indispensable. The sum of all this violent expenditure of nervous force and emotion was stability. Perhaps the bees in the hive behaved like Mediterranean woman in the half hour before they slept. She and Carry and the rest of them with their eternal good taste and economy of energy — did they really produce enough of the raw material for social life?

She suddenly folded Ecaterina in her arms, and comforted her with a kiss unused by Carry.

CHAPTER XIII

Home to Helwan

SERGEANT PRAYLE dismounted from a dusty truck, and entered the Field Security Depot. The billet was in a quiet Cairo square and known as the Bishop's House. What ecclesiastical purpose it had served, the army never discovered; but every spring, year after year, a congregation of ancient and episcopal bugs bore witness to the resurrection of the dead.

Prayle had passed a couple of weeks at the depot when his draft arrived from home. Cairo then had contrasted very pleasantly with the grim austerity of battered England, and had cheaply and easily quenched the thirst accumulated through six weeks of tropics and subtropics in the crowded slave holds of a troopship. The Army of the Middle East had seemed to him old-fashioned — it segregated officers and other ranks to a degree never attempted in England — yet it contrived to be gay. Many a snug little bar and restaurant bore a notice: RESERVED FOR WARRANT OFFICERS AND SERGEANTS ONLY.

He explored and appreciated Cairo again when his section stopped for reorganization on their way from the Western Desert to the Lebanon. Now the city had lost its glamour. To the sections in the field it represented a soft life of cinemas, amenities, approachable women and unlimited drink. They chose it for leave, but considered it an unmanly station, tainted by the proximity of G.H.Q. Sergeant Prayle strode into the depot with the air of a real soldier from the wide, open spaces.

Gathered up immediately by his acquaintances — who made it clear in the first five minutes that the Cairo underworld demanded a lot more brains than any open spaces — Sergeant Prayle felt a country cousin. Those N.C.O.s in passage through the depot, fresh from the desert formations or their listening posts in the Egyptian towns, knew everything: what the divisions thought, what the generals said, who had been sacked and why, who ought to have been shot and when. In the Lebanon, where fortunes were not directly tied to the desert campaign, the news had not seemed so catastrophic; Rommel's victory was a setback, and that was all. In Cairo it was a shame, a disappointment, a disaster. Every man felt that his personal failure had threatened the whole course of the war; and since, for the vast majority, there had been no personal failure whatever, the army was puzzled and bitter and crying out for leadership.

When the spate of conversation caused by a new and interested arrival had died down, Prayle was kept busy answering questions about the more picturesque members of his section, about the morale of the Lebanon and the control of the rich refugees from Egypt. Asked what the devil he was doing in Cairo anyway, he explained that he had been sent for to give his personal advice to the Commander in Chief, and thereby, even among his discreet colleagues, gained credit for discretion. The fact was that he had not the least idea who wanted him; nor had Captain Wyne known. His instructions were simply to report to such-and-such an office on such-and-such a floor in G.H.Q. He could not remember which it was without referring to his Movement Order.

In the morning Prayle approached, circumspectly, the two huge blocks of former flats that were G.H.Q. They were surrounded by formidable barriers of barbed wire, guarded by

Egyptian ghaffirs. Sergeant Prayle entered without being challenged, and looked up at the windows, porticoes and balconies where his infinitesimal fate was decided. Between the imposing gray pillars of the entrance he came to the conclusion that only if he had been a little dog could he have expressed the mixture of awe and impudence that he felt. He delivered a few cracking salutes to grim-faced, absent-minded officers hurrying in and out, and then wandered curiously about the buildings for half an hour before going up to his destination. G.H.Q. were certainly in a flap, he decided, but they did look purposeful. Good old army — good old country if it came to that — which always had to hit bottom before it did any work!

The office to which he reported was very small, and bore evidence of being hastily furnished for a new department of the staff. It had been a luxury bathroom. The fixtures were boxed in with plywood, and heaped with files. A staff sergeant was busily typing on the bathtub, with a fan revolving at the other end. He too, it could be seen, was a new intruder into the uniformity of G.H.Q. His shirt was open to the waist, showing a chest burned to the same shade of desert mahogany as his face.

"Sergeant Prayle. Told to report here."

"Oh, you're Prayle, are you?" answered the sergeant. "I've heard a lot about you."

He swept the perspiration from his countenance with a dripping arm, and cleared a space for a smile.

"Major Furney wants to see you," he said.

"Furney? What's he doing here? I thought he was Haile Selassie's snooper-in-chief."

"No. After they got him down here in such a hurry, they changed their minds, and put him on to checking wog labor instead."

"Lousy job," said Prayle feelingly. "They all look exactly alike, and they all use each other's passes. Is that what you do?"

"God, no! This isn't security. We use our brains here."

"Noggins Limited. Cut out the coupon and post this day."

"Eh?"

"Nothing. What's the racket, chum?"

"Just the opposite to you chaps."

"I see. Who's the big cheese? Furney?"

"For these parts, yes. Well, I'll tell him you're here."

Prayle passed through the bathroom into a larger office where the heat was more bearable. Major Guy had again protested against his surroundings. Instead of the usual khaki shirt tucked into his khaki shorts, he wore the gray flannel of the Indian Army. Round his shoulder and disappearing into his pocket was a remarkable lanyard of crimson and gold, on the end of which he kept his pince-nez. He had grown a little fatter, and looked a more integral part of the army than in Beirut. He rose from his desk and greeted Prayle affectionately.

"Good old Field Security! Always around when wanted! How's Beirut and the Hotel St. Georges?"

"Gone decent, sir. Spears Mission secretaries."

"And how did you while away this horrible winter? Security pub crawls?"

"No. I had a detachment on the Palestine frontier."

"Not much fun unless you speak Arabic."

"That's what I thought. So I learned it."

"Prayle, why haven't you a commission?" Furney exclaimed. "And don't say: 'Baton in the knapsack, sir!'"

"Recommended for one."

"Why so doubtful?"

"It's a good job — F.S. sergeant."

"You'd better hurry. There'll be no more direct commissions soon. They are going to start Officers' Cadet Training Units in the Middle East, and you'd never get through."

"Why not?" asked Prayle indignantly.

"Speaking as an old examiner, Sergeant — and we're all the same whether we're dons or colonels — I should find your answers irrelevant in viva voce, and unintelligible on paper. I should also observe that while your discipline and powers of leadership were first-class, you believed the lot to be so much hooey. And so I should lose a bloody good officer for Field Security. What does your commandant think?"

"Smiles kindly. Bats!"

"He?"

"No. Thinks I am."

"Couldn't be better. I know him. He always chooses officers who are a bit loopy. You wouldn't like to join us, would you?"

"Not if I have a chance in security. What do you do, sir?"

"We are organizing what will be left behind if Egypt goes."

"Is it going?"

"I don't think so for a moment. But it would be sad if Jerry were left alone in Cairo without any of us to help him."

"Have you got some good chaps?"

"Yes. And I have a useful couple in mind. You remember the mysterious Armande Herne?"

Prayle felt his face flush with resentment.

"Why didn't you do anything?"

"I couldn't, my dear man," Furney replied. "And apart from Mrs. Herne, do you suppose I wouldn't have given my right hand to save Montagne? I was always crying out their innocence. I stood on the roof of G.H.Q. and screamed it. I got the whole affair reviewed by the D.M.I. But those damned palace eunuchs had a convincing case on paper. Always paper! And they just said: 'Oh yes, it's Guy of course. Oh yes, *dear* Guy, *so* impetuous!' And, blast them, in a way they were right! I hadn't a single proof beyond my own certainty and Wyne's opinion — which meant yours. And so they went and black-listed Mrs. Herne, and the French put Montagne under close arrest. It was internment, really."

"He escaped, you know."

"I do know. He's in Cairo."

"Good man!" Prayle exclaimed enthusiastically. "We've been looking for him all over Syria and the Lebanon — not too hard. Do we know officially that he's here?"

"No, unofficially. I've been told I can have him provided the French don't find out."

"Sealed truck," said Prayle. "God help the Egyptians when he's let loose!"

"And his cover perfect, you see. Interned by the French as a fifth columnist — what more natural than that he should escape to the enemy? Mrs. Herne's cover is good, too."

"Poor little doings! Can't you leave her out?"

"She's dancing in a cabaret, you know."

"Butterflies," Prayle mumbled irritably.

He had kept himself informed of Armande's movements, and had filled up the gaps in his knowledge at the depot bar. He loathed the thought of her in cabaret, dancing half-naked, apparently, with some damned Rumanian tart. She, the un-approachable! Well, she wasn't unapproachable any longer. And that was a vile thought, if there ever was one! Why the devil shouldn't the poor kid earn her living any way she liked? His desire for her was tortured by the imagination of Ar-mande's beauty glowing more than ever in the meretricious adornments of the Casino, as well as by the thought of her exposed to all the outrageous suggestions of men like himself. He treasured the memory of those qualities in her that had most annoyed him. Kensington was a safeguard.

"Cabaret is not good enough for her," Furney added.

"And what the hell else could she do, sir?"

"I didn't mean it as a criticism. You suggested that I shouldn't bother her, but I think she might like to be bothered. A girl who could pull off that deal with Wadiah is simply wasted where she is. And she must know that she's wasted."

"She's browned off with the lot of us."

"Probably. But she's patriotic. You and I know that. And her cover is not bad. She is known to the Egyptian police to be black-listed. She stayed behind when she might have been evacuated. She could pass as a Frenchwoman, and I could fix her up with a French passport and all the papers to prove her movements for the last three years. It's a gift! That's what I wanted you for — to swear to my bona fides. Otherwise I doubt if she'd listen. As you say, she has had just about enough of Intelligence."

"I'll try to sell it, but no guarantee."

"Then suppose you go down to the Casino tonight, and feel out the situation?"

"Grand Dukes, and all that?" Prayle asked.

"Whatever you need to spend is all right. I wish to God I could have had a quarter of the funds for security that I have for this racket. And you might take Montagne with you so that they can recognize each other."

"With boots?"

"No, it's quite safe. He's grown a beard and he is dark as an Egyptian and his name is Makrisi. There's a little café in Boulak. I'll get him to meet you there at eight. And — " Furney hesitated, his donnish voice revealing an uneasiness or perhaps a mere dislike for change — "you might tell me your impression of him. He's not quite the same Montagne we knew."

Prayle made no reply. There was nothing polite that he could say. It seemed to him obvious that Montagne, humiliated, on the run, in disgrace, would not be just the same as the cocksure, incorruptibly left-wing security officer.

By the evening Sergeant Prayle was in a more festive mood. His worrying for and about and against Armande had receded into the background of his thoughts. The immediate future promised a lonely soldier's heaven at the expense of Major Furney's department. After a long spell in the wind-swept villages and black mud between Kuneitra and the springs of Jordan, he was prepared to enjoy any form of intoxication that Cairo might offer. He borrowed a white civilian suit — the Cairo City section was as well supplied with clothes as a theatrical touring company — and stuck a carnation in his buttonhole. Raffish, he decided, but genial.

The directions that Furney had given him were delightfully systematic — no nonsense of names that would not be legible at the street corners, and no turnings left and turnings right. He had only a little map after his own heart, marked with blue arrows and red crosses. The last blue arrow led him into a lane between crumbling walls of sun-dried mud; there he came upon a native café, patched with flattened petrol tins and roofed with straw, but well supplied with bottles. Passing through the main room, he found that the last red cross represented a small yard in which were a kitchen and a few tables under a single tree. There were no troops, no Europeans. The only customers were a pair of Coptic clerks who were drinking coffee. Sergeant Prayle ordered a bottle of the thick Delta wine, stretched his legs and looked up through the foliage at the moonlit sky with its shafts and vaultings of busy searchlights. Compassionately he meditated upon those two clerks, and the general tragedy of the literate in the Middle East. They were paid little more than the laborer, yet compelled to the expense of European clothes. No wonder that the Egyptian student, with such a careworn future before him, was continually in revolt!

"*Bon soir,* my policeman!"

Montagne's low voice was the first indication of his presence. He was in the act of sitting down.

He was the perfect small Christian employee, in broken shoes, dirty alpaca suit and frayed linen. They certainly learned a thing or two in the French service, Prayle thought. If there was anything wrong with his disguise, it was that he looked too well-fed — but well-fed he had never looked before. Only his deep, fanatical eyes were recognizable.

"Congratulations!" Prayle said. "I should never have known you."

"I also am of the Mediterranean," Montagne answered. "For us who were born in poverty it is not hard to appear poor."

"And my felicitations on your freedom! We were all so glad."

"That was easy. They wanted to put Lebanese guards over us. Well, we raised hell. And in the discussions I walked out."

Prayle and Montagne went over to the icebox and chose the raw materials of their meal. Montagne waited without impatience for the food to be cooked, sipping his wine and refusing Prayle's offer of a cigarette. He explained that lack of money had forced him to cut his smoking so low that now he no longer cared whether he smoked or not. His nerves were steady. Prayle, over the supper, felt for the underlying cause; he could only come to the instinctive and impossible conclusion that Montagne was more certain of his aim now that he could no longer have an aim at all.

"After your escape, how did you get clothes?" he asked. "I was interested professionally, you see."

"In these reasonable countries and in the spring — a sack and an old army jacket, they were quite enough. From such a person one does not demand his passport. I worked on the railway, and then when you began to check passes I rode a goods wagon down to Egypt."

"And here, how do you make a living?"

"If one has no pride," Montagne answered, "it is not difficult to live in Egypt."

"And how did Furney find you?"

"He did not attempt to find me. I found him. He is pleasant, your Furney, but a schoolmaster. Do you think he would bother himself with the disgraced?"

"He did, you know."

"So he told me, but he was hardly successful," said Montagne, sourly dismissing the subject. "I went to him because I wanted to join the French Army as a private, and no questions asked. That should not have been difficult for him to arrange. He said that he could not interfere with the French."

"Have a heart!" Prayle exclaimed. "You know very well what the French would have said if they suspected us of knowing where you were and keeping our traps shut."

"Perhaps. But it doesn't matter."

"I repeat — he tried to clear you."

"Tried? My good little secret policeman, I trusted him. That is a word you will never understand. Suppose that our positions had been reversed, and that he instead of I had been ruined by these Jews, I would have resigned my commission, I would have made the gesture of blowing my blasted brains out with his dossier upon my desk rather than assent to such injustice. He speaks as ever of his palace eunuchs, but he begins to smell of the seraglio himself."

They arrived at the Casino just before the show began. On the whole, Prayle gave the place his blessing; it was not one of those dives which would wreck Armande's health and complexion, and it was not primarily arranged for talking to the artistes in quiet corners. The Casino, he observed, was more a garden theater than a cabaret, and, if there had been no Armande and no duty, he would have dragged Montagne off to some other joint more likely to reward his long abstinence upon the desert hills.

The audience he could not love. Yet why in the world he should consider the lazy gentle Egyptians and Egyptian Europeans to be less desirable contacts for Armande than boiled shirts and brigadiers he could not tell. The trouble was, he decided, that whenever he thought of Armande he was slightly corrupted himself by her conventional background.

He thought of her often and vividly, as if she were in the next tent or a village down the road, likely to turn up at any moment. He could not deny that she had become an essential part of his life, though he preferred to ascribe her intrusion simply to their partnership in the disposal of Fouad. He treasured her last message as evidence, at least, of friendship: a message which Fairfather, delivering it quite casually one day when they met over a crazy hunt for parachutists on the slopes of Hermon, swore that she had uttered with decent repentance and in all sincerity — *Give him my love.*

"*Indigne!*" murmured Montagne with bitter emphasis.

— 238 —

He referred to the acrobats. Prayle had been enjoying the ingenious contortions of the father, mother and three boneless children, but Montagne carried down his sympathy with the performers to a deeper level. Yes, in a sense it was an infamous trade — the sad, brown faces, the black tights covered with dust from the stage, the sandy dust that blew in from the desert, unperceived, with the evening breeze; and, thinking of Armande upon the same stage, it seemed sordid that the human body should be so sprawled and twisted just for money.

Damn Montagne anyway! This new Montagne — and the old one, too, to some extent — was as bad as an earnest reformer for taking the pleasure out of anything one might be doing. Thank God that he appeared to approve of the next turn! Miss Fatima's rolypoly nakedness roused him to the remark:

"She works, that animal!"

But Mlle. Joliette failed to enchant. Montagne poured a whisky into the untidy gap between his beard and mustache and called her a *putain*.

Armande and Floarea floated onto the stage in their first number.

"And that — that is responsible," said Montagne, as if marveling that anyone so unimportant as a cabaret dancer, or, perhaps, anyone so unsubstantial as Armande, could have caused him disaster.

"She suffered too," Prayle reminded him.

"Yes, Furney explained to me. But, all the same, what folly! Well, she must love those Zionists as much as I do. I did not remember that she was so pretty. Her face is more open than it was."

As both girls were preserving a professional expression of innocent wistfulness, it was hard to see what he meant by open — not, in any case, an adjective which Prayle considered applicable to Armande. Her face was open as the sea at evening or a rich plain under slanting sun — open, if Montagne liked, but bringing first and overwhelmingly to mind the presence of mystery and detail unseen.

The dancers sank in a curtsey at the end of their waltz, and Prayle caught Armande's eye. She looked at him almost with resentment, her expression changing instantly to delighted surprise. She waved a hand to assure him she would come over after the show.

Prayle was contented. His little doings hadn't changed a bit. That moment of doubt, followed immediately by generosity, was like her. Of course the silly little piece would be ashamed to be kicking up her legs in front of a friend she used to patronize, and of course, one second afterwards, she would be happy that he was a friend and there.

Sergeant Prayle took a deep draught of his whisky and soda and relaxed. His meditations upon the essential innocence of Armande were rudely broken as the butterflies, wings flung up from shoulders to reveal the flashing whiteness of their bodies, alighted upon an imaginary flower.

"It appears to me," said Montagne, "that the days of sentimental friendship are past. You will amuse yourself this evening."

"Don't know," Prayle muttered. "Haven't appointed the Planning Committee yet."

Montagne's criticisms of the dancers became anatomical. Prayle listened, in his mind a tumult of swift and contradictory images which was as near as he ever got to anger. He was not annoyed with Montagne — being well aware that the Frenchman was deliberately trying to sting him into some absurdity of sentiment — but with Armande. She had no right to place herself in a false position where the exquisiteness of her slender body could be compared with other bodies. Young, incomparable! And, anyway, what was all this sudden prudery? She was perfectly decently dressed. Perfectly!

After the show Armande swept through the tables towards him, her movements followed by the turning of scores of deep brown, melancholy eyes. Prayle had never seen her so lovely, so spiritually unapproachable. She looked, he thought, like a priestess or like a willing sacrifice, a Jephthah's daughter. Her only ornament was a gold belt. The pleats of her soft white frock opened and closed, as she walked, over the smooth outlines of knee and thigh.

"Well, Sergeant Prayle?" she asked, as he rose to meet her.

It was a general humorous question, inviting comment on everything from her surroundings to his military career. He saw now what Montagne had meant by open. Her face had changed; it had preserved its delicacy, but was less mannered.

"Too good for this place," he answered, and then added, feeling obscurely that what he had said was a needless platitude: "Your dance, I mean."

Armande smiled. Sergeant Prayle in his white suit and carnation was delicious. He looked like some tall, spare colonial statesman out on the spree, his crooked face so full of intelligence, embarrassment and good will. His remark might have meant that her dance was too good for the Casino but that she was not. That interpretation she rejected. Prayle's courtesies were always subtle.

"This is Mr. Makrisi," he said.

Montagne put his hand on his heart, bowed and gabbled a compliment.

"Where did you learn such beautiful French?" Armande asked.

"In Paris, Madame."

"You must have been born there."

"I was," he answered shortly. "Well, my sergeant, I am off. Tomorrow at eleven. Same place."

"So soon?" Armande asked politely.

It was astonishing that a little employee of Mr. Makrisi's type should go before being driven away, especially with a chance of free drinks at the expense of Field Security. Armande stared into the deep, hard eyes that for a moment deliberately met her own.

"My wife is waiting for me," said Mr. Makrisi with the sudden, savage and alarming frankness of the Middle East. "When I am late, she makes me an intolerable scene."

As soon as he had gone, Armande remarked:

"I've seen him before somewhere, and he hadn't a beard. Should I or shouldn't I try to remember?"

"Just bring to boiling point and let it simmer," Prayle replied. "Who's the red admiral?"

"Floarea Pitescu. A rather lovely person in a way. Would you like to talk to her?"

Armande reproached herself for impulsive, foolish unselfishness. Prayle and Floarea would get on much too well together.

"Prefer fritillaries," he replied.

"Pancakes?"

"Butterflies. They flit over marshes, all tender colors. What will we drink? Does the management give you colored water in this place?"

"It does if we want it. But tonight," she said, acknowledging his loyalty with soft and merry eyes, "I would like a very long, very strong whisky and soda with lots of ice in it. Tell me about Fouad."

"Nothing to tell. We got away with it. He's a full corporal, I hear, and bursting with pride. Fun to be an Arab when there's a war on!"

Floarea and the Romanova came down the steps, and sat at a beflowered table. Armande made no signal. After a while they joined Miss Fatima and a party of South Africans in civilian dress.

"I like Auntie," said Prayle approvingly. "Circus horse retired. Does she take a commission?"

"Auntie does not," Armande replied. "But she shares whatever is going, and she deserves it."

Prayle grinned approvingly at her firmness.

"Doghouse for me," he said. "But a year ago Auntie — well, she wouldn't have been your type I'd have said."

"She trained me."

They sipped their drinks, and exchanged the bare facts of the recent past.

"Don't you dance?" Armande asked.

"No."

"Then what do you usually do in a place like this?"

"Play the fool on the floor if I get drunk enough."

"Did you never dance at home?"

"Not my style of beauty."

Sergeant Prayle, then, had never been in love; or, if he had, had never made any determined effort to win his beloved. Armande warmed to him. He was so certain that he was not attractive to women; yet attractive he was, if one looked, as it were, at the vitality of the drawing and not the caricature itself.

He had already changed the subject, that alarming subject of holding her in his arms to dance, and was lecturing with staccato incoherence. She was suddenly certain that Sergeant Prayle was profoundly interested in her, and doubtful about admitting it even to himself.

"Now don't get alarmed," he was saying. "It has nothing to do with security this time."

"What hasn't?"

"Weren't you listening?"

"I was thinking of something else. But tell me."

"Mr. Makrisi and I came to see you about a job. Cloak and dagger."

"I don't want to be involved in any more of it," she said.

"King and Country."

"But they don't need me."

"They do. It's all on the square. That's why I was sent for to Cairo — to give you my word that it's the real goods this time."

"And do *you* think it is?"

"So real that I hope you'll say no."

"I'm glad you think I'll say yes. So glad."

To Prayle the emotion in her voice was astounding. He had never dreamed that she cared what he thought of her. In fact he was sure that up to now, or up to, perhaps, some indefinable point in her private life, she never had cared. The whole essence of his relationship with her, since their first antagonistic interview, was that neither his appearance nor his opinions could be to her of the slightest importance. That conviction permitted him to remain a disapproving adorer, a fascinated but detached observer.

"I know you so well, Mrs. Herne," he said, his deep, tender voice expressing the melancholy of such useless knowledge.

"Why not Armande?"

"Always were, really."

"Well?" she asked merrily. "And am I to go on calling you Sergeant Prayle?"

"Just Prayle. No nickname."

"But what about your Christian name?"

"Damn awful."

"I might like it. What is it?"

"Percy."

"Yes, I wouldn't choose it any more than you," said Armande frankly. "Got any more?"

"Worse and worse. Dionysius."

"Percy Dionysius Prayle," she repeated with smiling respect. "It ought to have D.D. after it. An obscure but eminent scholar."

"Probably what Pa intended."

"What was he?"

"Under porter in an Oxford college."

"Ah!" Armande exclaimed, suddenly seeing in proper perspective her sergeant's classless intelligence, his social nihilism. "Well, I shall call you Dion."

"So did my mother. I've never had the face to propose it to anyone else."

"And what did you do when you grew up, Dion Prayle?"

"Nothing long."

"But what?"

"This and that. Mining. Knocking about. Company secretary. Good little companies — not enough capital. Bad little companies — got out before they bust. Abroad a lot. Going my own way, and taking anything that looked like being fun."

"What sort of fun?"

"Talking to people."

"To men, you mean?" she asked.

"Of course."

"Don't women count at all?"

"Not much. I just read what's in their little pans, and sheer off."

"Dion, you do talk such nonsense," she said. "Look at Floarea — can you read her little pan, as you call it?"

"Yes. What does she want?"

"I won't tell you. What's her character?"

"Just that. All that matters to her and the Boss is — what does she want?"

Armande considered the oracle. The answer was true. Floarea's value to herself, humanity and the Boss — yes, the dear idiot couldn't mean an earthly boss — depended entirely upon what she wanted. She was a fine creature because she wanted success in her profession, and did not wholly measure success in terms of money. If she had wanted luxury, she would be dishonest; if love, she might be a jealous horror like Mr. Makrisi's wife.

"What is it you and Mr. Makrisi wish me to do?" she asked.

"Not us. A G.H.Q. racket."

"Tell me."

Prayle from habit lowered his voice, though there was no chance of being overheard against the baaing of the dance band and the hum of conversation.

"They want you to stay behind if we lose Egypt."

"Yes," she said thoughtfully, "that is the real thing, isn't it? Then am I clear?"

"No, Armande. The black-listing is just what makes you useful — so long as it's widely known."

She shivered at the implication that everyone must know her secret; yet it was obvious that there her value and safety lay.

"But someone important must trust me?"

"Yes. He used to be in our game before he took to this. He

knows you are clear, but can't prove it. You must think we are all off our rockers. But it's not so easy. You did a spot of gunrunning, and you say you thought it was a nice, clean sport, all aboveboard and hunky-dory. That's the truth, but it's wildly improbable. Especially as you were just one big question mark in Beirut. And in Jerusalem — well, a nice little cash payment into your bank and no transfers to your account from London. So you see it was my opinion against a big, thick file. Montagne was in the same boat."

"What happened to Major Montagne?" she asked.

"Mr. Makrisi."

"Of course!" Armande exclaimed. "But he's not really so down-and-out, is he? I mean, Abu Tisein's inventions couldn't affect a security officer?"

"Couldn't they just!"

Prayle sketched for her Montagne's past; his escape, and his probable position as her immediate chief in the Cairo underground.

"And this man you spoke of couldn't clear him either?" she asked incredulously.

"He could have done more, I think. But what's one man against the army politicians? If the French had only court-martialed Montagne, our evidence would have been convincing. But they didn't. Montagne was a nuisance. It was a great chance to drop him in the pail and put the lid back quickly. So they just bunged him in a fortress. Sounds very correct and military, but the fortress was huts behind barbed wire. And our people said they couldn't interfere with internal discipline in the French Army, and went home to tea. I hope it choked them. But it wouldn't. Because, after all, you can only give a hint to your allies. You can't open their mouths and force them to ask questions if they don't want to."

— 247 —

"Poor, poor Montagne!" she said softly. "I didn't like him, but he was so inflexible and French and undaunted. Dion, I'll do everything I can for him. And he'll never be caught — well, if he doesn't plot just for the sake of plotting. I'm to be French too, I suppose?"

"Vichy sympathies. All your papers in order."

"Too many people know I'm British."

"Only in this joint. And you must leave it. All they can say afterwards is that you pretended to be British. We'll see that all your records disappear from the Egyptian police."

"Could I do it, Dion? Tell me the truth — should I have a chance?"

"You would. Think of my opposite number. Kraut security sergeant. Just occupied a town of a million, with nationalities all mixed up. If you're living quietly — not a dancer, of course — you'd go weeks and weeks before being questioned at all. And then: Papers in order? *Jawohl!* Can account for her time? *Bestimmt!* Bit hazy here and there? *Natürlich!* Feeling your way in a mist, Armande — that's security. If a cove has every bloody thing in order and an answer to every question, well, he's either a government official or there's something wrong. Motives, movements of real human beings, here and there they are bound to be vague. Vague. We're all liars, all self-deceivers.

"You won't be pulled in for serious interrogation unless you slip up. If you are, play Kensington. Look at the Gestapo sergeant as if he were a piece of mud. Then he'll think you're Churchill's French cousin, or something. Terrific sense of class the Krauts have. You'll get interrogated by a major with a monocle. Keep him interested, and he'll be so busy making excuses for Hitler that he'll forget half the questions he meant to ask. Security is only efficient in dealing with the crook and the little man. You're much too high-class and complicated. If

they get really suspicious, they'll just intern you and not bother
any more. Let's have another before the pub shuts."

"I think I deserve one."

"Very long and very strong again?"

"Yes. Oh, this heat! I can't think."

"You aren't supposed to. Not in Nature's plan. The thinking
season opens in November."

The waiter brought their drinks and presented the bill, for
Cairo night life stopped at one. Prayle gave him a lordly tip,
and having marked up the amount in blue pencil, carefully
folded the slip and put it in his wallet.

"That's on the house," he explained. "Item: To contacting
agents. Now I take over from the Bank of England. Where
shall we go?"

"Home to bed."

"Not yet. It won't be cool enough to sleep till dawn. And
we may not see each other again for a long time."

"Well — " she hesitated — "anyway, wait for me while I
change."

"Don't run out of the back door like the Hungarians."

"What Hungarians?"

"Used to staff places like this. All little Hungarian beauties.
Told boy-friend to wait in a taxi at the front door, and then
hopped out at the back and made a beeline for nearest limit-
less plain."

"Dion, you're sordid! Just for that, you shall wait in your
taxi and I'll be as long as possible. And what's more, the porter
will tell you it's no use waiting."

"Is it?"

"Work it out from my little pan, Sergeant."

Prayle left the Casino and endeavored to find a taxi with a
full petrol tank. When he was satisfied, he gave the driver fifty

piasters and delivered a speech on the admirable qualities of Egyptians and, above all, their capacity for unquestioning obedience. Then he took possession of his taxi and awaited Armande, chuckling for the first five minutes, and extremely anxious for the next ten. At last she came to him, hatless, comradely, and free as the night in a black silk frock printed with what he took to be chrysanthemums.

"Where shall we go?" he asked, when the taxi had been running some minutes.

Armande gave him her address.

"Yes, of course. But I thought it would do you good to go to Helwan first."

"Dion, Helwan is miles out of town," she protested.

"Don't like the Pyramids. Never did."

"But I will not go to Helwan."

"Jump out then."

"Dion, you are not to do this. Just because I —"

"Don't say it!"

"What was I going to say?"

"I don't know, but a suggestion that Armande Herne shouldn't be where she wants to be."

"She wants to be in bed."

"Wonk!"

"And stop making bloody silly exclamations!"

"Straight off the bat!" he said admiringly. "And sounded like an understatement. You're growing up."

"Has it ever occurred to you, Sergeant Prayle, that I might have been using 'bloody' to myself ever since I was a little girl, but had sufficient good taste not to do so aloud?"

"No, it hadn't."

"And now take me home, Dion dear, and don't quarrel with me."

The taxi was rumbling smoothly under an avenue of trees along the Nile. On the landward side of the road army lorries in two and threes, headlights blacked out, bonnet to tailboard, streamed from the Helwan camps to Cairo.

"He says he hasn't room to turn," explained Prayle after conversation with the driver. "Wait till we get to the round-about."

"All right."

The driver, hooting furiously, swung his taxi round to the left, and cut into the Cairo-bound traffic. The screech of brakes immediately behind them was taken up by the next lorry and the next, as the sound went diminishing up the road.

"Holding up the war," said Prayle disapprovingly, "just because you won't see the moon at Helwan."

"I can see it in the water," she laughed, glancing casually out of the window — and then exclaimed at the unexpected beauty.

The Nile was smooth and calm and moonlit as any other water, but it was hurrying. The river looked like an infinite length of silver silk pouring between the rollers of some vast machine where it had received a sheen more absolute than any brilliancy of nature.

"The worst of driving in convoy," Prayle remarked, "is that one can't stop."

"Yes. I wish we could."

They approached another traffic island. At the last moment Prayle snapped an order to the driver. The taxi came about like a yacht, rounded the island and started back in the direction of Helwan, accompanied by the curses of the lorry drivers on the other side of the road.

"Dion!" Armande protested.

"But you said you wanted to look at the moon again."

"I didn't!"

"Ah! Well, there's a place a little further up where we can stop."

Beyond the trees and striped by their moon shadows, a tongue of grass ran down to the water. Prayle opened the door of the taxi and offered his hand. His tall, white figure was compelling.

This dancing, stubborn mischievousness was all in the character of the sergeant she knew, all in his sixteenth-century face, yet, directed for the first time to herself instead of her circumstances, Armande found it unfamiliar. The odd rhythm of his speech was, she thought, more truly expressive of him than she had ever believed.

"You belong to the night," he said. "You aren't seen. And then the black and white of your head, the eagerness of you — they suddenly appear. Whenever you're excited or interested. You live in flashes. Why? What are you?"

"A soul in twilight," she answered. "But sometimes it looks across the river."

With a gesture she could neither foresee nor resist he smoothed her hair back from her temples, and as she turned to him, tender and surprised, he kissed her. She neither responded nor refused, fighting her excitement at this devastating, accumulated passion, exploded in an instant.

"Now we must go," she said.

She meant it to be a cold voice from a cold thought, but the voice trembled and she dared not think any thought at all.

"Like baby rabbits just beginning to nibble grass," he said.

"If you call yourself a baby rabbit — !"

"Your lips, I meant. Do they never say anything to themselves?"

"I don't listen to them."

Armande had only a moment to be angry with her body. Then, while she rested from his second kiss, there was left neither anger nor regret. She was reminding herself desperately that she was not in love and could not be in love.

"Armande," he said, "my darling, I wonder why I was ever frightened of you."

"Or I of you."

"Were you? I didn't know anybody had ever been afraid of me."

"Do you remember once saying to me *What else is there?*" she asked.

"No."

"When we first met. I told you to stop being coarse, and you said *What else is there?*"

"Meant it, I expect. There I am, watching them all lying and fussing and keeping up with the Joneses. Drink. Women. Battle. Anything to avoid the bitterness. And I love the bitterness. Don't want to die at all. And if they won't see things as they are, I make things a bit more as they are. Coarse? Well, but true. So what else is there?"

"This."

She took his head between her hands, and kissed his eyes, forehead and mouth.

"Was that coarse, Dion? Or bitter?"

His face was transfigured by joy and amazed surrender, but in the corners of the odd eyes and thin mouth she still perceived the ghost of irony. It hurt her, for she longed to wipe out that internal suffering which he pretended to enjoy.

"Well?" she repeated. "Was it, my dear?"

"But was it true?"

"Yes, for us two. All the possible truth."

She linked her arm in his and led him back to the car.

"We must turn at the next roundabout," she said when the taxi had started.

"We're halfway to Helwan."

"Dion, no!"

"I love you so. I have always loved you."

"I know, and I'm so glad. But I'm not a person to be loved. Remember what you used to think of me. It was nearly right."

"I want it to be nearly right. You I love. Armande, no might-be Armandes."

"Dion, we turn here."

"We'll go round and round all night, if you like."

Imperturbable as the driver, he passed on her order, and the taxi headed back to Cairo.

She relaxed on his shoulder, safe in the knowledge that in another quarter of an hour she would be home. Her lips answered his without thought of past or of so short a future.

"But I want you," he cried. "I will not let you go tonight."

"No!"

"Your breasts say yes."

She sat back in her corner with a sudden sense of shame — a cabaret girl taken out by a sergeant after the show.

"I'm not responsible," she answered angrily. "It's the heat, the moon, the whisky. Dion, for three years I have been faithful to my husband."

"Would he like you to be?" he asked.

"Of course. Well . . . why did you ask that?"

"I wondered. One watches. Of course some of us have been out here longer than the Crusaders. Still, is it only absence that nips off the marriages? New values at home. New values here."

"I don't want any new values."

"Don't you? In your own twilight, little lamp, don't you?

— 254 —

I know. I've watched you being bored with the lot of them. Of course you were. So desperately wanting to be needed that you gave yourself to all that nonsense in Beit Chabab. And all the while I needed you. Do now. Always shall."

"I can't help it."

"You can. I need you because you are the only human being I love, really love. Because I am dead without you. Isn't that a new value? Have you ever refused such a need of you?"

"Dion, that's not fair!"

"It is. You're not cruel. You just don't see. When you're needed, you aren't there."

"Dion, will you stop it?" she cried.

"No, I won't. I need you."

"It's impossible — some beastly, sordid hotel."

"No. A white room on the edge of the desert. And flowers. And when I ring the bell, a simple, sleepy, friendly black man to receive us."

"I will not. You've been there before."

"Of course. But alone."

"Promise me."

"All my life I have been alone. Don't you know it?"

"Yes."

Prayle held her across his heart as he leaned forward to order the driver:

"Back to Helwan, *habibi!*"

"No!"

"Shut up, Armande my beloved, shut up!"

"Dion, I shall never forgive myself."

"Tell me that tomorrow. At dawn. If you believe it."

Mr. Makrisi

No LONGER was the Middle East a fortress. The dusty beaters had driven the game out of their deserts into Tunisia, where the guns, appreciative of such excellent shooting, stood ready for the kill. After dark the streets of Cairo blazed again with light. Hotels and bazaars, picture palaces and native theaters, shone expensively, gaily or discreetly according to the wealth that war had presented to their owners. No longer did the café strategists discuss the virtues and failings of their garrison; no longer, indeed, had they more than spectators' interest in its fate. Half the width of Africa was between the Axis armies and the Levant, and in and over the eastern Mediterranean the power of the British was unchallengeable. Syrian and Egyptian, Arab and Jew, were free to attend to their domestic affairs.

Armande was happy as she had never been in all her life. Since Cairo had never been occupied, the underground organization had not been used for its original purpose; nevertheless, it had been busy. She began to suspect that recent jobs done for Mr. Makrisi were becoming pointless, and that her irregular wads of Egyptian pounds were no longer really earned; but her content, eager and warmhearted, was undisturbed. She had an object, and it was Dion Prayle.

That she had been won, in the first place, by his passion and gentleness as a lover she knew, but by what was she held? By the repeated glory of his swift visits to Cairo — that was un-doubted and no matter for self-questioning — and by what she described to herself as his isolation. Dion saw life steadily, but he did not, in her opinion, see it whole. He could appreciate, and none better, the beauty in a tree, a hippopotamus or the comments and aspirations of an Arab beggar; yet anything that the world appreciated, from poetry to social or monetary success, he treated with suspicion. Sweet it was that he should depend so utterly upon her for a sufficient companionship, but she wanted him to be more than a tense and often suffering observer of others. Human life was, in essence, artificial; it could not be forced into his preferential mold of the strong, the raw and the simple. Both he and she were fair products of their civilization, which had unvaryingly pursued the ideal of the aristocratic individual, open-minded, generous and urbane; and it was a triumph for that civilization that both of them had been produced from nothing. This, however, he would not see. He called it a triumph for the bloody Joneses; and by that conviction, he, who was so anxious to lose himself in humanity, cut himself off from humanity.

His commission had done him good. During those first precious days in Cairo and Helwan, he had accepted his com-mandant's offer. He was Captain Dion Prayle now (in his service it seemed to be understood that one only remained a lieutenant for a month or two) and, to her very private de-light, he looked the part. Sergeant Prayle was eccentric and misplaced; the same face on Captain Prayle was that of a hard-bitten original. Whether he really liked his commission she could not decide. He obviously adored and mothered his Field Security Section, but he complained that a sergeant's life had been more amusing. One had not, he said, to put up with the conversation of officers.

It was odd that her surrender to Dion should have made the writing of letters to John easier than before. At her first attempt she had been overwhelmed by a sense of disloyalty; this precluded all emotion and any soulful effort towards intimacy, while encouraging the transmission of mere news. John had seemed delighted, and had replied with a letter that certainly showed no sense of strain and, for him, was almost witty. Thereafter their long-distance relationship was simpler. John had ceased to be an unsatisfactory ambition, and become just a dear person with whom years ago she had lived.

To her amusement Dion Prayle was jealous. He maintained in obscure but uncompromising phrases that John should be told and that proceedings for divorce should be started; he could not be made to see that it was wicked to upset John in the steady course of his personal war, and that he might become careless of his life. It was not enough for Dion to lay it down that she had never been in love with John, and that by now he must suspect it. John was not the sort of person to suspect anything which was not in full view.

Armande waited in a secluded alley of the Cairo Zoo. She was fond of the zoo; its overhanging creepers, its vast African trees and running water made it the coolest of Egyptian gardens. She had chosen it as discreet and neutral ground for a first meeting with her chief. His request for a rendezvous was unexpected, and perplexing in that it had been passed to her by letter from Dion instead of through the normal channel of Mr. Makrisi. The meeting meant, she supposed, that she was to be thanked and that her employment was at an end.

No Gestapo could have got anything out of her, for she never saw cause or effect of what she did. She was often used as a postbox, and sometimes she was simply told to be away from her flat on certain dates. She would watch, and she would occasionally entertain. Once a high officer had been drunk in her flat, really drunk — he wasn't trusting his power to act — and had blurted out British intentions in the Dodecanese before some of Mr. Makrisi's guests. Makrisi, with his cold hatred of the enemy that always aroused her pity of them and for him, had told her that the evening's work sent two shiploads of Boches to the bottom of the Aegean.

It was about time, she admitted, that they closed down. The war was far away, and their branch of Intelligence could be left to the small and efficient band of professionals. Mr. Makrisi still seemed very busy, but she was not. She had no idea what he was up to; he was conspiratorial and uncommunicative.

Major Furney passed her seat, stopped to examine some decorative cranes in a paddock behind the bushes, repassed her and then sat down.

"It's curious, Mrs. Herne, that we have never actually met before," he said.

"Isn't it? I knew your face in Beirut, but not your name."

He thanked her very formally for her work. She couldn't help feeling as if she were leaving school with an elaborate certificate. She realized, however, why Dion liked Guy Furney. The precise face could not hide the fact that he enjoyed himself. He might lack depth of character, but not of insight.

"What I wanted to ask you," he said, "is — what are your personal relations to Mr. Makrisi?"

"Personal?"

"Yes."

"We have very little personal relationship. He's not a man one can help outside the game. I've darned his socks and looked after his diet a bit, but he doesn't — well, he doesn't encourage me."

"You like him, I suppose?" Furney asked.

"Oh, yes. I'm so sorry for him."

"I'm glad your loyalty isn't engaged in any way," he said with a smile of relief.

"My loyalty is exactly where it always has been, Major Furney."

"Yes," he answered with some embarrassment. "I know it and I knew it. But that question is now — academic. Mrs. Herne, I have given Mr. Makrisi no work whatever for weeks. Does that surprise you?"

"I suppose he has been making contacts for the future," she said.

"He has been busy?"

"Yes."

"I'm uneasy."

"Major Furney, it is utterly inconceivable," Armande answered directly, "that Major Montagne would work for the enemy."

"I'm happy you said that, though it only confirms what I too was sure of. But then, what is he doing?"

"I'm not in the picture enough to know."

"No, of course not. That was for your own safety, you see. Have you any idea whom he is seeing?"

"There have been some Poles," said Armande.

"Could they be Russians?"

"Not this lot."

"French? Jews?"

"He's the most bitter anti-Semite I ever met."

"It rankles, does it?"

"In the bottom of his heart and all through."

"Arabs?" Furney asked. "Has he anything to do with Arabs?"

"Naturally. All the time off and on. But you know who they are, I suppose. And there's no one new."

"Dion Prayle said — You know his extraordinary snap judgments?"

Armande did. It amused her that the Army should have picked up the Christian name which she had chosen for him. Dion, no longer self-conscious after her approval, had published himself as Dion.

"Well when I first put you and Montagne on the job, I asked him to give me his impression of Montagne. He said that he had an inner light, and it wasn't mine."

Armande warmed to Dion's words, coming secondhand out of past time. Darling Dion! Like some twisted medieval alchemist — incomprehensible, but so often right.

"That describes Montagne well," she said, smiling.

"But he's done splendidly for us. So have you."

"That doesn't mean we don't have a private life."

"No. And now there's time for it. Could he be playing for the French? He's never been particularly pro-British."

"He has not forgiven either French or British," said Armande slowly. "And he doesn't care what happens to either of us so long as we down Hitler. I hate that in him, but there it is."

"That sounds as if he might be a communist."

"He isn't, Major Furney. He despairs of politics. He could be an anarchist, except that he's too intelligent, fiendishly intelligent."

"Fiendishly? Inner light?" Furney repeated, a slight raising of his voice showing that he deprecated such exaggeration. "I wonder if you and Dion Prayle aren't too much impressed by that satanic look of his. He always had it, you know. Well, put a name to all your apocalyptic suspicions, will you?"

"How?"

"Watch him."

"I've no organization except his."

"I'll give you the start of one," he said. "Do you remember a certain Rashid, Rashid Abd-er-Rahman ibn Ajjueyn?"

"Rashid! Very well."

"He's devoted to you. He'd take your orders, and raise a few of his people to carry them out."

"Where is Major Honeymill?"

"D.S.O. Posthumous, I'm afraid."

"Oh, no! Poor Toots!" Armande protested, fighting the shock of sorrow and her tears. "I didn't know! I haven't spoken for months to anybody in the army but Dion."

"They were playing hell with Rommel's communications, and based on nothing themselves. They knew it couldn't go on forever."

"And Rashid got clear?"

"Yes. He was wounded. But he and the few who were left passed clean through a German division carrying Honeymill's body, and buried him at Derna. Rashid is out of hospital now, and at a loose end."

Armande compelled herself to concentrate.

"He fought against us in Palestine, you know," she warned him.

"That doesn't matter. Arabs give themselves to people, not causes. Rashid belongs to anyone he admires. Would you like him?"

"More than ever — if you're satisfied."

Major Furney looked at her primly over his glasses.

"I — er — don't upset him, will you?"

"I meant," she replied with a Mona Lisa smile, "that it's easier for me than it was to keep him as a friend."

"That's all then. You can ring me up and fix a meeting whenever you need to talk. Is there anything else that you think you are likely to want?"

"Could you help me to pay a debt?"

"How much?"

"Not that kind. A debt of friendship. You know the Rumanian I used to dance with at the Casino, and her mother?"

"Indeed I do. A pure Byzantine type. Most interesting."

"I want her to have a real chance. Aren't there empty planes going to South Africa?"

"There are. But I can't go shipping off pet cabaret girls. Only generals can do that."

"Suppose she had worked for you and her life were in danger?" Armande suggested.

"Is it?"

"Not in the least. But if it were, you'd put her on a plane."

"Oh my aunt! And her mother?"

"Yes."

"You guarantee them?"

"They keep right out of the war. All Floarea Pitescu wants is to dance in the capital of the winner. I think Johannesburg would be a good stop on the way."

"I can't do it. Really I can't," he said regretfully.

"Whisper, Major Furney. The simple soldiery will believe anything."

Armande could not keep back her tears. All this while she had forced down a grim, military cover upon her longing for a lonely minute in which to weep for Toots; and now, thinking with half her mind of that day when he had first met and comforted her, the memory of his voice and of his laughing words, which she had just used in his own tone, came back to her too vividly.

"I'm sorry. I'm so sorry, Mrs. Herne," Guy Furney was repeating. "In the end I'm just a mass of files like the rest of them. Give me their passports, and I'll do it. I promise you it shall be done."

He patted her hand in agitation. Armande choked on a hoarse sound that was neither a laugh nor a sob. She who had never deliberately used tears on a man was childishly, ironically, astonished to discover how effective they were.

Two days later Rashid came to see her. She sat him, gallantly protesting, down on a sofa while she mixed a drink of heroic size. Drinks, furniture, flat — none of them belonged to her. This floating life did not disturb her, for Dion Prayle represented the reality of past and future. Her present, wrapped in this chrysalis of government possessions, was unimportant.

Rashid had collected a Military Cross, and he pointed out the ribbon with a proud and reverent forefinger. Armande, too, was impressed, for the army, after nearly four years of fighting, had no medals later than the green and purple of the prewar Palestine campaign — and Rashid was most certainly not entitled to that.

He had none of the inhibitions of the British officer. He told the exploits of Honeymill's force in full and fantastic detail. The flashing eyes, the rhythmic sentences, the quick, stabbing movements of head and hands, while his seated body preserved its dignity, reminded her of storytellers in the bazaar. There were occasional mentions of Alexander and Montgomery, presiding or interfering like Homeric gods, but the war in the desert, as handed on to Arab poets of the future, was evidently to be a personal struggle between Rashid and Rommel.

"We fought with the British as equal to equal. We have beaten the Germans. And now we will deal with the Jews," declared Rashid as a peroration.

"Rashid Bey, shame on you!"

Rashid, unabashed, happily patted the unseen knife that lay upon his lean stomach.

"*Willah!*" he cried in his deep, gargling voice. "Only the British stand between the Jews and this! And the British are going. Everyone says so. Then we shall have Americans. I have seen them. They can fight. But they will not fight for the Jews as you did."

"Café talk, Rashid," she said in gentle reproof.

"I repeat what they say," he admitted. "Who am I to know the truth? Perhaps there will be no Americans. Perhaps the British will stay forever, and my home is ever open to them. But I think they will leave us alone with the Jews."

"And if you are — haven't they a secret army called the Hagana, and trained by us too? Are you so sure?"

"I am a soldier, Mrs. Armande. By God, I have no other trade, and I understand it. I know the Hagana. They will die like men. They will win every battle against us, but they cannot be everywhere at once. The Jews are surrounded by Islam. If we raid them, they can punish us. They will. But they cannot occupy, for there is nothing to occupy. How then will they force us to peace?"

"Damascus isn't far away."

"By God, Mrs. Armande, you should be a soldier! Your thought has the sharpness of the sword. Well, let them take Damascus — but they would need more warrior Jews than there are in the world to hold it! And meanwhile, Damascus is farther from Tel Aviv than Tel Aviv from Jordan."

She let Rashid rave himself out, aware that in the unfamiliar, exciting presence of a European woman he became intoxicated by his own personality. To Rashid, Armande guessed, she was real and solid and a friend, but incredible. It was hard to imagine a parallel experience for herself; to her and her like no social situation was wholly unprecedented. She could have talked to a black chieftain or a Siberian peasant with equal ease, knowing, instinctively, what was the common ground, and, historically, what were the obvious differences. Perhaps if the black chieftain had been educated at Oxford and yet wore no clothes at all, she would encounter something of what Rashid felt towards a woman with whom his intellect and emotions effortlessly marched, who yet broke every one of his traditions and conventions.

She told him as much as it was wise for him to know: that the British Secret Service (to him, who would be impressed by it, she used the unnecessarily dramatic name) wanted information about the movements and contacts of a Mr. Makrisi. When he was ready, he could come to her flat, meet this Mr. Makrisi and also leave with him, so that any men he might post in the street could recognize the person to be followed.

Armande herself knew where Mr. Makrisi was likely to be found at certain hours; thus, if she were not suspected, it was child's play to put Rashid's men back on his track when they lost it. She did not like this assignment; it tasted of treachery. She had, after all, worked with Montagne for some eight months, always loyally and sometimes admiringly. She was sure that Furney's uneasiness was justified — his vague suspicions squared too well with her own — but she hoped with all her heart that Montagne was not engaged in anything that need be taken overseriously, and that his activities could be unobtrusively checked in good time.

When she brought the two together, Rashid immediately

disliked Mr. Makrisi; he was so ceremoniously polite that it was obvious. She knew the reason. Mr. Makrisi could not keep out of his voice that faint irony with which the French, except for their rare spirits born to command, were wont to treat Arab peoples of whatever religion. Rashid might have put up with this from a Frenchman, simply assuming that it was one of the inevitable and unimportant European discourtesies, but he resented the tone in a little Egyptian clerk.

Fortunately their conversation was limited, for Rashid's Arabic was the classical tongue of northern Arabia, and Montagne's was his own personal adaptation from the Algerian. Armande was frequently called on to interpret through French and English.

"He won the war all alone, your friend," said Montagne.

"Perhaps. But you are not to annoy him," Armande answered.

"Annoy him? I? I adore the Tartarins. I envy them. Do you not know, even you," he cried bitterly, "how I wish that I had died at Bir Hachim?"

"What does he say of Bir Hachim?" asked Rashid.

"That the French, too, fought magnificently," Armande replied, not wishing to translate exactly and thus arouse a suspicion of Mr. Makrisi's true nationality.

Rashid, finding at last a subject upon which he could get to know his quarry, proceeded to map the battle with the aid of sofa cushions. Montagne added a rolled-up tablecloth to represent the enveloping Germans and Italians, and lumps of sugar for the minefields. As Rashid had actually seen the ground, and Montagne had read everything on the engagement that he could borrow from Furney, there was room for argument; Rashid, with proper subtlety, allowed Mr. Makrisi the best of it. Armande relaxed in her chair and let them play happily upon the floor. They left together, still discussing Bir Hachim, and on the friendliest terms.

During the next three weeks Rashid called several times at the flat for additional information on Mr. Makrisi, and once with a dashing, blustering demand for money to reward his men. He was evasive, difficult, exclamatory, claiming results but refusing to admit what they were. Armande, taught by Wadiah and clients at the Casino, knew her Arabs. It was not hard for her. Whether Christian or Moslem, they resembled European woman so much more than European man. They welcomed hypocrisy so long as it was pleasant; they surrendered instantly to a mixture of strength and courtesy, but felt an instinctive and unforgiving dislike of those who were incapable of either. She waited patiently and took pains that Rashid should be devoted to her as a woman, whatever he might think of her as an agent.

At last he came to report, grinning with such candor and confidence that Armande knew perfectly well he was determined to tell no more than half the truth.

"It was easy," he said. "He told me in the first week. He wanted me to work for the Arabs."

"Against whom?"

"The Jews, of course."

"That would be against us. Against me, Rashid Bey."

"I do not know. Perhaps. But who am I? What do you know of Makrisi's friends, Mrs. Armande?"

"Nothing," she answered, smiling. "I want you to tell me."

"Believe me, Mrs. Armande, I am out of politics. I am a soldier."

"You are all a soldier should be, Rashid Bey."

"By God, you are beautiful! I would give three hundred black goats to your father for you."

"But I am already married, my dear. And I have explained to you that our marriage is as serious as yours."

"Then we are friends for always. Brother and sister as if we had played in the same dust. And I will never betray you."

"Nor will I betray you, my brother Rashid."

"And you remember Major Toots," he continued with some agitation. "You know how I loved him. I will do nothing that he would not order."

Armande suddenly saw light. This magnificent creature, nervously advancing and retreating, was full of mistrust. He suspected that he was being double-crossed, and that, so far from being engaged to report on Mr. Makrisi, Makrisi was really engaged to report on him.

"Rashid," she said, "I too love the memory of Major Toots. I will never ask you to do anything that he would not order. Tell me — why do you think I doubted you?"

"By God, I thought no such thing!"

"But if you had thought so, why would you have thought it?"

Rashid grinned with delight at this courtesy.

"Why, Mrs. Armande? *Billah!* I will tell you why. Because your Makrisi incites me against the Jews, yet he makes secret visits to a house of Jews."

"What about it? Can't he have friends of all religions, as you and I?"

"Yes, but he is not open as you and I. My men have watched him. He goes secretly to this house. Two of the Jews he meets in a café near the station, also secretly, and once he gave them a small parcel. This is not mere friendship. This is what you told me to find. But what does it mean? Am I the hunter or the gazelle?"

"The hunter," she said, "and a very good one, my dear. I can't make any more of this than you, but we will see what they think higher up."

Armande decided to test Montagne herself before she made any report, and arranged, by a pretense of aimless boredom, for him to invite her to dinner at one of the small native eating places which he patronized. She had a cautious respect for Montagne's acute instinct for danger, sharpened by years of official and unofficial intrigue, but she reckoned that there would be nothing for him to suspect so long as she stayed within a part that was or had been natural to her. She gave deliberate expression to the worst in her — moody resentment of her treatment by Abu Tisein. She had, in fact, very little resentment left, only a broad, warm, healthy anger. It was absurd to brood over a petty black-listing by Security when she was the trusted agent of a department of Intelligence at least as secret and as important to the war.

It needed little effort of the imagination to throw herself back into the raw sensitivity of that Armande who had been the loveless, shrinking, black-listed dancer at the Casino. She was too clever openly to abuse Abu Tisein, but she became depressed and bitter over her wine, and allowed Montagne to draw his own conclusions. He drew them.

"In the jolly little dog kennel," he said, "where I hide myself among the excrement of my own thoughts, I pass my time in making a special study of Jewish politics. And I flatter myself that I have discovered the worst enemy of the Zionists. It is a good beginning for us."

"The Arab League?" she asked.

"The League? Never! The Arabs are intelligent, my child. They know that they have only to attack, for all the democracies to come down on the side of the Jews. No enemy of the

Zionists would pay a piaster to the Arabs. The Arabs are waiting. They know how to wait. The Jews do not.

"Jewish Palestine is an explosive, Armande. It can be made to destroy itself. And there is no lack of those who will supply . . ."

He held up finger and thumb two inches apart, as if they measured between them the length of a detonator. Armande recognized the gesture. In the privacy of her flat Montagne had a disconcerting habit, when fulminating against the Boche, of pulling out a detonator from its packing of cotton wool and exhorting it to carry out his final curses.

"Some for one motive, some for another will help them to blow themselves up. You and I, because we hate them. I have hated Franco. And Pétain. And the Catholics and monarchists who pervert my general . . ."

Armande watched his eyes. They should have been burning, but they were cold, even a little hazy, at the bottom of the deep sockets.

". . . But they were decent little hates — mere dislike, shall I say? — if I compare them to my hatred for this Jewish Agency. After Hitler and his crew are in hell, the Zionists will be the only National Socialists left in the world."

Armande's acting broke down in indignation.

"That isn't so," she cried. "They are nationalist and they are socialist, I know. But you cannot call them Nazis. They have to be strong in order to create."

"Strength through joy," spat Montagne, "and the same pretty tactics. We were in their way, eh? Little people in their way!"

Armande had ruined her chance of discovering more. She was sure that he was not suspicious, but ordinary common sense would prevent him telling any more of his anti-Zionist intrigue to a person who was not in sympathy. She led him gently through National Socialism into a discussion of Spanish politics.

There was now plenty to tell Guy Furney. She called him up. He asked her to lunch at a garden restaurant on the banks of the Nile, where the grilled pigeons were famous, and a table could be discreetly arranged among shrubs at a distance from other guests, who, for the most part, were respectable Egyptians enjoying family parties. Armande decided to look the humble and admiring employee in printed cotton. She had evolved an unconscious but consistent code for dealing with the quantity of free meals that came her way. If she was being entertained for herself, she did her best to please and excite her host; if she was fed as an agent of H. M. Government, she took pains to appear inconspicuous.

"That's a very clear story," said Furney when she had made her report. "Now let us see what facts there are — " He smiled at her as if to disclaim any superior intelligence. "We know (a) that Montagne blames the Jews for his misfortune. Personally I think he should blame me or the French or this damned G.H.Q. which shifted me out of Beirut at the beginning of the case. But there it is. (b) That all his fanaticism has been channeled into this personal grudge; in fact, that he's running amok. (c) That, in contradiction to all this, he is mixed up in an intrigue with Jews. Now it would all become much clearer if we knew what sort of Jews — Zionists, anti-Zionists, neutrals or just plain black market."

"Not that," Armande replied. "He cares nothing at all for money or comfort. He's just a bitter ascetic."

"My poor Montagne! I'd like to drop the whole thing, and force the French to court-martial him and clear him."

"Then why don't you?" she asked eagerly.

"Because I can't, Mrs. Herne. The difficulties are all greater than ever, for our relations with the French are worse. In Syria

there are mean, conceited little men on both sides. If I now
produce Montagne, there would be such a scandal between
allies that only the Cabinet could settle it. I'm not afraid of
being bust. It would make no difference to my career, and
they could easily put somebody in my chair who was just as
good and less of a nuisance. Dons — Lord, they could send the
whole lot of us back to the Senior Common Room! It wouldn't
make the slightest difference to the war, and it would save a
lot of office space. But this Montagne affair could poison relations for years. There's not enough back-slapping, Mrs. Herne,
not enough trust. Get a couple of genial back-slappers in high
places, and they'd have Montagne reinstated as a major this
week — if he didn't make it impossible himself, as he probably
would, by intolerable behavior. Did you ever know a chap
called Loujon?"

"Very well."

"Of course you did! I'd forgotten. Well, Loujon and I —
good Lord, leave me out of it! — Loujon and his opposite number in the Palestine police could have fixed up the whole affair
in a frontier pub, and nobody any the wiser. And next week
Loujon would have been down in Jerusalem asking for some
outrageous favor in return. And got it. In the days of peace,
Mrs. Herne, an official just assumed the good will of another.
There are only Americans left to do that now. And we say
they overdo it. You can't overdo it. By the way, returning to
Montagne's friends, what shape was the parcel he gave them?"

"I don't know."

"How I like to hear that! In the army there's a most un-
scholarly shame about saying 'I don't know.' Get Rashid to
clear that point up, will you? Now I have the addresses of
Montagne's enigmatic friends, and I'll find out their names.
Then, I am afraid, we shall have to pass the whole case over
to Security."

CHAPTER XV

Captains and Agents

CAPTAIN DION PRAYLE crossed and recrossed his long legs as he sat in a comfortable basket chair and discussed current business with Laurence Fairfather. Prayle's section had a roving commission in Trans-Jordan, which allowed him, if he wished, to drop in at conferences anywhere between Palestine and Bagdad. After the simplicity of desert frontiers, he felt a puzzled sense of hothouse romance in the Jerusalem Field Security office, which might, he admitted, be exaggerated by the after-effects of a considerable party, half artistic, half political, to which Fairfather had taken him the previous night.

Prayle was also listening to music, which affected him profoundly so long as it was unconventional. The sound of heavy lorries, shifting gears at the corner of King George Avenue, harmonized with an accordion record which was being played in the canteen next door. He wondered why all six-ton lorries seemed to strike the same combination of notes when the engine took up the drive in bottom gear, and why the moaning of many cogs in a gearbox should be in harmony with the many stops of the accordion, whatever it was playing. Law of averages, he supposed. When so many notes were struck simultaneously, the ear selected those chords which were most pleasant.

"Five miles from nearest pub," he said ironically.

Now that the troops were no longer kept busy in providing a front with its bodies and supplies, G.H.Q. was fussing about their morale. All the local newspapers had pilloried an advertisement in some English paper: *Lonely soldiers five miles from nearest pub want radio*. This was the subject of bitter mirth from the troops in Syria, Palestine and Egypt who had been out there three or four years without complaint, two thousand miles from the nearest pub.

"You have a slight hang-over, Dion," said Fairfather, "well earned in excellent civilian company. There's only one in fifty of us who ever have the chance. Anyway, the real trouble is sex."

Another newspaper report that 50,000 or 5000 or any multiple of Canadians had married British wives was also upsetting the troops. Except for a very small and enterprising minority they had no chance of any normal sexual life.

"Four years Confined to Brothels," Prayle agreed. "But why worry? Their morale is wonderful, and nothing is going to make it any better till they are sent home. Has uncle's loaf found any solution to our other problem?"

"It has," Fairfather replied. "I'm going to go and ask the Jewish Agency."

"Cuckoo!" said Prayle. "Den of lions."

"It's not. It's the Jewish Agency. And the Mandate says it shall take steps in consultation with His Britannic Majesty's Government (that's me, this time) to secure the co-operation of all Jews who are willing to assist in the establishment of the National Home."

"Den of lambs, then. But I still think it's cuckoo. Trip up, bo, and you'll get a bowler hat."

"Of course. And Palestine Headquarters know I wouldn't complain. That's why they have given me a free hand. I think I'd like Abu Tisein on this job."

"Not with me."

"Abu Tisein is a man of many crimes and virtues. Your Armande was only one of them. I know he's a bloody gun-runner but he talks sense about this country. Abu Tisein and I want to build the National Home, and we both agree, at any rate, on how it should not be done."

"Hand washing," said Prayle. "Like Pontius Pilate."

"At least he consulted the chief priests and elders."

"Have a heart, bo!" Prayle exclaimed. "Here's Montagne nipping up through Trans-Jordan, dressed as an Egyptian with a packet of filthy postcards under his arm, and you want to tell the Jewish Agency what we know and ask for co-operation. It's cuckoo!"

"What's he really carrying, Dion?"

"Detonators? Machine-gun parts? Something small and valuable."

"They could steal whatever they want in that line from the dumps and ordnance depots without any trouble at all. I think he's carrying money."

"Why not use the bank?"

"Bank transfers can be traced. I also suspect that Montagne or his backers want to be quite sure it reaches the right hands — and so the personal visit."

"The Agency are lousy with money," Prayle remarked.

"Exactly. So it isn't for them. And anyway Furney and Armande are quite certain that Montagne is working against the Agency. He's obviously contacting the Stern people or the Irgun Zvai Leumi, and don't ask me where one begins and the other ends. They took Italian money before the war, and they are taking it now from other Gentile sources. European Jewry is cut off and America hasn't started to contribute, so far as we know. Gentile, Dion! Anybody who is really prepared to start trouble for the British Empire can always get money."

"But are they prepared?"

"They have started assassinating police already. You come and see the Agency with me. They have a much better Intelligence Service than we have — when we're allowed to use it."

"Politics, bo. Not what we're paid for."

"God! I'd be bored to tears if I only did what I'm paid for."

Dion Prayle found it impossible to analyze his premonition. The business of shadowing and arresting Montagne was tricky, but it was unnecessary and undesirable to go stirring up any political mud. He had a mental picture of Laurence Fairfather trying to cut himself a lump of morass with some precise and delicate implement, and simply getting stuck.

"I don't like it, Laurence," he said. "Stick to your hobby."

"What's that?"

"Coffee-housing with the King's enemies."

"Ah, but I'm asked for action this time. They want to know where Montagne is going, and say he is not to be interfered with till he gets there. That's not a police job. It's pure army security. And the first thing to do is to see the Agency. I assume they know what I know and Montagne knows — that Irgun Zvai Leumi is their worst enemy. Whether they'll help is another matter, but they will certainly keep their national mouths shut. You'd better come with me. Useful contacts, and they won't eat you."

Prayle reluctantly agreed. His mind was not at all clear about the two wars which Furney long ago had mentioned, and he was skeptical when Laurence Fairfather pretended to accurate knowledge of the occasions for trusting and distrusting official Zionism.

The Jewish Agency building was a government office in miniature. It was low, massive and dignified, suggesting a bank and a fort. Prayle had always passed it with mentally averted eyes; to him the activities inside seemed to reach a superhuman standard of intrigue and of faith. The interior, with its gray stone and paneling, was restful. Fairfather exchanged some chat with the clerk at the slitlike reception desk — beneath the counter of which Prayle felt sure would be a Tommy gun — and turned back with a grin as they went upstairs.

"Ordinary chaps, just like you and me," he said encouragingly. "You're going to enjoy Josh."

Josh was dressed, with a proper degree of negligence, in light English tweed, and his face had a cultured diffidence which suggested an Oxford or Cambridge background. He was indistinguishable in type from one of the High Commissioner's young officials. Prayle's first reaction to such polish was suspicion — a suspicion entirely different from that which he had come prepared to feel. He reminded himself that this was the sort of man Armande would undoubtedly like, and that it was perfectly possible he had some brains.

Josh welcomed him unaffectedly and charmingly. He evidently knew something of Prayle's general duties along the frontier, and offered him the hospitality of any of the Jewish colonies from Dan to the Dead Sea; his face had a weary strength, while he talked, which showed him to be neither so young nor so conventional as he had appeared at first sight. Prayle guessed that this perfect façade of Anglicism must be extraordinarily useful to the Jewish Agency; the brigadiers would be impressed and cordial. Yet one could not say the manner was assumed. Whatever his opinions, this official was a whole and a fine whole.

"Coffee?" Josh asked, coming to business.

"We'd love some," Fairfather replied.

"Did you just bring Captain Prayle round to introduce him, or is there anything special?"

"Both. It's a long story, Josh. There's a gentleman called Montagne whom you will doubtless remember."

"Not my department, Laurence."

"I know. I'm not going to bring that up."

"He escaped in '42, didn't he?"

"Yes, he is now known as Makrisi."

"Makrisi!" Josh exclaimed.

"I thought you might be interested. Makrisi is traveling up through Trans-Jordan, pretending with great success to be an Egyptian peddler. He's watched all the way, but he doesn't know it. Imperialist secret police, Josh."

"They want some help as usual, I suppose?"

"They do. Makrisi is carrying what I believe to be money."

"It is money."

"Elders of Zion at it again, I see."

"Exactly, Laurence."

"Any information on the source of the cash?"

"I am not sure. Certainly Gentile."

Dion Prayle observed the friendship, the sad friendship, between these two men. This hard-drawn Josh made Laurence Fairfather seem a little flatulent. Yet each had his own mannerisms for attack and defense. Fairfather's pose of bold irresponsibility was frequently productive.

"Where's Makrisi going, Josh?"

"Why do you want to know?"

"Give me credit for some intelligence! I know he isn't working for the Agency."

"Thank God for that!" said Josh sardonically.

"All right. More cards on the table. Dion Prayle has watched — well, facilitated his journey as far as Deraa. From Deraa and over the Palestine roads we shall watch him together. But if he plays hide-and-seek with us in a town we shall lose him.

Our men haven't the experience. The police could possibly trace him right to his destination, but we rather want to keep this affair in the family. And so, Josh," he added sternly, "do you."

"Why?"

"Because you don't want a nice, open airing of the Montagne-Herne business. Who were those troops who collected Wadiah's arms, Josh?"

"It does seem a case where I could be allowed to co-operate."

"Come off it! You damn well know it is."

"What do you want?" Josh asked.

"I want Makrisi to deliver the money, and then I want the whole lot detained by the Hagana, and Makrisi handed over to me."

"Utterly impossible, Laurence. You know I can't use the Hagana against the Irgun Zvai Leumi."

"Appeasement," said Prayle.

"That is true," Josh admitted, giving him a swift glance. "But we hope that we can control them, and we know that you can't."

"Can you control them?" asked Fairfather.

"At any rate we are prepared to try," answered Josh non-committally. "But the point is this. We have given you some help already, and what happened? The first time the Palestine police interrogated the Irgun about the Hagana. The second time they let all their leaders escape from internment. If you police the country with a lot of inefficient anti-Semites, what do you expect? I wouldn't mind if they were efficient anti-Semites. At least we should have stability."

"But you wouldn't be working with the police. You'd be working with the army."

"I can't help it, Laurence."

"Well if I mayn't have some hot numbers from the Hagana, can I have Abu Tisein?"

"Why don't you arrest Makrisi now?" Josh asked.

"Because we have no case against him till he delivers that money. If we arrest him now, he is sure to produce a good story to account for it."

"I see. Well, you'd better ask Abu Tisein. He's in his office downstairs. I wouldn't mind so long as you both keep out of trouble."

Josh rang a bell and spoke in Hebrew to the clerk who entered. Dion Prayle drank his coffee and tried to settle his face to a cold politeness. Why on earth hadn't the Arabs bumped off Abu Tisein in the rebellion? But Abu Tisein himself supplied the answer. There was his mild, cordial, inquiring face poking round the door. No one with pleasant manners need ever die at the hands of Arabs.

David Nachmias greeted Fairfather with affection and Prayle with the slightest hesitation, which then was wiped away by a dignified and self-deprecatory smile. Prayle, with his acquired knowledge of the Arab, could make a more reasonable mental picture of Abu Tisein than he could of the ambiguous Josh. The man was a foul criminal, but just like some sheikh of the Beduw caught out in an atrocity that he couldn't deny but for which he couldn't be touched — gentle, disarming, showing his sense of guilt only in an exaggerated, but ever dignified, geniality, as much as to say that they were all scoundrels and who but God could apportion blame? David Nachmias might, of course, know nothing at all of Prayle's paper warfare against him for the sake of Armande, but Dion was certain that he did.

Abu Tisein lowered into a chair that dual solidity which

had earned him his nickname, and listened to a flow of Hebrew which sounded more like a speech than a story. Prayle noticed that Josh in Hebrew was far more fiery and animated than he was in English; probably he had long ago discovered that the English distrusted enthusiasm.

"What do you want me to do?" David Nachmias asked Fairfather.

"To go with us wherever Montagne is going."

"And then?"

"I shall take Montagne away. No possible scandals, David. He has done well for us, and we just want him to cool down. We might send him to East Africa, or give him a chance of dropping in France."

"And what about the people he has come to see?" asked Josh.

"Unless I recognize one of them as wanted for a crime, there's nothing I can do. Have you any idea who they are likely to be?"

"As individuals? No idea at all," Josh replied. "I just knew that Makrisi had been collecting funds for the Irgun Zvai Leumi. I didn't know he was Montagne, and I didn't know he was on his way up from Egypt."

"Forgive my suggestion, Captain Fairfather," said Abu Tisein slowly, "but I do not understand how your service can keep Montagne shadowed without him suspecting it."

"That's easy, David! We're not shadowing him. We're helping him. Mr. Makrisi has done good work for a certain department. When he pretended to have business at Deraa, they pretended to believe him and passed us the word. Dion Prayle, here, has even booked him a room at a disreputable hotel."

"But why not travel through Palestine?"

"Because the thought of a peculiar Gentile calling at the office doesn't please the Irgun one little bit — wherefore he feels safer traveling through Trans-Jordan."

"Yes," said Josh, "I think you are right. And Montagne must have insisted on coming in person. But, Laurence, there is one thing I can't understand — why is he doing this?"

"Because, Josh, he thinks the Jews have done him dirt."

"Revenge? Simple revenge?"

"Josh, I thank my God daily that I am not concerned with the sordid means by which that department of yours — the one you have nothing to do with — acquires arms. But they shouldn't get caught. And when they do get caught, they should not let the innocent suffer. And above all they shouldn't panic and tell David here that he's got to get them out of it or carry the can back himself. Am I right, David?"

"Your imagination, Captain Fairfather!" murmured Abu Tisein. "How I envy it!"

"Montagne looks very far ahead," said Josh thoughtfully.

To Dion Prayle revenge seemed an odd and fascinating emotion. He could not understand its power, for he was certain that whatever anyone did to him he would never be bothered with revenge; to add an evil to an evil was an objectless waste of time and energy. He himself seemed to be devoid of two impulses to action that were important to everyone else — getting on and getting one's own back. Revenge was all very well as a motive in history books, but surely no sane person today, beyond Germans and primitive blacks, could long trouble themselves for the sake of its fleeting satisfaction? But was Montagne sane? He had always lived in an exaggerated, personified world of his own. He simplified everything except his own suspicions.

"Do you agree that the Irgun is your worst enemy?" he asked Josh.

"No! **You** are!" Josh answered with sudden asperity. "If it were not for you these lunatic terrorists could never have existed."

"Before the war. Zionism. We were all proud of it and you," said Prayle peaceably. "Troops liked you, too. Hard to find an anti-Semite among the regulars who were here in '38. And now distrust on both sides. Why?"

"Because you will not see there are two points upon which we can never give way. Free immigration and the right to self-defense. When you prohibit both, you force us to illegality and you may force us to violence."

"And if we allowed both, we should force the Arabs to violence," Prayle retorted. "One hell of a price to pay for your nationalism!"

"Nationalism? Well, call it that if you like. But doesn't its quality count for you, Captain Prayle? Where did nationalism ever have the beauty and self-sacrifice of ours? When have you seen, since the Middle Ages, rich men giving up their possessions for the sake of an ideal? When have you seen lawyers, doctors, intellectuals and men who have got used to luxury in the dirtiest of commerce (which was all you would allow them) stripped to the waist and building and planting in a wilderness where there was nothing?"

"Western Desert," said Prayle irresistibly, and earned a glance of rebuke from Fairfather.

"That was for war," Josh replied, broadly accepting the remark as fair comment. "This is for a peaceful home. To give back their spirit to the most spiritual of nations. To create a home for the miserable, the downtrodden, the most tragically misunderstood people that ever were. Do you call that nationalism? Is it nationalism when the flower of our youth lives without reward, like your monks, and day by day completes

the impossible? You cannot beat such a spirit. A Jewish Pal
estine is inevitable. Nothing and nobody can stop it."

"But that, dear Josh," said Fairfather, "is exactly what I
always preach myself. So why hurry?"

"Because my people are in danger of extinction. Our chance
is now. Now! After the last war we were blind. The mass of
our people couldn't see the chance that had been offered. It
took Hitler to make them understand what Palestine meant
to us who live here. But after this war we will not make the
same mistake."

"Arabs?" asked Fairfather.

"They must give way."

"And there we are back at the beginning, aren't we, David?"

"When I was at school," said Abu Tisein, "we had a teacher
who used to tell us that Israel was the attendant of the King,
and his duty was to imitate the King."

"His first duty is to live," said Josh shortly.

Abu Tisein accompanied the two officers when they left the
Jewish Agency. He stumped along King George Avenue, discussing with Prayle the notables of Trans-Jordan, the help they
had given in founding the early Jewish settlements and the
strong bonds of friendship that still existed between individual
Arab and Jew. Abu Tisein's implicit belief was quite clear:
that the Jews were only in Palestine by favor of the British,
and that they could only continue by favor of the Arabs. In
listening to him, Dion Prayle was conscious of a nasty sense of
disloyalty to Armande. But David Nachmias was so courteous
and reasonable. It was at last easy to see how Armande had
been taken in by him. Only men such as Laurence Fairfather,
who seemed to live at ease in this world of interlocking and
contradictory loyalties, could dare to separate Abu Tisein into
his component parts and to claim recognition of his purposes.

CHAPTER XVI

Fight for Freedom

CAPTAIN PRAYLE lay on the hillside, looking down upon the Jordan Valley between Lake Hula and the Sea of Galilee. Whenever there was traffic on the hairpin bends of the road to Safad, he raised his field glasses; the slight movement of elbows stirred the scent of the sweet mountain herbs crushed by his body. Up the valley he could just see a shoulder of Hermon, shining a metallic yellow between the tenuous pillars of cloud that were distilled from its gorges by the cool of evening. To his right, three thousand feet below, the sea, reflecting the last of the sun, had turned a pale magenta, and along the Syrian shore parallel scarves of mist were of so frank a mauve that they reminded him of solemn high teas in childhood and the dress worn by a beloved great-aunt.

His mind ran on from one image of contemplation to another, for there was nothing to do but watch the road and attend at that spectacular performance staged by the atmosphere wherever the desert met the sown. At the head of the sea, black against the miracle-reflecting water, was the grove of poplar and cypress around the ruins of Capernaum and its synagogue. That was a sanctuary which he reverenced; there and there only in all Palestine he cherished certainty, unhindered by the touts and priests of organized Christianity, that he could see the same floor, the same stones that Christ had trod. Yet Capernaum was in no way an official Holy Place.

What a country for accepting profitable tradition! The Christians with their Holy Sepulcher, the Jews with their Wailing Wall, the Moslems with their footprints of the Prophet — and not a scrap of serious historical evidence to justify any of them! Perhaps tradition, right or wrong, was all that mattered, for human beings seemed so reluctant to worship without a visible object.

For him no visible object was necessary — well, to be fair, wasn't it? In four years of war he had lain on many hillsides, but never had his inquisitive thoughts played with the philosophy of worship. That they did so now was due, he recognized, to Armande. She was the visible object, through whom the physical beauty of the Jordan Valley became manifest as a spiritual beauty. Before he had loved her, his own soul and all that it observed had been incomplete; nor was completion yet, for nothing but marriage with Armande could quiet the observer's restlessness. Women — good Lord! What futile loyalties they had! A very good chap, her husband — but he suspected that this John had always brought out the worst in her, and they didn't love each other, and that was that. But would the darling admit it? No!

Prayle savagely cast her out of his mind. The longing for her offended against his independence. What had a woman to do with sunsets and miracles? What had she to do with the eternal? A visible object, very well — but bare and lovely Palestine was made for worship without intermediaries. Silent in the still evening it lay below him, and he was conscious of his infinite smallness; a wretched point upon the hillside that could only think of women.

True, the events of Palestinian history predisposed a man to worship; but, on a broader view, the country was fitted, chosen for the events. Palestine, for all its groves and terraced hills,

belonged to the desert where a man and his God walked alone
together; the land compelled humanity to be measured by a
greater rod than geography or history could supply. Whether
you struck a former comrade under the fifth rib in the efficient
arms drill of the Old Testament, whether you healed the sick,
whether you did your best, like Pontius Pilate, to give justice
to warring sects, or whether you taught peace and wisdom in
Safad over the hill, it had to be done on the scale of the eternal.

The Jews of Palestine, he decided, were so eager to avoid
thinking on the scale of the eternal. If they said that they could
not yet afford such a luxury, it would be forgivable; if they
insisted that new values must be created before the old could
return, he would agree. But they didn't. The vast majority
rejected for good and all the wisdom of their prophets and
scholars, laughed at it as unworldly. In fact they were off again,
irresistibly attracted, worshiping the gods of the heathen,
Power and Intrigue, Flags and the Firearm, and daring the
remorseless logic that sooner or later restored its soul to a
nation through disaster.

And that might be Mr. Makrisi, paddling up the hill astride
a donkey. Prayle steadied his elbows, and trained his glasses on
a bend of the road where the traveler would come into full
view. Makrisi had changed the clothes he wore at Deraa, but
that beard was his. A darkness between cheek and forehead,
which was undoubtedly the hollow of deep-set eyes, made his
identity certain. He was dressed in an old khaki jacket from
the last war and dusty Turkish trousers. It was unusual to see
so poor a villager or peddler with a beard, and, for disguise to
be perfect, he should have had a dusty wife marching behind
the donkey; but he would pass anywhere, so long as he did
not talk too much, as a Moghreby who had settled down in the
high borderland of Syria and Trans-Jordan.

All was going as it should. Laurence was at the Rosh Pina control post, Abu Tisein somewhere in Safad, himself halfway between the two; and there were twelve of their men scattered over the more distant road junctions so that Mr. Makrisi's trail, if he did the unexpected, could be quickly recovered.

Prayle waited for man and donkey to reappear round the last and most northerly bend in the road, where it passed through the edge of a plantation. They did not reappear. He consulted the map. There was nowhere Makrisi could go except a deserted camp site a few hundred yards from the road. Probably he had stopped to rest.

Then came Laurence Fairfather, swinging round the bends on a motorcycle and traveling much too fast. Prayle, watching like an anxious and impotent god what was about to happen to the mortals below him, observed that a civilian lorry on the wrong side of the road would reach the next corner at the same time as the motorcycle. He saw Fairfather take to the verge of the road in a cloud of dust, vanish behind the lorry, come out with a sickening wobble and recover speed. That imperturbable Laurence always showed off to himself on a motorcycle; it seemed to be the outlet for the wilder side of his character, and it was, Prayle thought, a damned sight more dangerous than drink.

Fairfather stopped at the top of the hill a hundred yards from the hidden Prayle. There he admired the view, sitting astride his bike. Prayle crawled towards the rendezvous under cover of sage and camel's-thorn, and came within speaking distance.

"If it's him on the donkey," he said, "he has stopped on the road."

Fairfather lit his pipe and continued to admire the view.

"I didn't pass him," he replied, without looking round.

"Have you the foggiest notion what you passed, bo?"

"Nothing at all but a lorry. I hope there are thorns in the soft underbelly."

"There are, damn you! Then he's turned off up the track to the old camp."

"All right. I'll get Abu Tisein. Let's meet at that patch of eucalyptus just over the crest. There's still plenty of light, and we should be able to see down into the camp from there."

Laurence put his pipe in his pocket, jumped on the kick start and vanished over the hill to Safad.

Dion Prayle had to walk. The section truck, which had dropped him near his present post, was five miles away at a road junction to the south. His route demanded careful planning, for a solitary British soldier on foot was a rare sight outside the camps and towns; if anyone but himself were on the watch, his sudden appearance on road or hillside might arouse suspicion. He waited for the dust of a passing truck to conceal his movement, then slipped across the road at the next bend and over the embankment at the farther side. From there he could reach the crest, unseen by any but the Arab fellahin far beneath him, working their little fields in Lower Galilee.

When he reached the grove of eucalyptus, Fairfather and David Nachmias were already there. Abu Tisein had left his car in Safad and traveled the short distance, over a rocky track, on the pillion of the motorcycle. He was smiling as if he had enjoyed it.

"Commended for gallantry," said Prayle. "At risk of death or permanent injury et cetera."

"I do not mind a new experience," replied Abu Tisein, "though I would prefer a horse. So much of my life is spent . . ." He made a slow, pacific gesture which seemed to imply long, patient hours of sitting in Arab tents and cafés, of waiting upon government officials and Agency politicians in leisurely Jerusalem. "I enjoy a day in the country."

Prayle knew instantly what he meant. It was the sort of phrase he would have used himself. A day in the country covered those dangerous journeys beyond the frontiers of neutral Turkey, or the first night in a new settlement when the joyous, singing colonists put up their tents on a patch of sand that would soon be a tidy village among its orange groves, or all the pleasures of active intrigue in the open air between Bagdad and Damascus.

"Shall we start?" asked Abu Tisein. "I think, if I may advise, that the edge of the grove is better avoided. The trees are thin and movement could be seen against the going down of the sun. Let us follow that stone wall. We can stand among the thorn at the end, and our heads will be hidden."

Prayle and Fairfather glanced at each other. Laurence indicated by an admiring and humorous lift of his eyebrow that he was perfectly willing to accept Abu Tisein's efficient leadership — it was the very gesture that Prayle had often seen pass between two men in the ranks when they were convinced that their officer was talking sense.

Without any sort of insistence David Nachmias quietly assumed command. Prayle was certain that if either of them had shown the minutest sign of questioning his right he would, as quietly and imperceptibly, have relinquished it. Abu Tisein's judgment of the ground was correct; from the wall, screened by bushes, they could see into the deserted camp. There were a few huts, all but one open to wind and weather. A civilian truck — that which had raised the dust for Prayle's crossing of the road — was parked on a strip of cracked asphalt. Makrisi's donkey, forelegs hobbled, browsed on a miniature forest of cabbage and carrot which had gone wild in the former mess garden.

"Are they likely to have put out sentries, David?" Fairfather asked.

"At the way in from the road. Not here. If we go quietly we shall reach the hut. What action do you propose then?"

"I just want Montagne."

"It may be dangerous."

"No. They won't make trouble with British troops."

"What makes you think that, Captain Fairfather?" asked Abu Tisein, the hard, golden flash of the desert in his brown eyes.

Fairfather looked at him in astonishment, and then smiled.

"My dear David, surely you don't think I doubt Jewish courage in this day and age? I simply meant that, however much we disagree, we are still comrades-in-arms."

"Still," Abu Tisein repeated. "Still. Yes, I think so. But the bond is weak. I will go alone and I will get Montagne for you."

"I can't do that, David."

"I am not altogether a civilian, you know."

"I should say not! You've risked your life more often than any of us. But I could never face Josh if I let you go alone and there was an incident."

"Yes, I understand. Then we must all go together."

"Orders, bo?" Prayle asked his senior, tapping the service .45 at his hip.

"Remember King's Regulations, Dion. I forget the precise and beautiful wording of the War Office, but, roughly speaking, if you plug a civilian before he plugs you, it's murder. And you won't be plugged. Am I right, David?"

"Yes," answered Abu Tisein. "But I am not sure that you will get Montagne."

"Why not?"

"You could never have followed him to this meeting unless you had known all his movements from the start."

"We certainly couldn't!"

"Then what," asked Abu Tisein, throwing open his arms as far as the surrounding thorn permitted, "will they think of Montagne?"

"I see. Then we'll have to make the interview snappy," said Fairfather. "Dion, it might — it might just be necessary to cover them to get Montagne away. But we'll go in peaceably."

Abu Tisein led them along the angle of two walls, bending low behind the roughly piled stones; they came out on a slope of sunburned, tussocky grass which led directly down into the camp, and gave silent and easy access to the closed hut on its windowless southern side.

Dion Prayle felt more and more dislike for the whole business; it was too full of psychological intangibles. To surprise a bunch of potential assassins, in blind confidence that they meant, as yet, to avoid trouble with the army, was hazarding too much on being able to fix one's exact position in the ever-changing fog of Jewish politics. This expedition of three was all wrong. They should either have called in a carload of police prepared to overwhelm all resistance — though in that case there would have been nobody to resist, for the police always managed to give ample warning of their coming — or else they should have left the job to Abu Tisein. And that, though logical, was, by any standard of behavior, impossible.

They reached the door of the hut unseen and unchallenged. Laurence flung it open and went in. There were four men seated at a table talking to Montagne. They were dressed as

Arab soldiers of the British Army. All had their Arab head-cloth drawn lightly across the lower part of the face. On the table was a small, open attaché case stuffed with bank notes, Egyptian and Palestinian. During the first two seconds of amazement and a third while hands moved down to pockets and up again with pistols, Abu Tisein was speaking quietly in Hebrew.

A man wearing a red and white checked headcloth, who sat next to Montagne, said in English:

"Put your arms on the table."

Facing four pistols at a range of two yards, there was no option. The leader unloaded the two service revolvers and handed them back again. Another man ran his hands over the three of them, looking for additional arms. Prayle's still neutral opinion of David Nachmias changed to admiration on seeing that he carried no weapon at all.

"What do you want here?"

The leader spoke a cultured English with some trace of a Slav accent.

"Not you," Fairfather answered in a friendly tone. "I'm not a policeman. I don't know who you are and I don't want to know. My business is with Mr. Makrisi."

"A rescue party. No, Captain Fairfather."

"You know me then?"

"By sight and reputation. They say you are fond of justice."

"I hope so."

"Watch it!"

Mr. Makrisi was seated at his side, silent and uncaring. With a smooth, efficient, horribly merciful flow of hand and arm, the leader shot him through the back of the skull.

Dion Prayle felt his knees trembling and tried to control them. He was no more afraid than one who sees a deadly accident in the street, but the shock of this cold-blooded execution surpassed anything his emotions could endure without some physical reaction. Montagne, so vividly alive, for the madder the man, the more alive, was sliding off his chair onto the floor and kicking when he got there. Kick. Twitch. Kick. Twitch. Impersonal as a clock. Prayle pulled himself together with deliberate thoughts of half-dead matter that he had seen and trodden in around Dunkirk. None of it had the horror of this clean bullet. Germans, Russians — they did this sort of thing. God knew, perhaps everybody in occupied Europe was doing it! Where could they find the men to do it? And how? How?

"That is what will happen to your agents," said the man in the red and white checks.

His voice carried no threat. It was a tone of regret, as if asking why they did not accept the inevitable.

"He was nobody's agent but yours," Prayle retorted fiercely.

"No? Not in Egypt?"

"Didn't even know he was suspected! Isn't that proof of it?" asked Prayle, pointing to the money on the table.

"It is proof of nothing."

Abu Tisein let loose a flood of Hebrew, through which his sultry anger rumbled, courteous and incalculably dangerous. He stood square to the table, not tense as a European, but with all the muscles of his powerful body relaxed in the contempt of the stronger for the weaker.

"I am sorry," he said, turning to Prayle and Fairfather from the table he had so completely dominated. "I was telling them merely that they are unworthy to be Jews."

One of the four men called him by some insulting name; the voice was shrill and unsure, and Prayle gained the impression that the speaker was very young. It was hard to tell his age from the burning black eyes above the headcloth, but the slight figure, the clear, ivory forehead, suggested a boy of not more than fifteen. He was playing with his pistol. Prayle hated carelessness with arms.

"I wish you'd tell that boy to leave his gun alone," he said.

"Afraid, Englishman?"

"Of course I am," answered Prayle testily. "So would you be if you had any sense. He's pointing it at you now."

"Lunatics who fight with children!" scoffed Abu Tisein.

"*Rak Ivrit!*" ordered the leader.

"No! To you I will not speak Hebrew."

"Ashamed, you spy?"

"Yes. Ashamed. I and my father and our fathers before us, they spoke Hebrew while you gargled in your Yiddish like — like sick sheep. I speak the language of these officers because they are guests in my country."

"And because you take their money," the man sneered.

"David Nachmias," said Fairfather firmly, "has no more taken our money than you did — if any of you are really in the army."

"I have no quarrel with you. I know that you do not wish to be here," the leader declared, as if repeating a slogan of faith. "You would rather be at home."

"As a matter of fact," Fairfather replied, "I would rather be here than anywhere else. But I suppose that is hardly a shooting matter?"

The man seemed disconcerted by this reasonable reply.

"So long as you go when we require it," he answered.

"Good God, bo!" Prayle exclaimed. "Can't you see that attitude will bring more of us?"

"The worse for them!"

"And for you!"

"We accept that," answered the man in the red checks

proudly. "For us, in our fight for freedom, death is nothing."

"Hell!" said Dion, exasperated. "So I see! But does it do any good?"

"Be quiet! I have not finished with your other spy yet."

Prayle gave Abu Tisein a half smile, involuntarily expressing his sense of the absurdity of the charge. Spy David Nachmias had certainly been, except on his own people; but the word when applied to that bold, quadrangular figure was so small, so emptily dramatic.

The leader again attacked in bitter Hebrew. David Nachmias calmly heard him out.

"Crawl to them?" he said reflectively. "Crawl to them? Is it crawling to speak a language that all can understand? Because our manners were too gracious when we were slaves, as you call us, is it a reason for having none in our own country?"

He was silent for a moment, then began to defend his courage, boastful yet dignified as an old Emir justifying his leadership to his followers.

"I, Abu Tisein as they name me, I have gone out to my death too often to believe I am a coward. I have dealt with the Gestapo face to face. Sometimes they knew I was a Jew, but I brought money. Sometimes they thought I was an Arab, and gave me money. I served the British, and I led out those of our people whom I could save.

"I have founded colonies. I have filled Eretz Israel with men and women, and arms for their defense. I have fought all my life against Turks, against Arabs, against British. And all of them were my friends. You — you have stolen our sword and refused our wisdom. You hide there in those British uniforms, and who taught you? I did! But I never put a man in their uniform to make war on them. When we fight, it shall be under our own flag and in our own uniform. And never — I tell you, never — whatever threats may be made, whatever words may fly in anger, never will we murder the British. What do you gain by your childishness? That man who lies there, whom you shot, I killed him long ago. I killed him by making a mistake. His blood is on my head, but what leader of men cannot say the same? It was only a crime against my brother. But also, for the sake of my people, I did not bear witness when I could have done so. And that is a crime against God."

Abu Tisein grimly regarded Montagne's body, now only a shapeless mass on the floor of the darkening hut.

"Without law! Without law!" he cried, as if in a lament. Then with the first gesture of his whole speech he stabbed a finger towards the table.

It was clear that only the leader and the youth understood his slow English — understood so keenly that they listened. Of the other two, one leaned forward puzzling out the alien speech, and the fourth, probably a newcomer to Palestine, sat dully awaiting orders and scratching the sand-fly bites on his arms.

"When will you understand that we have law? I am not the servant of the British Government. I am the servant of your government, of our government. We are the representatives of the living, and of the dead who longed to see us here. And Eretz Israel is ours. We have won it by our work, our blood, our cunning, and with the friendship of the British. You — where were you when I was dancing in the streets of Tel Aviv? Yes, I dancing — for joy that at last we had founded our city. The police whom you kill, I kissed that day. I cannot forget it. I hate them as you do. But I cannot forget it. When will you understand that you have your leaders, freely elected? When will you understand that we know all you know, feel all that you feel? You talk of freedom and democracy, but you do not know what they mean. The people can have no freedom if their will is not obeyed. Obey your government, your own Jewish Government. And if still you do not understand, then remember what you heard as children: You shall not separate yourselves from your people."

"We do obey," said the leader, impressed to the point of argument. "But your methods are futile and useless. We only do for you what you dare not do for yourselves."

"Dare not? And with ten thousand trained men instead of your handful of hysterical, suicidal . . . Bah! And with our own money! Where did that come from?" asked Abu Tisein, pointing to the case of bank notes.

"I do not care where it came from. I shall use it in our fight for freedom."

"Your fight!" cried David Nachmias ironically. "Your little fight, when all the power of Jew and Gentile is strained to the limit against the greatest enemy our race ever had! What do you know? What do you care? For you Hitler and the British are all one. Have none of you lost parents, wives, children? Have none of you seen what I have seen?"

"And what have you seen, safe here in Palestine?" cried the boy. "My father was killed. My mother was killed. Taken away by police like these police!"

"Then let us tell you how to take revenge. Revenge is not this way. Look, boy! There is that money, and you are told not to care where it has come from. Can you not see that you are mad not to listen to us who know? That money — it could be from the teeth of your mother."

The boy jumped up. He was shorter and slighter than he had seemed at the table. He waved his pistol, pointing it wildly at himself, at enemies imaginary, real; shouting defiance and misery in the raucous Hebrew of his half-broken voice. His rancor seemed to find its outlet in the compassionate face of David Nachmias. He gesticulated towards him with wild reproaches, the pistol in his hand a power, a talisman against further hurt and further pity. It went off.

Prayle and Fairfather jumped forward to catch Abu Tisein's body, and were stopped short by guns jammed hard into their stomachs. The boy looked at the blood with timid curiosity; then raised his eyes, flashing. They could see him forcing pride into his eyes. The leader took away his pistol, and wiped it carefully; he closed Abu Tisein's hand around the butt, and placed his limp finger within the trigger guard.

Dion Prayle assumed that he and Fairfather would be the next. With his hands up he stood there, to his astonishment, thinking. Prayle, observer, watched events happening to Prayle, alien body. The pair of eyes that faced him were completely expressionless, neither hard, nor fanatical, nor pitying. No British soldier had eyes like those. The man was an automaton, obeying, and sacrificing all his emotions for the satisfaction of obedience. The best chance for Prayle, body, was to stand still. Commandos might have some trick for being quicker than the human finger, but a surer safety lay in those political intangibles. Dion looked across at the man opposite Fairfather. That one was more human; he seemed pleased to have something better to do than scratch himself.

The red and white headcloth gave out its orders. Prayle strained his intelligence to guess the meaning of the Hebrew from its faint resemblance to Arabic. Then the man spoke in English.

"Captain Fairfather, I shall lock you both in this hut while we go. I hope you will realize that we too can be merciful to our enemies, and that you will be grateful."

"If you think I'm not going to try to bring you to justice for these bloody murders . . ." stormed Fairfather.

"Captain, I am sure you will try. But what you British believe I do not care. And what the Jews believe — you will see."

"They'll believe anything!" Fairfather exclaimed contemptuously.

"Yes," said the man, "a people in utter misery will believe anything. I am now going to cover you myself, while my friends take away the bodies. One against two — so if you make the slightest movement I shall shoot."

His three companions picked up the body of Abu Tisein, carefully resting on his chest the hand that held the pistol, and carried it out. Then they returned for Montagne.

"Keep looking straight to your front," ordered the leader. "I am now going to the door, but I can kill you just as easily from behind. When you hear the door shut and locked, you may move. Try the windows, if you like, but they are steel and rusted up."

He closed the suitcase, picked it up and passed out of their field of vision. They heard the clicks of latch and lock. The engine of the lorry roared.

Prayle put down his hands, and felt in his pocket.

"Cigarette?" he said, offering his case to Fairfather.

"Thank you, Dion."

They lit up.

"That's better," said Fairfather. "I was feeling slightly sick."

"So did I when they shot Montagne. After that — well, it was all a solid piece."

"Poor David! Poor, dear David!"

"Do you think the little bastard meant to shoot him?"

"Dion, I don't know. *I didn't mean it* — it's what they all say from Hitler to some moron who waves a pistol at his girl-friend. God, how David let 'em have it!"

"Not a man to be angry."

"Never saw him angry before."

"I've got the number of the lorry."

"It's quite certainly a different one now," said Laurence.

"Yes. Efficiency on the scale of modern industry. Shall we have a bang at the door, bo? I think he was right about those windows."

"Let's swing the table at it, and save my aged shoulder."

The door gave at their second charge. They were outside in the cool darkness of the Galilee hills. There were no sounds but the evening breeze stirring the scrub, and the munching of Montagne's donkey in the deserted garden.

Epilogue

"I am leaving Field Security," he wrote. *"Open for business shortly at G.H.Q."*

It meant months of Dion — no more fantastic, unexpected evenings splitting the bearable continuity of life into meaningless sections of before and after; no more separations to be followed by those damnable days when Armande felt that he had vanished, when she was convinced that his life or health was in danger, when she was terrified by the sudden mobility of his army life. Her obsession was that he might be posted to India. She feared India for its distance, for his possible infidelities. There were so many women who could love and read her Dion better — no, none better, but they might make him think so. He was just the sort of man to fall for some delicious and misunderstood Oriental who could persuade him that she cared for nothing but reality — in his sense, of course.

At G.H.Q. All his free hours for her. She longed for him so, for again loneliness threatened her in this world of men. The government flat would be hers for another month, and then the present job was over. Guy Furney's manner had been abrupt. He told her that Montagne had disappeared and was presumed dead. He seemed to feel his death most bitterly, and to hold it against her, as if resenting the efficiency with which his orders had been carried out. Or was it that he, too, found her dangerous, that he blamed her for the whole trouble from beginning to end?

She put the precious letter in her bag, and went out, idly and happily, into the streets of Cairo. In the shops the display of intimate garments and summer frocks was alluring, though too expensive for any but Egyptians. She needed nothing and reminded herself, when she hesitated before an occasional temptation, that she was only wondering what Dion would think of her choice. He seemed to like — and she suspected that most men agreed with him — a demure formality outside and extreme vulgarity underneath. At last she could resist no longer, and merrily bought for his delight.

She wandered into that garden café upon which she had looked down during her first morning in Cairo, where, weeks later, she had taken her decision to dance with Floarea. Over strawberries and cream she considered and tried to plan the months ahead with Dion. Her mood changed to severe responsibility. Love could not be allowed just to flow and find its level. It was like Intelligence; it needed proper channels — on condition that the hand which cleared them was never too obviously observed at work.

No longer could this affair be passed off to conscience as a lovely and unreal ecstasy, of no importance to any but the two dreamers. It had to be preserved. That necessity involved, at once, all the threads that bound her as a woman to everyone she thought about, loved or tolerated. Threads binding Dion existed too, though he was pleased to believe that they did not. Yet it was Dion who insisted that John should be told. His motives were absurd, but of course scrupulous as himself; they seemed to be a mixture of inhuman love for absolute truth and loyalty to an unknown companion-in-arms; they were quite different from her own desire, to her simple and practical, that Dion and she should become an easier part of their environment.

John need not exactly be told in so many words; she would just indicate that she was worried whether the profounder motives for their union were any longer valid, and leave him to read between the lines. The hint, without alarming him into despair, would start him wondering if after the war their marriage should continue, hoping that it could, and slowly realizing that it could not.

In the afternoon she composed an evasive letter which would reveal to John her disturbed emotions. There were certain phrases that she knew he would take as danger signals; in the forgotten days of 1940, when she wrote from Paris and Beirut, those phrases, which then implied nothing more than temporary depression, had never failed to arouse his anxiety. She determined to keep the letter a day or two for cool revision. Two hours later, in a panic lest she should tear it up, she posted it by air mail.

A week passed slowly for she was always expecting Dion. Correspondence from the military to a civilian, within the Middle East, traveled by devious routes of its own and remained in pigeonholes under the disapproving eyes of censors or sorting clerks. Whatever warning Dion gave her of his arrival, he had always come and spent the precious hours with her and gone before his letter arrived. For the whole week she left her front door open when she was out, and hurried home, with exasperated excitement, in case he should be waiting.

When at last he appeared, it was at a reasonable hour, after lunch, in the heat of the day. He was neat, polished and cool as if he had been on his way to an interview with a general. She would have preferred him to show his longing by bursting in on her dusty and unshaven from the road, but her beloved was still sensitive about his personal appearance. As if it mattered! She teased and adored him for his childishness until he revealed, as well she knew, that his passionate impatience was satisfying as her own. Armande rejoiced in the incontinence and beauty of her naked body, caressed, while her lover of a moment since lay still, by the warm wind that blew through the shutters of the flat.

Then she touched his face with her fingers, feeling for imaginary differences that the eyes could not detect.

"You've been worrying, beloved," she said. "What really has brought you down to Egypt?"

"Shipped down river for promotion," he answered lazily.

"But how splendid! A major?"

"A genuine phony major."

"My clever love! How did you do it?"

"Got the sack."

"Darling, don't be discreet. Tell me!"

"Just usual army practice. Man embarrasses us. Must be a clever chap to do that, but don't want him here. How shall we get rid of him? Well, sir, why not promote the bastard?"

"Dion!"

"Best racket in the British Army, my soul. It supplies just as many good officers as bad ones. Can't say that of any other system."

"Talk to me properly. Tell me!"

"How much have you heard?" he asked.

"Nothing. Just Guy Furney being hollow and superior. He said that you had all done a good job and that Montagne was presumed dead."

"Presumed?" he exclaimed, sitting up and turning round to her. "Did Furney say that?"

"That or some other word."

"He couldn't be deader. And they know it. Presumed! Just because his body hasn't turned up! Furney had better stop laughing at his palace eunuchs. It's taken them four years of war to get his off, but they've done it!"

"Dion, you're disgusting."

"Kensington," he murmured.

"If you ever say that to me again, I'll — I'll bite you."

"What would Ma think if she saw you in that condition?"

"She's the only person who has, Dion. And . . ."

"Ow! You beastly little foreigner!"

"And black-listed. And vicious. And in love. Put me inside under 18 B, my Dion, my darling!"

When the sun had gone down behind the tall blocks in the center of Cairo, and the cool, green scent from the shadowed backwaters of the Nile began to drift through the eastern windows of the flat, Dion wandered out of the bedroom and mixed two long drinks from the plentiful remains of the departmental stock of liquor. When he came back, Armande was sitting before her mirror, her black hair demurely coiled, her body innocent and hieratic in a crimson and gold Bokhara dressing gown.

"Dion, now tell me all of what happened," she said.

"I was just going to tell you when you interrupted."

"You — !"

"Now be a good girl, and drink your medicine."

He began to tell the story. Armande linked her arm in his, and led him into the living room. She sat opposite him, her love of his mouth and of every twisted phrase overwhelming her interest. She even resented that she had to listen so long to something so impersonal, something that belonged to one and not to both of them. Then, as he dealt in his obscure understatements with events in the hut, fear for him stabbed her imagination as agonizingly as if she had been present.

At the death of Abu Tisein she exclaimed in pity, but it

was a moment before her preoccupation with the fate of Dion would let her remember; then she had nothing but sorrow for the end of such robust vitality. She thought of him as he was in Beirut, with Madame. That poor woman! It might so easily have been Dion and not David Nachmias. Poor, broken woman! She must write . . .

"And so they just told us to bust the door down when we felt like hopping it," he ended. "And then, Armande, we found, thank God, that they had put Laurence's motorcycle out of action! So we walked to Safad police station and stirred up the cops."

"David Nachmias!" she sighed. "Whatever he was — what a loss to them all in Palestine!"

"The cops found him next morning at Tiberias in his own car. Hand stiff round the gun. And no fingerprints but his own on the steering wheel. Ingenious devils — must have towed him there."

"But why bother when you knew the truth?"

"Convention, darling. Seems to be generally accepted in the Holy Land that Jews never kill Jews. They are found to have bumped themselves off."

"Nobody who knew Abu Tisein could ever believe he killed himself," she said.

"No. Laurence of course popped straight across to his tame Zionist. Man he called Josh. I never got hold of his other name. He nearly broke down when he came out. All starry-eyed. He said they weren't quite sure what to believe. They weren't quite sure. The poor devils! God, what distrust of the world! That Irgun man was about right when he said they would believe anything. But our own people haven't their excuse."

"What do you mean, Dion?" she asked, shocked.

There had been a faint smell of perfidy in the whole chain of official reaction ever since Furney's coolness.

"We were the cat's whiskers to start with. After all we were successful, and all hush-hush. And there was nothing on earth we could have done to save Abu Tisein. Then G.H.Q. began to give Palestine hell. There's a little egg called Rains at G.H.Q. You wouldn't know him. He's a brigadier now. He said Abu Tisein had been invaluable, and the Field Security had sacrificed him. He didn't like the gunplay at all. He thought we started it. But Palestine backed us to the limit. They insisted that what we said had happened, had happened. They told them where they could put their *presumed*. So we were just sacked and promoted. Laurence is going to Sicily as an economic expert. Oranges and lemons, you see. Had 'em in Palestine, and they have 'em there. Me, I'm liaising with Algiers. I said I wanted a job with lots of colored pencils. So it had to be G.H.Q. And here we are together in the dream city by the Nile. Gin, horse dung, and the idle military."

"Tell me, darling," she said, ignoring his lightheartedness, "am I to blame for all this? Am I?"

"You? Why? Most of it falls on Abu Tisein. Some on me. A bit for Furney. And a fine slimy lump for Mr. Bloody Brigadier Rains. Not much left for you, my soul."

"I'll never get mixed up in it again," she said with a shiver of her shoulders. "We stink, as Laurence Fairfather once said."

"Only a little. There are lots of us to keep it nice and shiny."

"But I'm not . . . I don't belong. What shall I do, Dion? What use am I?"

"Simple, darling — like everything you make the biggest fuss about. Join the A.T.S. They're over here in thousands now and busy recruiting."

"What about the black list?"

"Oh Lord! I'd forgotten that. Well, be a W.A.A.F. You'd look a pippin in their comic lid."

"Can I?"

"Don't worry. The R.A.F. have never been known to read a black list. They haven't time."

"Sure?"

"Quite sure."

"And you won't go far away from me?"

"Not till you are certain of yourself. That won't be long. It's fulfillment for you."

"Yes," she answered slowly. "Fulfillment for me. I think it would be. To lose myself in the mass — all of myself that isn't you. Not to be ashamed and proud and all without reason. Just to serve. I will do that, Dion."

"Then cheer up, my sweet. There's a fortnight's leave ahead."

Armande clung to him, and shook off the past by a long silence in his arms.

"You'll stay here," she said. "All the fortnight."

"Here?" asked Dion, heaven in one eye and doubt in the other. "Wouldn't His Majesty object?"

"I'm his representative till the end of the month."

"Scandal?"

"I'm below scandal, darling."

"I wish," he said, "that you had written to your husband."

"I have. So there!"

"Good girl! What did you say?"

"This and that. Enough."

"An Armande letter, I suppose."

"What's that?"

"Beautiful feelings. No facts."

"They weren't at all beautiful," she said, distressed.

Dion Prayle moved his valise and suitcase into the flat. Armande had determined not only to lose herself in love, but to guide it towards permanence. Within a week she had forgotten tact and management, since she had no occasion for either. There was only ease. Her Dion was gentle, even at his most eccentric, and never a bore. As spectators of the world, they saw the same; as participants their minor tastes differed. He would not learn to dance. He avoided the fashionable. In compensation, he could extract from the simplicity of man or woman, of restaurant or public place, riches of amusement for both.

They had lived together for ten days when John's answer arrived. Armande opened it in privacy. She found herself in such a turmoil of annoyance and modesty that she said nothing.

She drank two stiff Martinis before lunch and sulked.

"Planning Committee still hard at it?" asked Dion, having given his mixture time to work.

"Yes."

"Top Secret or just Confidential?"

"Neither," Armande snapped. "I've heard from John."

"Ah! Got a girl, I suppose?"

"Yes. How on earth did you know? I think he might have tried to be faithful. I did."

"That little loaf," he said, "is stuffed so full of hypocrisy that — "

"Hypocrisy? Me?" she asked indignantly. "Read it, Dion!"

She handed him the letter. Dion composed his face into a serious expression, fixed it, and read.

John was glad that she had given him an opening. It was, he said, just like her. John hoped she would not be hurt. He had wanted to tell her long ago, but felt that while she was serving her country in the Middle East it was his duty not to let her be upset. He was in love. An American girl in their

naval service. He was sure that Armande would adore her.
There had never been anyone quite like her. . . .

"Well, well!" said Dion cautiously.

"But you don't understand," Armande insisted. "A little
American isn't at all the right woman for John. She'd be
exasperated by him in a week."

"I can just imagine John," he said, "if he knew you were
going to marry a primitive sergeant with vulgar tastes."

"I'm not going to marry a sergeant."

"Promotion of the body, not the spirit."

"Marriage, Dion? For us?"

"You know. It's in the prayer book. For the satisfaction of
lust and the procreation of children. Or I may have got it
wrong somewhere. Don't tell me you haven't been thinking
about it!"

"Yes, I have," she admitted. "All day and all night when
you were not here. Dion darling, yes, I think so — but can't
we go on as we are till the war ends?"

"We'll have to — considering the queue for the divorce
courts."

"And then? Oh Dion, I should love life with you! But what
sort of life?"

"What we can make for ourselves. We don't know. 1944.
1945. Victory, they say. But we don't know what it will be like.
We shall be out on our feet, and the other fellow on the slab.
Then we get handed back to the politicians. Cutting here and
patching there. You and I — two living, unimportant cells.
Chuck us in the hospital ash can? Use us to make a bit of
healthy tissue? We shan't know. We can't choose. But at least
there will be two of us."